Introduction

An Acquired Taste by Susan K. Downs

JJ Taylor disdains those hippie-musician types. . .until a guitar-wielding minstrel shows up at the bookstore where she works and strums his way into her fortressed heart. On a whim, Camden Coffees CEO, Branson D. Smythe, has passed himself off as guitarist David Smith to perform for the grand opening of his new coffee shop, located in one of his family's bookst [illegible] he convince JJ to love him as a pe [illegible] the wealthy entrepreneur he really i [illegible]

The Perfect Blend by Anita Higman

The Café Rose is a place for gre [illegible] love. Jacques, the owner and matchmaker of the Café Rose, seats his friend, Hamilton Wakefield, with loner Kasey Morland. Her business life is a mess, and since Hamilton is an entrepreneur, he lets Kasey know he's just the man to straighten her out! Sparks fly, coffee is poured, and romance is in the air. Will their clashing personalities turn into a bitter brew, or will Hamilton and Kasey discover they are instead, the perfect blend?

Breaking New Grounds by DiAnn Mills

Kae Alice and Gene have been friends since they were fifteen. Now, in their seventies, their friendship has grown from a comfortable relationship to a deep, abiding love. They tease, reminisce about the fifties, volunteer their time at a retirement center, and transport the sick to their doctors. Unfortunately neither one can admit their feelings, and time is running out! Then Gene decides he has to speak his heart, but the result may tear them apart forever.

Coffee Scoop by Kathleen Miller Y'Barbo

Religion reporter Carrie Collins wants to make her mark in journalism. A chance meeting with the American owner of a Costa Rican coffee company aboard a flight between Los Angeles and Austin provides Carrie with the story of a lifetime: exposing a business claiming to be a ministry. Can she investigate what looks to be another fraud perpetrated on innocent Christians without giving away her intentions and eventually her heart?

fresh-brewed love

Four Novellas Share a Cup of Kindness. . .

with a Dollop of Romance

Susan K. Downs
Anita Higman
DiAnn Mills
Kathleen Miller Y'Barbo

ISBN 1-59310-603-3

Cover art by Jesse Reisch

Interior art by Julie Doll

Published by Barbour Publishing, Inc., P.O. Box 719, Uhrichsville, Ohio 44683, www.barbourbooks.com

Our mission is to publish and distribute inspirational products offering exceptional value and biblical encouragement to the masses.

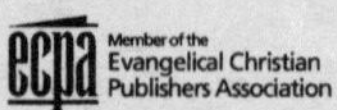

Printed in the United States of America.
5 4 3 2 1

an acquired taste

by Susan K. Downs
with Nancy Toback

Dedication

To my dear pal and writing buddy, Nancy. When God ordained our paths to cross, He blessed me with a true friend. You always seem to know just the right thing to say or do to cheer me up when I'm down. . .to motivate me when I feel like giving up. . .to come alongside and share the load when it's too heavy for me to bear alone. Thank you for allowing the Lord to use you to minister to me in a thousand different ways—and always when I needed it most.

Every time you cross my mind,
I break out in exclamations of thanks to God.
Each exclamation is a trigger to prayer.
I find myself praying for you with a glad heart.
PHILIPPIANS 1: 3–4 THE MESSAGE

Chapter 1

If JJ Taylor had her way, coffee would be outlawed, banned from society as an illegal drug. At the very least, there should be a prohibition on consuming the foul drink in her bookstore.

The aroma of fresh-brewed grounds permeated the air and masked her favorite bookstore scents—printer's ink, paper, bookbinding glue, all buried by a smell of coffee beans.

JJ whisked her feather duster across the stocked shelves of the TRAVEL section and shot a furtive glance toward the café. With a sinking heart, she observed her coworkers sampling disgusting variations of the drinkable mud from paper cups. The heartiest caffeine-induced laughter came from those who had, in private conversations, shared in her consternation over the café's opening.

Well, she was no hypocrite.

JJ turned her back on the Camden Corners Café pre-grand-opening festivities, pushed her glasses up the bridge of her nose, and returned to the task of dusting. If only she could have a word with the infamous Mr. Branson Smythe,

the owner's son and architect of the coffee café brainchild. But in the three years she had worked at Camden Corners Books, she had yet to see him. He could've been one of the suits trailing head honcho B. D. Smythe when they'd come to oversee construction of the café. But on those occasions, she had been too resentful—and intimidated—to approach the ominous owner of the nationwide megabookstore chain.

The upper management powers that be of Camden Corners hadn't bothered to consult a peon assistant manager like herself prior to knocking down walls and renovating their flagship bookstore to accommodate an in-house coffee café.

If she ever did have a face-to-face with the illustrious Branson Smythe, she would rattle off a long list of reasons (her personal distaste for the bitter drink notwithstanding) why she opposed a coffee café on the premises of Camden Corners Books. The unsavory characters that frequented coffeehouses topped her list. They weren't the kind of folks she wanted as patrons of their establishment—antisocial sorts, like her own parents—who would sit for hours and read books they never intended to buy, damaging the merchandise with their coffee stains and pastry crumbs.

With a swish of the feather duster, JJ sent a sawdust cloud floating into the bookstore's stratosphere only to rain down on the shelves all over again. She chided herself for her less-than-Christian thoughts.

She would have to learn to cope with this change.

Or quit.

And she wasn't about to do that.

Her stomach clinched when she even entertained the thought

of abandoning her goal of climbing the Camden Corners Books corporate totem pole. Next year, she would graduate with her M.B.A., thanks to the company's scholarship program. She had finished her coursework and needed only to finish her master's thesis; then she would be done. Armed with her degree, plus her stellar employment record with the bookstore, she stood a good chance of landing her dream job in marketing at Camden Corners Books corporate headquarters—if, in light of these latest unpleasant developments, she could hang on in her present position until then.

She must somehow overcome her aversion to coffee, temporarily at least, even though the stinking brew dredged up buried memories from her better-left-forgotten past.

"Miss Taylor, line two." The page cut into the Muzak rendition of an old John Denver tune. The instrumental track picked up again at the "West Virginia, Mountain Mama" part. She suddenly felt the threat of tears. When she was a kid, her grandma used to sing the chorus of the golden oldie tune whenever they crossed the river from Ohio to West Virginia on their way to family reunions at her uncle Frank's.

Both Grandma and Frank had been gone for years now. And her mother, in a nursing home, was virtually gone, too, thanks to her drug-junkie lifestyle that had brought on a stroke and left her incapacitated at age fifty-five.

On her way to the phone, JJ stooped to pick up a napkin from the carpeted floor. Day One of the café's opening, and the bookstore already looked a shambles. She pulled in a deep breath, fought off the myriad of emotions percolating in her chest, and punched the flashing phone button.

"Hi, JJ, it's Kara," her manager blurted before JJ had a chance to say hello.

"Kara, where are you?" *And why aren't you here?* JJ shot a look of disapproval at a woman carrying a coffee cup between her teeth while leafing through an expensive hardcover book.

"Sorry, I was called in to attend a last-minute meeting at corporate HQ. But listen, the musician for the grand opening will be arriving in the next couple of hours to set up for tonight's performance."

JJ felt a sweat break out on her brow. She'd dealt with enough musicians to last her two lifetimes. "Right."

"Be on the lookout for a tall, good-looking guy." Kara giggled. "And give him a rousing welcome. Make him feel comfortable and show him where to go to set up for his performance."

A rousing welcome? Apparently Kara couldn't distinguish between a musician and a VIP. "I'm sure he'll be happy for the work." *Even without a rousing welcome,* she was tempted to add.

"Gotta go, girl, but catch you later," Kara said.

"Wait, what's his name?" JJ heard the *click* of the disconnect, huffed out a breath, and set down the phone. She'd give him a rousing welcome all right. She would point him in the right direction and wait for Kara to come in and do all the rousing.

Nobody would recognize him in these grungy clothes. Branson Smythe examined his new look in the mirrored sliding doors of his walk-in closet. He flashed a smile at his reflection. The black holey T-shirt did the trick. For the next couple of weekends he would pass himself off as David Smith—his middle name and the common spelling of his last name.

David Smith, the guitar-wielding entertainer at Camden Corners Café.

Branson nodded his approval once more, then stepped out of the master bedroom and down the hall to his spacious home theater. The room still exhibited his ex-wife's rich—i.e., expensive—tastes in decorating. "Hey, Mike."

His racquetball partner and good buddy shifted from his prone position on the overstuffed leather sofa he occupied. Two other matching contemporary sofas sat empty on the theater-style tiers that rose behind the ground-level viewing area.

"How do I look?" Branson spread his arms.

Mike gave him a slit-eyed once-over, and shook his head. "Like *Extreme Makeover* in reverse?"

Branson laughed. "Good. Exactly what I was going for."

"I know but. . ." Mike added a tongue cluck of disapproval. ". . .if B. D. finds out, he's going to be hacked."

The words of warning struck a chord of worry in him, but Branson shrugged. "Sometimes I think you're more intimidated by my father than I am." Even the impossible-to-please B. D. thought the world of Mike Ellis.

Branson crossed the room to the corner kitchenette, grabbed a soda from the minifridge, and popped the can's tab. He leaned on the island's countertop and studied Mike while his friend trained his gaze on the wide-screen, flat-panel TV.

He doubted Mike was appreciating the device's high-definition quality. He recognized the signs of those invisible churning cogs inside Mike's clean-cut, conservative head. Any second now, another objection would spew from

Mike-the-lawyer's mouth, and he would proceed to present his argument.

With a *click* of the remote control, Mike silenced the TV.

Here it comes, Branson mused.

"I'm still not clear as to your motivation." Mike slapped his thighs and rose from the sofa, then meandered to the kitchenette's counter. A frown pulled at his lips and wrinkles creased his brow. "Frankly, this impersonation thing seems wacky to me, if not downright devious."

Branson had grappled with those very thoughts, but he had based his decision on sound reasoning. "Think of it this way, I'm protecting my business interests. Camden Coffees is *my* baby. If I strut in there like the owner that—"

"That you are," Mike said.

"Like the owner that I am, I won't get a real feel for how the place is going over with the public and the staff. And my father expects me to take the corporation to the next level of business success. Camden Coffees has got to work." He wouldn't vocalize the core reason for his decision to play coffeehouse minstrel. For once in his life, he wanted to be judged according to his personality and talent rather than his value in terms of fiscal worth. Besides, the role play would be fun.

"Yeah, well, I still think this idea of yours is a big mistake, but good luck with the gig tonight." Mike shook his head. "Hey, I've gotta run. Don't bother seeing me to the door. I know my way out. . . ." He pivoted and started to walk off but paused and turned back toward Branson. "If B. D. finds out. . ." Mike pointed his index finger at Branson in perfect lawyer posturing. "I mean, *when* he finds out, remember, I'm innocent of any wrongdoing in this deal."

Branson laughed. "Sorry, bud, but you won't get off that easy. If my dad's the judge, you will be ruled guilty by association." He watched Mike walk away and couldn't resist one last barb. "Remind me never to hire you as my defense attorney," he shouted to his friend's retreating form.

Mike returned to the doorway and poked his head into the room. "Need I remind you that I'm not now, nor ever will be, a defense attorney?" He grinned. "And I don't foresee you ever again needing my assistance with divorce proceedings." Mike shook his head. "What's that old saying, 'Once burned, twice shy'? If you ever do marry again, it won't be to a gold digger like Heidi—regardless of what your father says." He glanced at his watch. "Yikes, look at the time. I've really gotta go." His heels clicked across the marbled floor of the entryway as he hurried to go.

Branson left his pop can on the countertop and followed Mike to the front door. "I do believe my father learned his lesson on advising me in matters of love and marriage partners. He still blames himself for the fact that the woman he chose as my perfect mate ran off with my best friend. Even my mother, the ever-doting and submissive June Cleaver of a wife that she is, couldn't resist telling my father 'I told you so' when our marriage failed. Although, I suspect Dad was more upset about my giving Heidi the Jag without putting up a fight than he was about my broken heart. He has yet to get over the fact that she was smart enough to find that little loophole in the prenups he had us sign."

Mike clapped him on the shoulder. "I personally think

you should have let me do battle with her attorneys over that car. You're way too nice a guy. She didn't deserve a single red cent from you after the way she used, abused, and dissed you. But we've already been round and round on that one. No use reopening old wounds." He slipped through the open door and tossed a wave over his shoulder as he headed to his car. "I'll catch you later, pal."

Branson nodded and blew out a long, slow breath as he closed and locked the door. The realization still stung. . .Heidi had only wanted him for his money.

For once, he would like to be appreciated for his talent and abilities, not his bank balance. This plan wasn't meant to be devious but more like a grand social experiment.

Branson scrubbed his hand over his day-old beard and shook his head, but the effort failed to dislodge an unpleasant memory. The set of his father's jaw, the tone of his voice when he had signed their business agreement, still haunted Branson's thoughts.

"Any of your shenanigans, Son, and this deal is off."

His father hadn't needed to warn him. Branson had noted all the sticking points in their contract before he signed on the dotted line. On the other hand, this "gig" of his, as Mike referred to it, would last for only four weekends in October. Ol' B. D. and his mom would be in Europe for the next six weeks. Everything would run smoothly, and his father would finally see him as an entrepreneur in his own right.

What could possibly go wrong?

Chapter 2

JJ perched on a miniature chair and strained to read *The Cat in the Hat* aloud to the children over the hiss and gurgle of the silver and brass coffeemakers. If she raised her voice another notch, she would be shouting the tale at them.

She could no longer hitch her career dreams to the Camden Corners Books' bandwagon. The new coffee café's grand opening festivities were just getting underway, and she was already tempted to throw in the towel.

JJ looked over her shoulder, glared at Minnie behind the café counter, and tsked her disapproval.

Minnie met her gaze and shrugged, as if to say, "It's not my fault." The appropriately named petite girl with the squeaky voice had every right to her silent argument. Culpability for ruining the bookstore's peaceful ambiance lay solely on the shoulders of the café's creator—Mr. Branson Smythe III.

After offering Minnie an apologetic smile, JJ touched the notepad in her blazer pocket. She'd made her list and checked it twice. The grapevine news reported that, in his father's absence, Branson Smythe would soon grace the premises of the store. She was armed and ready for his appearance. Her plan to corner the hotshot junior exec and enumerate on her itemized list of café evils would finally come to pass.

JJ returned her attention to the toddlers gathered at her feet on colorful mats. "Can you all hear me okay?"

Each of the five children bobbed their heads. A red-haired boy, freckles smattered across his nose, offered a smile up at her. "I can hears you real good, Miss Taylor."

JJ wondered if he could sense the frustration bubbling just beneath the surface. "Good, I. . ." Her voice caught. Oh dear, all she needed was to lapse into a crying jag in front of these youngsters.

She pulled in a long, shaky breath. "Okay, then, let's continue."

The security monitor at the front door buzzed. No doubt, another zombie in need of a caffeine fix had just made a grand entrance.

JJ fought to focus on story time, but from the corner of her eye, she caught sight of a derelict as he trudged into the bookstore and over to the book stacks.

The bum, in desperate need of a shave, pretended to read while sneaking peeks at the café. By the looks of him, he'd fallen into his seedy lifestyle and onto hard times at a younger age than most.

JJ tried to see beneath his grunge and guessed the fella's age to be close to her own. Dressed in a hole-riddled black T-shirt and torn jeans, he looked like one of the Kirkwood Avenue undesirables who made their homes in cardboard boxes under the railroad viaduct.

Just as she feared, the café was a magnet for all the wrong kinds.

From her peripheral vision, JJ observed him flipping through a book's pages. He employed a feigned interest in literature as an obvious ploy to case the joint.

When she reached the last page of *The Cat in the Hat*, JJ sighed and relaxed her stiff shoulders. "The end," she managed with a smile, then rushed through polite good-byes and rose from her chair.

She grabbed the stack of romance novels she had meant to shelve earlier, then made her way to within a few feet of the drifter. His type didn't scare her. Her parents and their zoned-out friends had been made of the same stuff.

JJ approached him, cleared her throat, and forced a smile. "May I help you?"

He closed the book in his hand with a slap.

JJ jumped, tilted her chin, and regained her composure. "You're in the *LITERATURE* section."

If her emphasis on *literature* insulted him, he showed no signs of it. But at least she had let him know his antics didn't fool her one bit. His appreciation of the classics surely rivaled her love of coffee.

"Is there something specific I can help you—?"

"Hi, there." He set the book atop a shelf, then stuck out his hand. "I'm David Smith."

Right, and I'm Jane Doe. JJ stared at his hand and fought the urge to recoil. Who in their right mind expected a handshake from a store clerk? She shifted the paperbacks in her arms to her left side and made a mental note to tell Branson Smythe that, thanks to him, her new job description included humoring coffeehouse freaks.

Reluctant to make physical contact with the tall, dark, and dangerous man in scruffy clothes, she drew a breath and made quick work of shaking his hand. His hand felt strong, yet smooth. A distress signal flashed across her mind as she checked him out. His muscular build suggested he was a laborer—probably a card-carrying member of a chain gang—but his hands weren't callused. No tattoos. No pierced body parts. At least none she could see.

And he smelled good. Too good.

Every instinct borne of her miserable childhood screamed trouble.

"Nice to meet you. . ." David Smith left the question of how to address her hanging in the air.

"My name is Miss Taylor, and I'm the assistant manager here." She nodded to her ID badge that verified both her name—JJ Taylor—and her position. "If you should need any help. . ."

She didn't bother finishing her sentence as her words obviously fell on deaf ears. Mr. Smith's focus had turned to the café again.

JJ inched her way backward down the aisle, reluctant to take her eyes off the so-called Mr. Smith.

Stooped in front of the ROMANCE shelf, she puzzled over the incongruities of this David Smith fellow. He might be on a controlled substance, a sociopath who thought the world was a yo-yo, and he held the string.

"How's the café doing?"

JJ looked up at him from her crouched posture by the bottom

shelf. News of the café's success must have spread to every criminal in town. At nearly five dollars a pop for a lousy cup of coffee, even feebleminded druggies could deduce that the new Camden Corners Café was an easy target with a large stash of cash on hand.

JJ stood upright. The paperbacks slipped out of her arms and spilled onto the floor. She stared down at the kaleidoscope of colorful covers, each promising romance—a nonexistent commodity in her life. She redirected her gaze to David.

His lips lifted at one corner in a half smile. His dark brown gaze drifted over her face.

She tried her best to match his gaze, stand up to his stare. This suspicious character acted way too bold for a common viaduct troll. The heat of a blush inched up JJ's neck.

He won the stare-down.

She looked away.

David indicated the books on the floor with a jut of his chin. "Let me help you with those—"

"I don't need any help, thanks." She straightened and pulled her shoulders back.

With a mild shrug, David returned his attention to the café. "You haven't answered my question."

She had intentionally ignored it. JJ's pulse sped. "Question?"

"The café." He ran his tongue inside his cheek and appeared to be thinking. Calculating. "How's business?"

"Oh, um. . ." This Incredible Hulk of a guy could lift Minnie with one hand and toss her across the room before he emptied the register.

JJ swallowed hard. She despised lying, but Minnie's life

could be at stake. "Frankly, I don't believe the café is doing too good." *Not doing me any good, at least. That much is the absolute truth.* She looked down and shook her head. "Not good at all." She wanted to add there was no money in the register but thought it might be overkill.

David slammed his fist into his palm. "You've got to be kidding!"

JJ felt the blood drain from her face. He'd seen through her bluff. She was Java Jo again, the little girl named for the coffeehouse, the Java Joint, where her parents first met. Back then, she invented stories to save her hide from the sting of a belt. She stared at him, mute, her legs shaking.

David scrubbed his hand over his shadowed jawline. Without removing his dark gaze from her face, he pointed toward the café. "I see customers waiting in line. A *lot* of them."

JJ whipped off her eyeglasses. Using the corner of her wool blazer, she buffed the lenses, buying time until she could find a way to signal Minnie of trouble. If only her manager, Kara Kroll, would return early from her meeting at corporate HQ.

JJ eased her glasses back on and focused on poor, unsuspecting Minnie. Minnie was laughing with a customer, blissfully unaware that these might be her final moments. "Yes, I see what you're saying. . .but that's because. . .they're giving away free coffee this morning." *Well, they* were *giving away free coffee to the employees earlier. . .and the stretch might very well avert a crime.*

"Free coffee?" The muscles in the bum's jaw ticked.

JJ's breath caught at the incredulous note in his voice.

"There's no profit in that." He scowled and shook his head. "How am I going to. . ." He paused midsentence, as though he'd caught himself about to say something he shouldn't. He buried his volatile emotions behind a pasted smile.

Her pulse roared in her ears. She had to stay calm. She dared not incite this new breed of thief bold enough to be angered over an empty register. She had to try another tack with him. But what? How?

David waved his hand.

JJ flinched.

"On the other hand. . ." He shook his head. "If they aren't paying for coffee, I guess the customers will have more cash in their pockets to give to me."

A scream welled in her throat. She used all the fortitude she could muster to swallow it back down.

It wouldn't do to create a panic in the store if one could be averted. She could see both of his hands. He had yet to make any sudden moves to reach for a weapon. Until he did, she had to stay calm. If only she could figure out a way to call for help without alarming the other customers.

JJ scowled and glared at her suspect through hooded eyes.

She couldn't read the expression he sent her in return.

"You know, in tips. . .gratuities. . ."

JJ took a step back. Then another.

Tips? For what? His good looks? She had to reach a phone and dial 9-1-1 without agitating him lest he resort to a hostage situation. This poor David fellow was either strung out on drugs, drunk, or plain crazy. Delusional. She could almost hear the loose screws rattling around in his head.

"David!"

Branson caught sight of Kara Kroll, the plus-size store

manager, barreling down the aisle toward him and Miss Taylor.

He waved at Kara. Her arrival came not a moment too soon. Another second alone with JJ Taylor, and he might have confessed his true identity. The prim and proper clerk should work for the district attorney's office.

"Hey, Kara." Branson smiled and fell into her bear hug. Locked in Kara's embrace, he caught a glimpse of the stunned expression on JJ's face.

Kara stepped back and exchanged glances with JJ. "Have you two already met?" Without waiting for a response, she waved her hand and dismissed her own query. "Never mind," she said. "Allow me to do the honors." Kara nodded toward Miss Taylor. "David, this is my assistant manager, JJ." She patted Branson on the sleeve, then gave his arm a little squeeze. "And JJ, this is David Smith, our featured guitarist for the café's grand opening festivities." Her voice ended on a high note, as though she expected her scowling coworker to give him a rousing welcome.

"Guitarist?" JJ whispered. Her fair skin took on a rosy glow. "Oh. I see."

Branson noted the contrast between the two women and suppressed a laugh. His thoughts returned to the free coffee and how much money he was losing. A sobering contemplation.

"What's this free coffee deal?" he asked, meeting Kara's confused glare.

"Huh?" Kara shook her head, sending wisps of platinum blond hair across her moon-shaped face. "Nobody around here is getting free coffee." She placed her fisted hand on her ample hip.

"I apologize. I thought. . ." JJ dropped to one knee and started to gather the books from the floor.

Branson felt something jab his heart. He felt sorry for her. No rhyme. No reason. But when she'd taken off her glasses, he thought he glimpsed sadness in her dark blue eyes. He'd be the first to admit he had no clue when it came to understanding the opposite sex. Still. . .

Kara looped her arm through his. "Let's get going. I'll show you the setup for tonight."

"Cool." As he walked away, he couldn't resist one last look at JJ. He turned and caught her staring up at him. She averted her gaze in response to his smile.

Kara squeezed his arm. "Well, how'd I do?" she whispered.

Branson winked. He appreciated Kara's enthusiastic effort at keeping his little secret. "You did great," he said to the accompaniment of her giggles.

Reluctant to put a damper on Kara's delight, he stifled the urge to ask questions about JJ. The poor girl had either been misinformed, or she had lied outright about the free coffee. Why? Did her chilly response to him have everything to do with his crummy clothes and her assumption that he was a nobody? So far, his grand social experiment had succeeded only in putting a sizable dent in his ego.

Chapter 3

At 6:00 p.m. sharp, as per the manager's instructions, the bookstore was closed for one hour to prepare for the café's grand opening. JJ prepped the café with Kara, then unlocked Camden Corners' front door at 7:00 p.m. She lingered beside the glass door as a sudden rain shower pelted the city. Thankfully, she'd completed her work and wouldn't need to stay for the café's grand opening—"Good Music, Good Books, Good Friends, Great Coffee Night."

Lightning flashed across the darkened sky, and a clap of thunder shook the windowpanes.

JJ shuddered. A memory tore loose from the recesses of her mind, sinking her stomach. She hurried toward the inventory room to collect her things, but thoughts of a long-ago rainy day flooded her mind.

Nine-year-old Java Jo stood in Guido's Deli, trembling. She knew the evils of stealing but wanted to invite her best friend, Lisa, home. Java Jo stuffed the can of scouring powder under her coat. She ran the two blocks to her home, asking God to forgive her. She hadn't stolen sweets, she'd reasoned.

She only wanted to clean the house.

She scrubbed the chipped Formica counter in her parents' filthy apartment till her hands grew raw red. Despite her efforts, she couldn't remove the permanent scars—circular coffee stains, cigarette burns, and splotches of her mom's hair dye. The apartment reeked of burnt coffee and marijuana. And roaches zoomed across the kitchen in broad daylight.

Java Jo never did invite Lisa over, nor any of her other friends. Even if, by some miracle, she could have transformed the apartment, her parents still proved her worst embarrassment of all.

JJ's heart swelled with sorrow. By God's grace alone, she'd built a totally new life. Camden Corners Books was a big part of her new life. Yet the opening of the café had revived the buried and unwelcome memories, and her only option seemed to be to give Kara her two weeks' notice.

"How's it going?"

JJ's fingers froze on the zipper of her briefcase. At the sight of David Smith, her pulse kicked up a notch. In one sweeping glance, she took in his rain-dampened dark hair and the black guitar case that he'd had to run out into the storm to retrieve from his car.

"You scared me," JJ said.

David's dark gaze rested on her, in that same cool, confident way she'd noted earlier today. "Sorry if I startled you," he answered.

"No big deal." JJ swung her briefcase off the chair. "I was just leaving."

David spread his arms. "Was it something I said?"

The similarities between David and her father struck her as uncanny. Her dad used to make a joke of everything, too. JJ gripped the handle of her briefcase tighter. "Nothing you said." In case David thought his presence unsettled her, JJ pushed a smile to her face.

"Could you stay?" David propped his guitar case against the wooden table and smiled. "For a little while at least?" He dragged his fingers through his dark hair, splattering water on carton boxes.

"Stay?" If she were able to communicate with her mom, JJ would offer her a heartfelt apology. She'd always thought of her mother as weak-willed, but if her father exuded half the charm of David Smith, she could understand how her mom had fallen under his spell. "Why?"

"We've got four customers in the café." David's chest rose and fell on a deep breath. "And two of them look like they're half-asleep." He laughed. "It's kind of embarrassing playing to a virtually empty room."

She shouldn't feel sympathy for him, but she did. She understood these artsy types for what they really were—hopeless dreamers. "Did you ever consider another line of work?" The words popped out of her mouth. As if her useless admonition had the power to change him. The look of amusement in David's eyes confirmed her conviction.

"It might surprise you." David crossed his arms over his broad chest. "But I'm already a productive member of society."

JJ snorted a cynical laugh. "Sorry, it's just that my father was a musician. . . ." A shadow passed across her heart, warning her to keep her mouth shut.

David's brows lifted. "No kidding, what did he play?"

"Guitar." *And he, too, thought he was a "productive member of society."* "He died when I was very young. . . ." JJ averted her gaze, unable to account for why she kept babbling to this perfect stranger.

"Sorry to hear that." David's dark eyes held a genuine look of sympathy.

"It's no big deal," JJ blurted. In answer to the look of surprise on his face, she raised her hand. "I mean, I hardly even remember him."

Kara popped into the inventory room, saving her from another exhausting exchange with the musician. "Hey, you two." Kara punched the air with her fisted hand. "It's show time!"

"Not for me," JJ said. "I'm out of here." She squeezed past David, then nodded at Kara. "See you tomorrow."

Kara's large frame blocked the doorway. "I need you here, JJ."

Trapped and feeling dizzy, JJ resisted the urge to push past her manager. "What? Why?"

"Helen just called in sick." Kara looked past her to David. "The good news for you is, since the rain's let up, a crowd of customers has arrived." She glanced back at JJ and tilted her head, looking apologetic. "Unfortunately for you, I can't handle them without your help."

"Hmm." Branson grabbed his guitar. "I guess I'd better get out there, then. We'll talk later."

"Right." Kara patted his arm. "Good luck, *David.*"

"Thanks, but luck has nothing to do with it." Though Kara claimed to be an atheist, Branson felt the need to vocalize the truth stirring in his heart. "I'm relying on the Lord to get me through this, totally and completely."

"Um, I see. Well, whatever. . ." Kara shrugged, then made a hasty exit.

Branson hovered in the doorway, hugging his guitar to his chest like a shield, cognizant of the murmurs and laughter coming from the café. His idea of passing himself off as David Smith no longer seemed clever or fun.

In his mind's eye, he could see his father's glare of disapproval. If the Camden Coffees franchise didn't succeed, he would never gain the respect of B. D.—and that's all he'd ever wanted.

Branson stepped into the café and onto the platform. He positioned himself on the barstool, to the accompaniment of mild applause, and gave a nod of appreciation.

The second he caught sight of JJ, standing in the bookstore with her back to him, his heart warned him that his nerves had more to do with his wanting to impress her than his desire to please the crowd.

"I'm David Smith." Branson strummed a couple of warm-up notes. He saw JJ make a half turn, though she still didn't face him. "And I'd like to dedicate this first song to JJ Taylor." He kept his eyes trained on her, hoping she'd look his way so he could offer her a smile. But when she finally glanced at him, his smile died before it reached his lips.

JJ clapped her hand over her mouth, horror written in her eyes, and spun toward the café.

Chapter 4

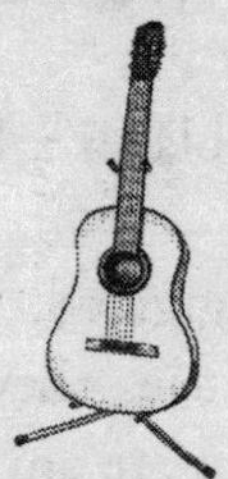

What is he doing? Her pulse pounded in her ears like drummed accompaniment to the chords David strummed on his guitar.

JJ stumbled backward, searching for cover. She pulled her gaze from David's smiling face, ducked behind a bookshelf, and dropped onto a step stool. Couldn't the crazy musician take a hint? She had sent David enough bad vibes, as her father used to say, to leave no question as to her disapproval.

The music penetrating her ears brought on a fresh wave of indignation.

In perfect tone and pitch, David crooned the words to the seventies Carole King song "You've Got a Friend."

The lyrics were endearing—between friends. But David and she were virtual strangers. She had no desire to relive the dark days of her childhood via a friendship with this down-and-out musician. Or any musician.

Sincerity laced David's words as he continued to extol in song the benefits and blessings of friendship in a cold, cruel world. Sympathy washed over her, and JJ shook her head. The poor, deluded musician probably thought he would make it big some day.

A touch on her shoulder sent JJ scrambling to her feet.

"Are you okay?" Wide-eyed, Kara pushed strands of platinum hair off her face.

"I'm fine." JJ gave her blazer a hard tug. "Sorry, I know I should be helping you."

"Not a problem." Kara giggled. "Most of the customers are so caught up in David's music, they are waiting for an intermission to order anything more anyway."

"Of course." The groupies would soon start coming just to see him, like they had with her father. Women used to hang all over her dad, and her mom would shrug and say, *"That's show biz."*

JJ cleared her throat. "Well, we'd better get back to work." At times like these, she didn't feel a bit snobbish or disloyal for building a life in direct contrast to her parents'.

"Whenever you're ready." Kara leaned around the corner of the bookshelf and gave a thumbs-up.

JJ followed her, suspecting Kara was smitten with the itinerant minstrel. Who could blame her? David's rough edges couldn't hide his natural good looks or winsome charm. But if Kara had lived Java Jo's life, she would know the bottomless depths of a musician's ego, and she'd run as fast and as far from David Smith as her legs would carry her.

Kara slipped behind the café counter, leaving JJ to collect paper menus, checkmarked with customers' orders. As JJ weaved her way around the tables, she willed herself not to look in David's direction. She must have given him the wrong impression earlier, causing him to dedicate "You've Got a Friend" to her. This time, if David approached her, she would not allow her mouth to get ahead of her brain.

While serving the customers, JJ observed their heads bobbing, feet tapping, to David's medley of seventies tunes. She readily identified each song and its artist within the first few chords. She had picked up the useless skill during her dad's late-night jam sessions, while straining to concentrate on her homework.

JJ swiped another menu from the table and fought to rein in her troubling thoughts. It wasn't right to blame David, the vagabond musician, for ruining the bookstore—and her life.

A surge of anger bubbled inside her. JJ strummed her fingers on the countertop while waiting for the noisy machines to spit out a café latte and an espresso. First thing Monday morning, she would phone Branson Smythe and give him a piece of her mind.

"I'm going to take five." David's announcement broke into her thoughts.

A collective groan of disappointment came from the audience. JJ was tempted to shush the customers as she took an extra-large latte from Kara and placed the mug on the serving tray.

David would probably step off the stage and start schmoozing the customers. But if the macho musician did come over to her, she would keep the conversation short and sweet.

From out of the corner of her eye, JJ saw David approaching. He unclipped his cell phone from his belt and looked at the device, apparently checking for messages. He lifted his gaze in time to catch her staring at him. Her stomach did a slow roll, for which she had no explanation.

JJ glanced away, trying to sort her emotions.

David smiled. "Did I do okay?" He asked the question as though they were friends and her opinion really mattered to him.

"Fine." JJ nodded. "Good." She clamped her mouth shut, lest she gush a string of compliments that would encourage him not to get a real job.

David sighed. "You're a tough sell, JJ Taylor."

JJ stared at him, mute. Her gaze dropped to David's ragged T-shirt, then took in the shiny cell phone in his hand. She felt the sensible JJ returning. David probably owed his condition to a drug or alcohol problem, and he needed a cell phone to line up his clandestine transactions.

"Hmm, no comment?" David reached over the counter, took the espresso from Kara, and set it on JJ's serving tray. "Can I buy you a cup of coffee?"

"I hate coffee!" JJ punctuated her words with a wave, and her overzealous rebuff sent her hand smashing against his.

In slow-motion horror, his cell phone flew from his grasp and plopped into the giant mug of steaming latte. Froth splattered across her tray.

JJ gasped. They stared into the muddy liquid like lifeguards waiting for a swimmer's head to bob to the surface before they dove in for a rescue.

David sighed. "There seems to be no sign of it."

JJ summoned the courage to look him in the eye. "But I—I saw it go in there." She sighed. "I'm really sorry. I'll pay for it."

Although, by her way of thinking, a down-and-out musician had no business owning a cell phone in the first place.

David shrugged. "I couldn't let you do that. Smart phones cost a small fortune. Hey, accidents happen." He grabbed a plastic stirrer and poked around in the cup.

JJ's stomach sank. She had budgeted her bill payments down to her last dollar this month. "A small fortune?" She watched him continue to trawl through the latte with the stirrer. "No sense trying to rescue it now. Once these things are immersed—"

"Drowned," David corrected.

He needn't make matters worse. "Like I said, I'm sorry." JJ tilted her chin. "Just let me know how much it costs, and I'll pay you on. . ." She squinted, doing math calisthenics. "I can pay you next Friday. Would that be all right?"

"Five hundred dollars," David muttered and abandoned the stirrer.

Five hundred dollars? Her hearted pounded with renewed panic. "Can I break it up into. . .five payments?"

With his head tilted, David folded his muscular arms and seemed to consider her pathetic offer. "How about a trade?" he asked in that cool, composed voice of his.

JJ removed her glasses and glared at him. "What do you mean?" She was certain she read humor in his dark eyes.

"Instead of paying me, we share a cup of coffee together." David smiled.

JJ raised her hand in protest. "I told you—"

"I know. You hate coffee. But that's the deal, take it or leave it. You have a latte with me, right here, right now, and we forget about my cell phone."

What a very strange man. Her heart pounded so hard, she feared David could hear it. But she simply did not have five hundred dollars to spare. JJ dragged in a shaky breath, pushed her glasses back in place, and looked at the grinning musician. "Okay. Deal."

After he helped JJ serve two tables, Branson asked Kara to take over JJ's duties. She readily agreed. Maybe too readily. Unlike JJ, Kara Kroll knew he was Branson Smythe, CEO of Camden Coffees.

If B. D. could overhear his musings, he'd be wearing a smug smile. His father's caveat was that a man without position and money was a nobody. A nothing. A nameless face among the masses.

"You ought to be grateful you were born with a silver spoon in your mouth, Son."

But the Smythe family silver left behind a bitter aftertaste, which overpowered the sweetest of riches. Only the success of Camden Coffees would guarantee him the chance to strike out on his own and wiggle out from under B. D.'s thumb.

Branson leaned against the counter, waiting for Kara to make two lattes. He glanced at the corner table, where JJ sat like a death-row inmate, prepared for a lethal injection of caffeine. Her crime—and the only reason they'd be sharing the same table—was that she had destroyed his smart phone.

He was being judged as David now, according to his personality and talent rather than his fiscal net worth. . .and batting zero with JJ Taylor. So much for disproving his father's grim assertion that he owed any and all of his success to the Smythe family name and fortune.

Guilt wormed its way into his conscience. One-upping B. D. had little to do with wanting JJ to like him. In the three years since Heidi ran off with Paul Wirth, and their subsequent—and as far as Branson was concerned, unwelcome—divorce, he had many opportunities to date, but no woman had piqued his interest.

Branson cut a glance at JJ. She was attractive all right, but he couldn't pinpoint exactly why he was drawn to her.

"Here you go." Kara's voice broke into his thoughts.

Branson grabbed the coffees and winked. "Thanks." He turned and headed toward JJ, feeling like a loan shark about to collect from a panicked debtor. *Great way to start a friendship.*

"Two lattes," Branson said, setting the mugs on the table. He pulled out a chair, sat down, and then raised his cup in a toast. "Are you ready?"

With her one hand clutching her blazer lapel, JJ shivered. "How much of it must I drink?"

"Only five hundred dollars' worth." Branson smiled, and to his great relief, JJ laughed. In that split second, with her blue eyes dazzling, he sensed a fun-loving JJ hiding behind the conservative clothes and black-rimmed eyeglasses. It was as though she deliberately dressed to conceal her beauty.

She raised the coffee mug to her lips, and everything in him wanted to let her off the hook. But if he released her now, there was no telling if he'd ever have another chance for a one-on-one with her.

JJ met his gaze. "Can I hold my nose while I drink?"

The look of worry written on her heart-shaped face almost made him fold, but he cocked a brow, feigning indignation. "I'm afraid that would be cheating."

"Fine, then." JJ cleared her throat and raised the cup to her lips again.

Branson scooted to the edge of his seat, his gaze glued to JJ's face. He hadn't thought to inquire why she hated coffee. What if coffee made her sick? Or maybe she had religious convictions against caffeinated drinks. She might've believed he would really accept five hundred dollars from her, and in desperation, accepted his offer. After all, how much could she be earning here? He made a mental note to give JJ a raise. Then he opened his mouth to tell her the deal was off.

But she tipped back her head and gulped the latte.

Branson held his breath, waiting for her reaction. "You don't have to finish it," he said, full of guilt. "I was only kidding."

"No, no." JJ tucked her shiny dark hair behind her ears. "I always keep my word." She licked her lips and smiled. "Besides, it's really rather good."

"Now wait a sec." Branson rested his back against the chair as truth dawned. She must have claimed to hate coffee as a polite way to wiggle out of his invitation.

JJ took another gulp, confirming his suspicion.

Branson sighed. "Okay, out with the truth. You don't really hate coffee, do you?"

"I *did* hate it," she blurted, her voice full of conviction. "But this is more like hot chocolate than the kind of coffee my folks used to drink. I practically grew up in a hippie-style coffeehouse and. . ." JJ pressed her lips together, as though she'd just divulged a terrible secret.

He told himself to stop staring at her, but he wanted to probe for more. Branson slid the napkin from under his cup and reached across the table to wipe off her latte mustache. "You've got some foam—"

JJ flinched. "I'll get it myself."

"Right." He'd gone to the trouble of taking on the David persona in order to get honest feedback on the café from employees and patrons. Instead of flirting with JJ, he needed to get down to business.

Branson scrubbed his hand over his unshaven face. "Do you like working here?"

A small line formed between her pretty brows. "I used to." JJ shook her head and sighed. "But that was before they opened this crummy café. I hope this latest harebrained free-enterprise experiment flops sooner rather than later, so life can return to normal around here."

Her words stung like a physical slap. Branson clasped his hands on the tabletop in a feeble attempt at composure. "What's wrong with the café?" The edge in his voice betrayed his true feelings.

"Oh no, what am I thinking?" JJ pressed her hand to her cheek. "You play here. I'm so sorry."

If he hoped to get to the truth, he'd best think of himself as David, the detached observer. Branson shrugged. "No big deal."

"Right, right, you can get a job in any club or café." JJ waved her hand. "But I loved the bookstore before the café opened." She glanced around, as though trying to conjure up a picture of the way it used to be. "By the way, do you see anybody buying books?"

Branson shifted in his seat. "No, but—"

"Exactly. They're destroying books with their sticky fingers, reading them as if they're in a library, but they're not buying books."

Branson massaged the taut muscles at the back of his neck, compelled to say something in defense of the café without revealing his true identity. "Part of my boring day job is marketing research." He saw JJ's eyes go round with surprise but forged ahead. "Based on my knowledge, I'm certain the café will increase book sales."

JJ shook her head. "No, I've been working here for three years, and I believe I have pretty good intuition when sales are up or down. I strongly suspect today's receipts will show a noticeable drop in sales. They're reading but not buying."

He tried to force down the irritation building in his chest. "The largest bookseller chains have cafés in their stores. Are their stats all wrong?"

"I only know what's good for Camden Corners Books." JJ smiled without humor. "And come Monday morning, I'm going to give the café franchise owner a piece of my mind."

Branson's back went ramrod straight. "I don't think that's a good idea." He could picture JJ, traipsing through the Camden Corners' corporate offices to the top floor's executive suites, the walls of which were lined with photos of him and his family. His gig would be up for sure. "What do you intend to do, burst into his office like a blazing fireball?"

JJ tilted her head and blinked. The thought that she might be reconsidering her plan sparked hope in his heart.

"I'm not going to *see* him. I'm going to phone him, just to let him know that he ruined the bookstore."

Branson leaned across the table, prepared to plead. "If you like your job, you ought to give the café a chance. It might grow on you, just like the latte."

"Thanks for caring. . .really." JJ rested her cheek against her fisted hand and smiled. "But I don't think so."

"You can't determine much yet. The café has only been open a day." Branson watched for any sign that he was getting through to her. He was considered a skillful negotiator, even by his father's standards. But JJ showed no sign of budging. "What if you get the boss ticked off and you lose your job?"

JJ nodded. "I already considered that." Her voice was a mere whisper. "But if things don't improve drastically around here, I may quit anyway."

He was powerless to stop her. His heart sank with the realization. He had to do something to persuade her not to walk away from her job. He could tell by just the short amount of time he'd observed her work that she was a valuable asset to the company. He should've heeded Mike's warnings and not gone through with this impersonation thing. If he could speak to JJ as Branson Smythe, he was certain he could talk her into staying.

His only hope was to take her phone call Monday morning and pray she wouldn't recognize his voice.

"You're on," JJ said, pointing.

"Pardon?" Branson turned to see Kara waving him back up to the stage. He groaned. He wasn't up to singing right now, but he stood and grabbed his guitar. “See you later, JJ. I'm glad to have met you.”

She removed her glasses and smiled. Even after I ruined your phone? I still feel just awful about that." She shook her head.

"Ah, forget about the phone," Branson said, swiping his hand through the air as though he could dismiss her protests as he might wave off a pesky fly. "Thanks for sharing a cup of coffee with me."

JJ nodded. “Any time.”

He turned and walked toward the platform, prepared to do whatever it took to win over JJ Taylor.

Chapter 5

At one minute past three o'clock on Monday afternoon, JJ pushed through the bookstore's front glass doors and stepped past the bargain book tables and onto the busy sidewalk. She hiked her soft-sided briefcase, which doubled as her purse, up onto her shoulder. Even in midafternoon and broad daylight, she no longer dared leave work by way of the alley. There were simply too many weirdos hanging around the place these days—thanks to Branson Smythe's coffee-café brainchild. She shuddered and buried her hands in the pockets of her gray wool sweater.

Tilting her face into the brisk autumn breeze, she made her way toward the bus stop en route to her weekly visit with her mother at the Buckeye Towers Nursing Home. Every Monday for the past ten months, Kara had honored JJ's request not to schedule her for work after 3:00 p.m.—no questions asked. JJ had also been given Sundays off so she could attend church. She knew if she were forced to find another job, the chances of her next employer being so indulgent were slim. And another thought had been nagging at the back of her mind. Ethically, she couldn't allow the corporation to pay for her graduate degree if she up and quit so close to graduating. Yet, it would take her a lifetime to pay back Camden Corners for the cost of her education.

She could see a bus waiting for the light to change at the corner intersection, and she picked up her pace to beat the bus to the stop.

When she came within a few yards of her destination, JJ faltered in her footrace to the bus. There, leaning against the bus route signpost, stood one of the seedy characters who had spent all afternoon sprawled across an overstuffed chair in their café, reading a previous customer's deserted newspaper. He looked straight at her as if she had called out his name.

A chill feathered down her spine and into her extremities. The slouching man stood in desperate need of a haircut; his jeans and biker T-shirt bore that slept-in look. His rheumy-eyed stare held a repulsive glint.

Was this creep stalking her?

She shook her head to dislodge the farfetched worry. Her nerves were getting the best of her. She had to calm down. She couldn't keep on suspecting every casually dressed café customer of ill intent. Hadn't her encounter with David Smith reiterated the hazards of jumping to negative conclusions based on first impressions? Even so, a girl could never be too careful. If the store insisted on continuing with this coffeeshop fiasco, they ought to look into hiring a real, live security guard in addition to the video surveillance system they used. It would only take one violent crime perpetrated on the store premises to mire the corporation in bad press and, very possibly, costly civil litigation. Then, they would all be out of a job—from B. D. Smythe and his highfalutin son, Branson, on down.

JJ held back a few feet from the other passengers who waited to board the approaching bus. With squealing brakes, the lumbering vehicle pulled up alongside the curb, and its accordion doors swung open. The louse from the bookstore pushed himself away from his resting place and cast another long glance JJ's way before he climbed onto the bus. The huddle of other boarding riders filed in behind him. When all but JJ had embarked, the driver looked at her, his chin lowered and his eyebrows raised.

A sudden urge struck her to walk the mile or so to her mother's nursing home. She waved the driver off, and he nodded, then pulled the lever to close the doors. The bus seemed to sigh and groan when it eased back into traffic. As it passed, JJ's gaze again met that of the louse from the café. She frowned and swallowed hard against her flash-dried throat. Her tongue stuck to the roof of her mouth. She fisted her trembling hands as she crossed to the other side of Grant Avenue.

She determined then and there to petition—no, demand—that the store hire an in-house security guard. One who would see her to the bus stop if need be. She couldn't live with this kind of fear. She scribbled a mental note to add this new demand to her list of complaints she planned to raise with Branson Smythe—when she finally garnered the courage to phone him.

Yeah. Right. Who was she, JJ-the-Coward, trying to kid?

For all her bravado, she hadn't been able to carry through on her threats to call the head honcho of Camden Coffees.

During her lunch break, she'd made a halfhearted attempt to call his office, punching in all but the last digit of his phone number. But she'd chickened out and dropped the receiver back on its cradle as though it were burning her hand. The questions David had posed to her during her coerced latte sampling kept scrolling through her mind.

What would she do if she angered Mr. Smythe and he up and fired her on the spot? How could she manage if she couldn't find another job right away? She lived paycheck-to-paycheck as it was. She wouldn't manage as long as a month without income and still meet her financial obligations.

She had best restrain herself for the time being, even if it meant enduring a miserable work environment. At all costs, she would do whatever she could to avoid following in her parents' deadbeat footsteps, forced to take charity or apply for welfare.

For weeks after her mother's stroke, she dreaded seeing her. "Sherry Taylor is in a semivegetative state," Dr. Gordon had announced matter-of-factly, while Leo Barnes, her mom's live-in boyfriend, kept his glassy-eyed glare on a shapely nurse.

At first, JJ had to contend with her bottled-up anger—knowing her mother had committed slow suicide with drugs and alcohol. Her outrage produced guilt, then a mood of resigned hopelessness. She fought a continual battle between the reality of her mother's condition and her own belief in God's power and ability to change lives.

JJ had personally experienced the miracle of a fresh start when, as a college sophomore, she gave her life to Christ and accepted His forgiveness for her sins. Yet she also knew full well the devastating effects of free will when a person rejected the gift of eternal life offered to all who believe in Him. She'd seen how the wages of sin destroyed her parents' lives and brought death to her father. But as long as her mother still lived, JJ prayed she would have the opportunity to lead her to Christ.

JJ drew a breath of the crisp air and tuned her ears to the dry leaves scraping the pavement and crunching beneath her feet. She now looked forward to Mondays, despite Dr. Gordon's grim diagnosis. She'd grown to see beyond her mom's paralysis, to the attentive spark in her blue eyes. When JJ would give her mother updates on her life or read to her from the Bible, she believed, in her heart, her mother could hear her.

At the busy intersection, JJ waited in a sea of strangers for the traffic light to flash green. Her heart sped at the sight of the glass-tower building in the distance—home of the Camden corporate enterprises.

JJ hustled across the avenue, debating whether or not to enter Branson Smythe's domain and give him a piece of her mind. She slowed her steps, reached the building's dark glass doors, and halted. Before she could talk herself out of it, and while the strength of her convictions heated her face, JJ pushed through the revolving door.

In a sweeping glance, she took in the magnificent lobby, tiled floor-to-ceiling in dazzling white marble. It had been a couple of years since she'd come here to leave a package with security, but nothing had changed in the interim. She was, again, captivated to the core and wanted more than ever to be a part of this bustling scene.

The stability of a job at Camden Corners' Corp is what she'd strived for all these years. Each of her carefully plotted steps brought her closer to a professional position within the company headquarters—and further from her unstable past.

She had almost allowed anger to pervert her judgment and wreck her best opportunity for a financially secure future. But she would not allow the café, the damaged merchandise, or even a potential stalker to offset her dreams.

JJ crossed the lobby and caught the eye of a stooped security guard, standing behind a wooden podium.

The man nodded her way, and she meandered over to him, still not knowing exactly what she would say to Branson Smythe if she got in to see him. Maybe she would merely suggest Mr. Smythe ensure his employees' safety by hiring a security guard in the café during evening hours. Nothing threatening or accusing. Just a simple request.

"Hi. I'm JJ Taylor, and I'm here to see Branson Smythe." Her voice warbled, but the guard wagged his head. Her nails bit into her palms as she waited for an explanation.

"Did you have an appointment?" he asked.

"Not really, but—"

"I figured." He winked, then pointed to the doors. "Mr. Smythe left about an hour ago."

JJ nodded. "Thanks. Thanks, anyway." She pivoted and fast-walked straight ahead.

Once outside, she realized her legs were shaking. She stared, unseeing, at a shadow box window display of bestsellers, trying to gather her wits. What if Branson Smythe had been in his office? Would she have had the courage to follow through on her plans? Though she'd never met him, she had a strong mental impression of the hotshot young exec—sitting on the edge of his desk, looking down his aristocratic nose at her, and wearing a grin of disdain. She'd heard he was an only child, and she couldn't even fathom his pampered, privileged youth. The café was probably just another of his toys, soon to be forgotten when the next big moneymaking scheme came along. Perhaps she'd do well to bide her time.

She walked away from the corporate headquarters and down the busy sidewalk. Her breathing slowed to somewhat normal, and the clothes in a boutique window drew her attention. *What a stunning dress!* She never wore red, but she wished she had a special occasion to attend for an excuse to buy this gown. JJ wandered into the store, if only to determine if the fabric felt as silky as it looked on the mannequin. She stood at the rack, then ran her hand down the tea length garment, to the price tag. She stared long and hard before she realized the dress wasn't seventy dollars but seven hundred.

"May I help you?"

JJ shook her head and smiled. "Just looking."

"Let me see—" With squinted eyes and a strand of her dyed-black hair swooping over her forehead, the saleswoman tilted her head. Even standing several feet away, JJ could taste the woman's perfume at the back of her throat.

"You must be a four, correct? Perhaps a six?" the clerk asked in an elegant French accent.

What was she doing in here? "Usually a four, but I can't take the time to try it on today. I've got to leave. . .now." She felt like Little Red Riding Hood, who'd made one too many stops on her way to Granny's house.

While the saleslady was still speaking, JJ hastened to the

door. Her visit with her mom would be a respite from this chaos.

JJ entered the nursing home, crept past the unattended desk on the first floor, and continued down the long corridor toward her mother's room. At this time of day, there were rarely any visitors, but the eerie silence sent a shudder up her spine.

She'd learned the majority of patients didn't get visitors, and she'd often stop in their rooms to try to cheer them up. But not today.

Today she would sprinkle her mom's bed with lavender talcum powder, and while she brushed her thinning hair, she'd tell her all about the crazy musician she'd met at the café.

JJ smiled. Despite her parents' messed-up lives, they had obviously been in love with one another. Her mom would get a kick out of hearing that David was good-looking and charming like her dad, even though her dad never used to bother with appearances as far as his clothing was concerned any more than David did now.

The door to her mother's room was closed.

"Strange," JJ whispered, but there was no need for her to go dizzy with panic.

She wrapped her fingers around the knob and told herself she'd see her mom when she opened the door. Same as every Monday.

A sorrowful moan echoed through the corridor. With her hand pressed to her hammering heart, JJ spun around, but saw no one.

She turned back to the door and pushed it open.

Frozen in the entryway, she fought for breaths. Her briefcase slipped from her fingers and crashed to the floor.

She stared at the stripped mattress, curled over the rusted bedsprings, and willed strength into her limbs. In a flash, she was at the dresser, yanking open each and every drawer.

Empty.

JJ pressed her hands to her head and slid to the floor. "No, Mommy. . .no!"

Chapter 6

From his window seat in the gym's health bar, Branson witnessed his nightmare come true—and was powerless to do anything to stop it.

He watched JJ pass through Camden's doors and into the lobby, and his heart sank. She would slip past Walter, the elderly guard, undetected, and he'd be found out. He'd desperately wanted the chance to explain to her why he'd played the David role, but now—

"What's up with you?" Mike shoveled the last of his spinach salad onto his fork. "Seriously, you're out of it today."

Branson shook his head. "I just saw JJ go into my building."

"Ouch." Mike rested his fork on the plate and stared. "I'm sorry on two counts, but mostly because you like her so much," he said without inflection.

Branson's denial died on his tongue. JJ was all he'd talked about before, during, and after their racquetball game today, and Mike had been only too eager to point that out to him.

Mike wagged his head. "I knew there'd be ramifications."

"Shh." Branson saw JJ come out of the building, and relief

washed through him. "She didn't get past Walter after all."

Mike swiveled in his seat. "Which one is she?"

"Gray sweater, dark hair, black-rimmed glasses, standing in front of Lorette's Boutique." Branson pushed aside his plate of untouched tuna wrap and smiled. He had to force himself not to rush out the gym door, cross the street, and confess his true identity. And *if* JJ forgave him, he would ask her out.

"Aha, I see." Mike turned back to him, grinning. "Attractive. Very pretty." He cleared his throat and sobered. "But how much do you know about her?"

Next to nothing. "I know she's been working at the bookstore for three years. According to Kara, JJ needs only to finish her master's project or thesis and she'll have her M.B.A. She's a hard worker." He also knew she cut out early every Monday, but since it raised his own suspicions, he could only imagine what Mike would make of it.

Mike looked at his wristwatch. "It's nearly three thirty. Why isn't she at work now?"

But of course he would ask. Branson shrugged. "Folks might ask the same thing about you and me." He laughed and waved Mike off before he could lodge a protest. "I know what you're thinking. A gal in her position doesn't have the luxury of setting her own schedule. All I know is that she takes off every Monday at three o'clock. Kara doesn't know the reason why. Just that JJ has what she calls a 'standing appointment.' "

Mike released a long, low whistle, then rested his back against the chair. "Bear with me a minute, but what if she's seeing a married man?"

"Are you nuts?" Branson pushed back from the table. "JJ's

not that kind of woman. I can tell." But he had toyed with the idea that JJ had a boyfriend, or worse, a fiancé.

"Know her family background?"

Branson bristled. "I knew all there was to know about Heidi's family background. My father even had the chutzpah to run a security clearance, unbeknownst to either me or Heidi. A lot of good that did me."

Mike clucked his tongue. "You haven't answered my question."

While forming a response, he watched JJ enter the boutique. "Nope, I know nothing about her family, and neither does Kara. So sue me." He laughed.

"A man in your position had better know the facts, Smythe."

Branson waved his hand. "You're always in lawyer mode. Give it a rest, will ya?" He signaled the waitress over and requested the check.

"I'll pay, you go ahead." Mike glanced around before speaking again. "Call me paranoid, but I suggest you follow her."

Branson stood and tossed his napkin on the table. "You *are* paranoid, but I've got to get back to work. Thanks for the game and for lunch."

He strode to the front door and waited until JJ was a safe distance from the boutique before he exited the gym. As much as he'd scoffed at Mike's suggestion, he stood motionless, watching JJ, and fighting an overwhelming temptation to follow her.

Branson shivered. What was he thinking? He had to get back to the office. Moonlighting as a musician had taken its toll. He'd be buried in work up to his eyeballs if he continued to spread himself too thin.

He stepped off the curb and looked to his left, checking for traffic. But what snagged his attention was his ex-wife, striding up Grant Avenue like she owned it.

Branson drew his hood up over his head, sprinted across the street, and headed into the boutique for cover. Ever since he was a kid, he'd been dodging into Miss L's store where she'd sneak him candy from the glass bowl on her desk. But today, he wanted only to avoid Heidi.

Branson pushed his sweatshirt hood away from his head when he stepped inside.

"Bran-sone!" she screeched in her French accent. She stood gaping at him with her hand pressed to her throat. "You nearly give me a heart attack."

"Sorry, ma'am." He glanced over his shoulder.

"What? Somebody is following you?"

Perish the thought. Branson shook his head. "A little while ago, a woman came in here." Ignoring her suspicious frown, he smiled. "Very pretty with dark hair and eyeglasses. Do you remember her?"

Miss L rolled her eyes. "I certainly do. She was looking at zat dress," she said, pointing. "Then she scampers out of here like a scared rabbit."

"Is that you, Branson?"

He didn't need to look to recognize the throaty voice of his ex-wife, Heidi.

"I'll take the dress," Branson said before turning. "Hello, Heidi, how are you?"

Neither woman acknowledged the other, though he wasn't surprised. He had introduced Heidi to Miss L after their engagement, and while Heidi had tried on clothing, Miss L grabbed his arm and whispered, "Mistake, Bran-sone. Big mistake." How he wished he would've heeded the woman's advice instead of his father's.

Heidi tucked her bottom lip under a perfect row of veneers—on which he'd spent a small fortune. "I just knew it was you, you handsome creature." Her gaze slipped to the dress Miss L was holding. "Ooh, somebody's got expensive taste." She punctuated with a sarcastic laugh.

"Wrap it up, will you?" Branson said.

Always quick on the uptake, Miss L smiled. "For you, Bran-sone, anything." She winked. "Your lady friend is size four, yes? Very beautiful." She floated off, leaving a cloud of flowery perfume in her wake.

Heidi's brows lifted. "A bit loud, isn't it?"

"Loud?"

Heidi groaned and glanced around as though she had an audience, or wished for one. "You know, the dress? Someone must be looking for attention."

He'd been too intent on avoiding his ex to compare the ultraconservative JJ with the sultry red dress. "She's not an attention seeker, if that's what you're getting at," he countered, instantly regretting his denial. He certainly didn't owe Heidi any explanations. Though what he knew about JJ he could fit into a thimble. Maybe she had a flashy alter ego when she was off the time clock.

"No matter." Heidi clamped her bony fingers around his

wrist. "How about a drink?"

"You know I gave up drinking when I became a Christian. . . ." He found himself comparing the look in her blue eyes with JJ's. While JJ was guarded, Heidi was crafty. How had he missed all the cues before Heidi marched down St. Mark's aisle toward him?

"Ah, well, I thought you might be over that goody-two-shoes kick by now." With a jerk of her head, Heidi flipped her long bleached hair over her shoulder. "You know, if you had paid as much attention to me as you do that religion of yours, we might still be married. You're way too young to be such a stuffed shirt."

Branson shook off the insult, determined not to let it get to him. He knew in his heart he had done all he could to save their marriage. It was Heidi who refused to work on salvaging their relationship. When Branson put his foot down and refused to throw money at her sinful pursuits, she turned her attentions to an easy mark with a bank account sufficient to cover her expensive tastes—his ex-best friend and former drinking buddy, Paul Wirth. "Someday you'll learn that the joys of faith, friends, and family far outweigh the fast-lane living and party life you're so fond of now. Until then, I'll keep praying for you." Branson knew from experience there was no use trying to convince Heidi of her need for salvation. He had to trust the Holy Spirit to work in her life.

"So, how are things going with you and Paul?"

She released his wrist and sighed. "I think I made a big mistake, Branson."

He felt nothing but pity for this woman who had, once

upon a time, been his precious wife—not only his marriage partner but also the love of his life. He had been willing to forgive her adulterous affair, had offered to start over again, but Heidi persisted in going through with the divorce, claiming she and Paul were soul mates. Branson drew a breath and averted his gaze. He couldn't bring himself to express condolences that her affair didn't result in happily ever after.

"That's rough, Heidi."

"Bran-sone?" Miss L stepped between them and handed him the lavender shopping bag.

"Oh." Branson reached into his back pocket for his wallet.

Miss L raised her hand. "You pay me later." She lowered her lids and sashayed toward the register.

Heidi sidled up to him, looped her arm through his, and smiled. Every muscle in his body tensed.

Branson slid his arm from her grip. "I really need to get going. . . ."

Heidi tilted her head. It was the look she used when she wanted to convince him to do something he didn't want to do. "Branson, can you spare me just a few minutes? I really need to talk."

No. He wasn't angry anymore—but he could never trust Heidi again. He'd forgiven her, but there was nothing more to discuss between the two of them. Branson shook his head. "Sorry, Heidi, I'm not the one you should be talking to anymore. That's Paul's role now. And I really do have to go."

She snorted a laugh. "What was I thinking? I've got better things to do myself than share my troubles with you." Heidi turned on her heel and proceeded out the door, leaving him with a profound sense of sadness.

He'd bought the red dress only to wound Heidi. Not a very Christlike thing to do. Branson looked over his shoulder at Miss L, who was eyeing him intently. "Will you put the dress on hold for me until tomorrow? I'm not sure that—"

"I understand," Miss L said quickly.

"Thanks." Branson waved. He left the store wondering if he could ever trust another woman after Heidi's betrayal.

But JJ was different. She had no idea who he actually was, and if she liked him as David, it meant she had no ulterior motives. Although, a couple of smiles from JJ did not a relationship make.

He had just stepped onto the elevator when his new cell phone began to vibrate and buzz on its belt clip. He unhooked the phone from the clip and glanced at the number of the incoming call before punching the CONNECT button. "Dad? I'm in an elevator. If I lose the signal, I'll call you right back." He was tempted to pray for a dropped call. Why had he rushed right out and replaced his latte-soaked smart phone?

"Where have you been?"

Branson exited the elevator and padded past his secretary, over the red carpet to his office. "What's up, Dad?"

"I'm about ready to crawl under the covers."

"Bed?" Branson scowled, then remembered the time difference.

Static crackled over the line, but his father's message came through loud, clear, and demanding. "I want the stats on the café," he shouted, "before I go to bed."

Branson dropped into his black leather chair and summoned

a confident voice. "I was tied up all morning with coffee bean distributors. But I'll work on getting the sales figures for you right away."

"I'll call you back in half an hour." B. D. grumbled something else, which Branson couldn't make out, then disconnected the call.

Heidi created one kind of anxiety in him, and B. D. another. Even Mike, as well meaning as he was, had him wary about JJ.

Branson dialed the bookstore and was relieved when Kara answered. Along with the sales figures for the café, he asked her to fax him JJ's employment file. Perhaps he'd glean something of importance from JJ's records.

"I don't have all the café's stats yet," Kara said. "But I can fax you JJ's file. . .if you really want it."

He ignored the censure in Kara's voice. "Yes, fax it over, please." Branson cleared his throat. "And I'll be in later to go over the sales figures with you."

His father wouldn't be happy to learn about the delay in sending him the café's stats. Maybe he could maneuver another phone-meets-latte accident before B. D. returned his call. The thought made Branson smile as he pictured JJ sipping her mug of penance. She was one sweet gal. Not at all a tiger-woman like Heidi.

Within minutes, he watched the pages of JJ's employment records feeding through the fax machine. He dropped the pages into a file folder and paced the office, tapping the palm of his hand with the spine of the file.

What did he think he was doing? He paused and stared at the folder, then continued to pace. If he didn't trust JJ, or any other woman, he should simply employ the option of steering clear of relationships. Jesus said, "Do unto others as you would have them do unto you." Would he want someone snooping in his records, investigating him without permission?

Branson shook his head, then crossed the room to the paper shredder. *When in doubt, take the high road.*

After the machine chewed up all evidence of JJ's file, Branson nodded. *Thank You for Your wisdom, Lord.*

JJ sat in Dr. Gordon's office, her body still quaking. "Nobody phoned to let me know my mother had been moved to another room."

"Sorry, the order to call you must have gotten lost somewhere along the chain of command." Dr. Gordon glanced up from the chart on his desk and pulled off his glasses. He didn't look a bit repentant for scaring the daylights out of her. "You should be relieved, at least there's some hope."

Hope. Her harried discussion with Dr. Schiff had left her with more questions than answers. JJ scooted to the edge of her seat. "These treatments are experimental. Is there any chance my mom's condition will get worse instead of better?"

"Let's put it this way." Dr. Gordon ran his hand over his balding head, and she got the disturbing impression that he was stalling for time. "Without these treatments, there's no chance your mother's condition will ever improve."

JJ clasped her hands on her lap. If only she had a sibling or her father were still alive. She desperately needed someone to help her shoulder the burden of this decision. David and his reassuring smile popped into her mind unbidden. She might even break her code of silence, tell him about her sick mom—that and nothing more—and ask his opinion.

But she was sitting here alone, and there was no sense dreaming of a rescuer. JJ sent up a silent plea to God for wisdom. She waited for His peace to come in before nodding. "All right then. How much will the treatments cost?"

Dr. Gordon released an audible breath. "That's the downside to this treatment. Since it's an experimental program, Medicaid won't cover the costs of the meds. I'd say you're looking at ten thousand or so of out-of-pocket expense."

She felt like the oxygen had been sucked out of the room. Where would she get that kind of money? If Kara would let her work extra shifts, even some nights in the café, she might be able to eek out a hundred dollars a week or so to put toward the expense, but she'd be paying down the balance for years to come. And that was assuming they'd let her pay it out over time. If not, she would have to decline the experimental treatments. She couldn't live with herself if she didn't allow them to at least try to help her mom.

She'd have to rely on the Lord to provide, as He had always provided for her needs up till now. JJ stood. "I don't know how, but I'll figure out some way to cover the expense."

With his hand outstretched, Dr. Gordon got to his feet. "Hey, you never know, your mother might get well enough for you to take her home."

Chapter 7

Branson sat shoulder-to-shoulder beside Kara in her cramped office in the inventory room.

"I'm giving my notice," he announced.

Kara grinned. "What?"

"Seriously. I can't play at the café anymore. The idea wasn't one of my brightest to begin with."

He had to get back to his office full-time lest the work on his desk spill into the hallways. Then there was JJ, who'd awakened in him a desire to pursue at least a friendship with her. One based on total honesty. "We'll hire a real musician this time."

"Um, not good. Take it from someone who frequents clubs and coffeehouses. My friends and I expect to see the singer or group billed when we walk in. And all week long, customers have been coming in asking for *you.*" Kara slid the folder on the desk closer to him. "These are the sales stats you asked for."

"Thanks." Branson tapped his fingers on the file and summoned a casual tone. "So, what do you think JJ will say when she finds out who I really am?"

Kara shook her head. "Maybe you ought to hold off telling her for at least a couple of days."

The idea of delaying the inevitable appealed to him. Branson flipped open the file. "Why's that?"

Kara glanced over her shoulder before meeting his gaze again. "JJ came in here this morning really shaken up, you know?"

A pang of guilt hit. Perhaps JJ already suspected him of trying to dupe her. "Upset? About what?"

Kara's mouth turned down in a sympathetic frown. "She said she needed money for a medical procedure and asked me to give her extra hours."

A spasm of worry tightened his stomach. He eyed Kara, awaiting the details, but quickly lost patience. "What? Is JJ sick?"

"Sorry." Kara shrugged. "She didn't say. But I tried to alleviate some of her worry by telling her about the hourly pay raise."

"You didn't let on that Branson Smythe was behind it, did you?"

"No, of course not." Kara sighed. "It's your call, but I sense this isn't the best time to break your news to JJ."

"A medical procedure," Branson muttered. "Well, give JJ the extra hours. I don't care if it means we're overstaffed."

Kara patted his arm. "You've always been a great boss, Branson. I love reporting directly to you instead of—"

"My dad?" Branson shook his head. He would like to have been able to defend his father, but who knew better than he that B. D. was a hard taskmaster who ruled with an iron fist? B. D. was a great believer in negative reinforcement.

"Anyway, it ends up that I gave JJ a few evening shifts because we needed her." Kara gave him a sly grin. "You really like JJ, don't you?"

So much for not wearing his heart on his sleeve. Without comment, Branson returned his attention to the stats, determined to talk with JJ as soon as he finished up. He studied the figures with a combination of elation and dread. "Sales in the bookstore and the café nearly doubled the nights I played."

"Yeah, I know." Kara cleared her throat. "That's what I was trying to tell you. We promised the customers a month of David Smith. They really enjoy your music. Besides, a lot of them have been asking if you'll play weeknights, too."

Branson sighed. "Great." He could fax the sales figures to his father now or stall for time, play a couple of nights during the week, and present B. D. with even more promising results later in the week. He closed the folder and got to his feet. "Hold off faxing these to my father, okay?"

"Sure." Kara stood. "Are you going to tell JJ you're you-know-who?"

Kara's exaggerated effort at espionage made him laugh. "I don't know." Branson reached for the doorknob and hesitated. If JJ needed money, he could send it to her anonymously. But if he revealed his true identity, she'd know right off he was the donor and ultimately refuse his help. "No, I'd better wait on that."

"Good idea." Kara smiled. "And are you still going to quit?"

He had to give Camden Coffees his best shot. Branson shook his head. "My father won't be returning till mid-November." He winked to cover his trepidation. "Book me up till then, and we'll add a couple of weeknights to my *gig*."

Kara laughed. "Cool."

Branson exited the office feeling anything but cool and walked through the bookstore in search of JJ. He'd never intended to weave such a tangled web, but his situation was growing more complicated by the day. He should've heeded Mike's logical advice.

He caught sight of JJ, sitting alone at a table in the café, her chin resting on her hand. It hit him that he'd be devastated if the medical procedure entailed a serious issue with her health. The salad sitting on the table in front of her looked untouched. Branson sent up a silent prayer for her health and meandered over to her table, resolving to get the truth from her. "May I join you?"

JJ looked up at him as though he'd awoken her from a dream. "Oh. . .David. Hi." Her welcoming smile warmed his heart. "Sure, have a seat," she said.

"Thanks." Branson settled into a chair, then scooted closer to her. "So, JJ, how's it going? Everything good? You feeling all right?" His gaze went to the salad. "Is that your lunch?"

JJ laughed. "Yes, I'm feeling fine. And, yes, this is my lunch."

"Well, you haven't eaten any of it." Branson swiped the plastic fork off the table, then removed its wrapper. "Don't let me stop you."

Shaking her head, she took the fork from him. "Okay, what's this all about?"

He searched his mind for words that wouldn't betray what Kara had told him. "I'm going to be playing at the café a couple of weeknights now."

"Congratulations, David." JJ pushed the salad around the plate. "I'll be working Tuesday, Wednesday, and Thursday nights myself starting this week."

Branson made a mental note to play on those particular nights. "You're going to work three nights, in addition to being here six days a week?"

JJ forked salad into her mouth, held up her hand, and nodded. "I have to do it. I really need the—"

"Money?" Branson searched her face as if the answers were written there. "Because I can lend you some."

"Absolutely not!" JJ shook her head adamantly. "How could you afford. . . I mean, I wouldn't think of it, but I appreciate your offer. Truly, I do. I'm sure if I work as if everything depends on me and pray as if everything depends on God, the Lord will provide for us somehow."

Branson clamped his hands so tight his knuckles cracked. "Did you get a rent increase or something?"

JJ set down her fork and shook her head. "I may as well tell you." She looked directly into his eyes and a long silence ensued. The exchange told him his heart was in trouble. Deep trouble.

"It's my mother," JJ finally whispered. "She's sick."

Instinctively, Branson reached across the table and held her hands. "I'm so sorry to hear that, JJ. What happened?"

At least an hour had gone by since she'd spoken to David, and her mind was still reeling. Trying to sort out her scattered emotions, JJ sank onto a step stool and continued shelving books. She had never been one to share her private affairs and concerns with others, not even with her church friends, yet she'd practically poured out her life history to David. And he hadn't judged her.

She'd spent years trying to run from her past for fear of rejection, but when she finally told it all, the worst had not happened. In fact, far from it.

David had totally disarmed her when he offered to loan her money. Poor guy. She'd always suspected that the "marketing research day job" he referred to amounted to nothing more than telemarketing for a fly-by-night mortgage company. He couldn't be earning more than minimum wage at that. He probably couldn't pay his own bills. But the compassion in his dark brown eyes had melted her heart and prompted her to bare her soul. She'd felt the peace of God—as though the Lord Himself had given her permission to pour out her feelings to David.

Her throat choked with gratitude at David's offer to accompany her on her next visit to the nursing home. Never in her life had she met anyone as kind and caring. Though, she had to admit, she'd never given anyone else much of an opportunity to help her. She worked hard to keep up a good front and allowed others to see her only as a strong, independent woman.

JJ sighed and meandered down the bookstore aisle. Though she could manage alone, she was sick of pretending she didn't want a strong shoulder to lean on. Yes, she could turn to her heavenly Father for strength and comfort. And she did. Often. But when David—a flesh-and-blood man—had wrapped his warm hands around hers, a sensation swept over her that, until that moment, she had never felt before. She felt safe. Protected. Secure. She didn't want him to let go—not ever. For years she'd shunned her deepest desire to be loved and cherished by a man, judging her need as a sign of weakness.

But she was tired of pretending. And until today, she dared not put a name to what stirred in her heart.

She wanted a husband—a man to whom she could give her heart.

JJ closed her eyes. *Oh, Lord, please help me. I don't want to have these feelings for David.* The silent confession made her face burn.

Chapter 8

A few minutes before 3:00 p.m., Branson pulled up in front of the bookstore in the Rent-a-Wreck car he had rented for the day. He'd thought he was oh-so-smart to come up with the idea of driving up to meet JJ in this clunker of a sedan—until he couldn't locate the switch to turn on the windshield wipers.

He had to get them working before JJ came out of Camden Corners. Then again, maybe he should confess everything today and be done with the charade. But the thought of living without JJ as a part of his days left him feeling cold and empty. There had to be a way he could break the news of his identity to her without JJ feeling as though she'd been betrayed. Now that he'd gained JJ's trust and she had confided in him about her family history, she would loathe him all the more when he broke the news that he was Branson Smythe. She had revealed her heart's innermost secrets to her boss, as far as JJ was concerned—the man whom JJ referred to as the "hotshot exec" of Camden Coffees. If he told her now that he was Branson, he didn't have a prayer that she would allow him into her life.

While sneaking peeks at the store, Branson managed to get the hazard lights blinking and interior lights on, plus a flashing blue light that indicated the brights were activated. The vehicle looked like a Christmas tree, but still no wipers.

Casting another quick glance at the store's glass doors, he yanked open the glove compartment and sifted through a pile of oil-change receipts in search of the car's owner's manual. Just when he felt the vinyl cover of the sought-after book, he saw JJ exit the store and pop open her umbrella.

Branson leaned on the car horn. At first she squinted at him with a confused frown. He hadn't told her he'd be here today, so she couldn't very well be expected to recognize him right away. When, at last, the light of recognition gleamed in her eyes, she dashed over to the car, smiling.

Branson rolled down the window. "Get in," he said.

JJ shook her head. "I'm heading to the nursing home now."

"I know." Branson pointed to the passenger seat. "I'm going with you."

JJ opened her mouth, closed it, and then nodded.

Branson quickly resumed his search for the switch to turn on the wiper blades while JJ came around the front of the car. Still no luck, and he couldn't see a thing through the muddy windshield.

JJ closed the car door and sighed. "Thanks, David."

"You're welcome." He looked over at her and shrugged. "I can never remember where to find the switch for the wipers in this car."

"Really?" JJ slid closer to him and squinted at the dash. She punched a black button, bringing the wipers to life. "I guess you've got more important things floating around in that head of yours," she said, sending a curious glance his way. "My mom used to have a car just like this one, back in the day when she still drove."

"Um. Thanks." Branson managed a smile and searched his mind for a change of topic. "How's your mother doing since the treatments?"

"It's only been three weeks." JJ rubbed her hands together and sighed. "I don't want to set my expectations too high, but I'm thrilled with the latest news. The doctor called last night and said my mother's able to respond to questions. She blinks to indicate yes or no."

Stopped at the red light, Branson looked over at her smiling face. "That's positively awesome, JJ. God is so good."

"Yes, He is." JJ gave him a lingering look.

Lost in her dark blue gaze, only the honking behind him told him the light had changed. He returned his attention to the road, then stepped on the accelerator.

They continued in silence on the short drive to the nursing home, save the ruckus going on in his head. He'd come up with ten different scenarios on how he could initiate a kiss with JJ, but before he mustered the boldness to carry out his plans, they were walking toward her mother's room.

Dr. Schiff had asked that JJ come to his office after her visit with her mom. She padded down the long corridor with David at her side. "You don't have to come in to see the doctor if you don't want to."

"I don't mind at all," David said.

JJ nodded. She'd come to rely on David so quickly. Too quickly? Even her mom's crooked smile told her she approved of David. What if things started to unravel between them? The passing thought soured her stomach. Before she could ponder the worst, they were venturing into Dr. Schiff's office.

"Sit down, please," the doctor offered.

They both dropped into the chairs in front of his desk. JJ smiled. "Doctor, I have to thank you for all you're doing for my mother. I can't believe she's able to respond to my questions with yes and no." JJ's heart grew so full, she thought she might cry.

Dr. Schiff smiled. "Well then, I'm glad you're sitting. I've got even more great news for the two of you."

JJ felt her face warm at the suggestion that they were a couple. She glanced at David, and he winked at her. She bit back a smile and refocused her attention on Dr. Schiff. "More good news?"

The doctor held out a sheet of paper. "Take a look at this."

JJ took the page from him and held it so that David could see, too. Why the doctor had given her a photocopied invoice and receipt in the amount of ten thousand dollars was a mystery. She first looked at David, who was scrubbing his hand over his jawline; then she lifted her gaze to the doctor and frowned. "I don't understand."

Dr. Schiff pointed. "That donation came to us anonymously, on behalf of your mother."

JJ gasped. "That's impossible. We don't know anybody

with that kind of money." She looked at David, but he was busy inspecting his fingernails. "Does the money go toward my mom's treatments? I don't understand."

"Yes." Dr. Schiff smiled. "The donor indicated that if these funds aren't enough to cover your mother's treatments, we are to send the bills to a certain P.O. Box, and they'll see that the balance is paid."

JJ closed her eyes. "Oh my. Who would be so kind to have. . ." She turned and saw David standing near the door with his hands in his pockets, staring at the floor.

"I'm sorry for keeping you, David."

"No problem," David said, but he glanced at his wristwatch, and JJ got to her feet.

Chapter 9

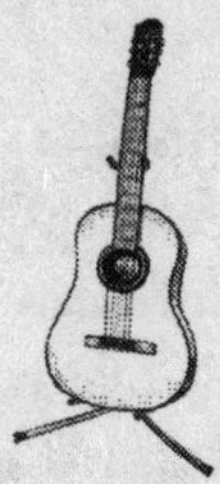

JJ dug a tunnel in the whipped cream of her peppermint mocha and took a sip. The hot drink burned the back of her throat as it went down, but the pain didn't compare to the ache in her heart. Just when she had acquired a taste for the hot drink, her standing coffee dates with David were coming to an end.

Tomorrow would be David's last night as the featured musician at Camden Corners Café.

She looked up at David on stage, singing his gentle ballad. The sight of him, even in his ragged tie-dyed T-shirt, couldn't diminish her smile or the love for him she felt flowing from her heart. No, he hadn't met her expectations of the ideal man when they'd first met. Far from it. In fact, he'd embodied the antithesis of all she dreamed her true love would be. But the more she came to know him, the more he'd proven her preconceived notions wrong.

He had broken through her defenses, shattered her prejudices against musicians and their ilk. And, if she was serious about following through with this crazy idea, it was now or never.

Last night, after tossing and turning, wide awake, in her bed for hours on end, she'd finally thrown back the covers and started pacing and praying. The day she'd dreaded for weeks now loomed on the horizon. She had to find a way to keep David in her life.

Amid this midnight turmoil, a song to her beloved welled from the depths of her soul and spilled onto a blank page. Her fingers raced to transcribe the lyrics of her heart's cry.

The ability to play music by ear, a dormant talent she had inherited from her father, returned as naturally as a long-abandoned skill of bike riding. She had dusted off and tuned the relic of her dad's guitar. Then she closed her eyes and sang her new song to David as though he were right beside her.

But now—now she was in the café. Not alone in her apartment. Where would she find the courage to get on stage in front of the customers and staff to dedicate her song to the man with whom she had fallen madly in love?

JJ retrieved the paper from the pocket of her blazer and unfolded it. Her hands perspired and bled the ink from the red marker across the page, blurring the lyrics. Tonight, if she could make it up on stage without collapsing, she would tell David with her song. . .

I love you.

David hopped down from the platform, his guitar slung over his broad shoulders, and made his way toward her.

JJ uttered a silent plea for mercy. *Lord, please help me.* She struggled out of her chair on wobbly legs and managed a smile.

"What's up?" David ran his gaze over her face, frowned, and then patted her cheek. "Hey, you all right?"

She desperately wanted to ask, "Should I risk this? Do you love me, David?" Maybe she'd be better off to ask him outright and forgo the embarrassment of singing it in front of a crowd.

"I'm fine." JJ clasped her hands and cleared her throat. "You won't believe this, but. . ." She swallowed past the sudden dryness in her throat. "I have a song I want to sing." She looked into his contemplative dark eyes, and heat seared her face.

"You?" David dipped his chin in question. He must've read the stark terror on her face, because he slipped his guitar off his shoulder without missing a beat. "What? Right now?"

Now or never. JJ nodded.

David held the guitar out to her. "Well, then. Go for it, JJ."

Surely his nonchalance proved he had no inkling of her intent. JJ locked her knees lest her legs buckle. She still had time to back out, tell him she was kidding. But her hands reached for the guitar as if of their own accord. The instrument felt double its normal weight. Trembling, she looked over David's shoulder to the exit and saw herself pushing through the doors. But if she bolted now, she'd never stop running. "Will you stay and listen?"

David winked and without preamble pressed his lips to the corner of her mouth. His tender kiss emboldened her. "I wouldn't miss this for the world."

Her heart hammered wildly, but she told herself that David's kiss must be a sign that she should go through with this madness.

JJ turned and made her way to the platform. The sound of muttering and clanking dishes filled her ears as she mounted the stool. She strummed a few chords, testing her ability to make music in front of the crowd. She still wanted to bolt. But she leaned toward the mike. "Good evening, everyone, my name is JJ Taylor."

Her erratic pulse drummed in her ears as the café grew quieter by degrees. Under the gawking scrutiny of the onlookers, she felt like an accident victim. For what seemed an eternity, she stared out into the sea of faces, her mouth refusing to work.

JJ shifted on the stool and looked directly at David. From his seat at a table on her far left, he gave her a thumbs-up and a smile, and she knew it would be all right.

"Um." JJ coughed. "I—I wrote this song. . .last night." She strummed the melody. "And I want to dedicate this to a special friend. I'm sure he'll know who he is."

JJ looked at David again, and the lyrics, meant only for him, journeyed from her heart to her lips.

"I've been rehearsing all my life how not to love you. . . ."

David's smiled faded. His dark brows pulled together.

JJ forced herself to go on. "And when you walked into my world, I built a fortress 'round my heart."

David stared at her intently. Goose bumps rippled over her skin.

"But you showed me love, and my defenses crumbled."

The silence in the café was deafening. David was looking down, shaking his head. Her heart plummeted.

JJ closed her eyes. "But I must confess—I love you more each passing day. . . ."

She opened her eyes to see David. Writing. His head bent

over the table. What could he possibly be writing at a time like this?

JJ ignored the tidal wave of doubt threatening to take her under and continued to profess her love for David with her foolish song.

The familiar faces in the café swam in her blurred vision.

Kara, her hand pressed to her cheek, averted her gaze. Wide-eyed Minnie stood with her mouth ajar.

She trained her gaze to her hands as she strummed the chords of "David's Song" on his guitar. But when she looked up again, hoping to find courage, confirmation, in his eyes. . . he was gone, his place at the table empty.

A frantic scan of the store proved fruitless.

Despite the familiar faces, she'd never felt more alone in her life.

And she would never be able to face David again.

Chapter 10

Branson sat in his car in the Camden Corners Books' parking lot, working up the nerve to come clean with JJ. A blanket of snow had accumulated on the windshield, but he still hadn't thought of a nice way to admit he'd deceived her.

Father, forgive me.

Branson pounded the steering wheel with the heels of his hands. If only he'd sought God's approval instead of B. D.'s, none of this would've happened.

What do I do now, Lord?

The results of his ruse had caught up with him—hit him in the face with brutal force. Of all the idiotic things he'd done to prove he was a somebody apart from his father, role-playing the part of David had been his most pathetic.

JJ would feel betrayed when he confessed his lie to her. Just when he was willing to take a chance on love again, he would lose the one woman he knew, in his heart, was the only woman in the world for him.

A cold knot formed in the pit of his stomach. JJ already

perceived Branson Smythe as the "spoiled rich kid" who'd ruined the bookstore with his trendy café. Now he would add to JJ's list of Branson–inflicted crimes that of his masquerading as David.

After all he'd done to break through JJ's defenses, to win her love, he had wiped out his progress in one fell swoop. It must've taken everything for shy JJ to get up there and sing her beautiful song. Her voice, the lyrics, sank so deeply into his heart he couldn't bear to look her in the eye. He'd run from her last night, acting the coward as he tried to explain his departure in a note he'd hastily scribbled on a napkin and left with Kara to deliver to JJ.

She would never love him—not him as the Branson she despised. JJ's song was meant for David-the-musician. Not Branson–the–fraud. Branson tugged at the knot in his tie and sighed. Yes, it was David she loved.

But if somehow he could get her to see beyond his name to the man she'd grown to love in the past two months, she would realize that even minus the ragged clothes, he was more like David than the hotshot exec JJ imagined Branson to be.

Who was he trying to kid? He would be a fool to think he could strut into the café, apologize for his deception, and all would be forgiven.

Yet he wanted more than her forgiveness. He wanted to win JJ's heart.

He had to go in there, tell her everything, and trust the Lord with the consequences. Branson hopped out of his car and slammed the door shut.

He trudged through the snow and stopped just outside

the interior doors, where he watched JJ shelving books. The depth of his love for her amazed him, though he shouldn't be surprised. From the moment he'd met JJ, his heart beat in a thrilling new rhythm.

Branson entered the store on a deep breath. He caught sight of Kara, who motioned for him to come over to her. He signaled her with a shake of his head. Whatever she wanted to tell him would have to wait.

When he reached within an arm's length of JJ, Branson cleared his throat.

"I'll be right with you," she said with her back to him.

Branson ran his gaze over her dark hair and slim figure. He resisted the urge to pull her into his arms. To kiss her before blurting his confession, knowing it could be their last kiss. He clamped his hands behind his back and waited.

"May I help you?" she asked, and turned. JJ's mouth dropped open. Her eyes registered shock.

Everything he'd rehearsed flew out of his head. "JJ, I'm sorry. I'm truly sorry about what happened last night." Branson reached toward her, but she shrank back.

"Don't apologize, David." A breathless laugh escaped her and her face flushed. "You look different—nice. Really good." JJ waved her hand. "What I want to say is *I* should apologize to you. I embarrassed you with my stupid little song."

"Is that what you think?" Branson shook his head. "Didn't you get my note? I told you your voice, your song, were awesome. I was honored, JJ. I just needed a little time to think things through—decide how to tell you the truth. . . ."

She interrupted him, lifting her shoulders in a shrug. "I

don't know what possessed me to get up there and—"

"I do." He moved closer to her. To his relief, she didn't back away. "You did it because you know. . ." His gaze locked on her dark blue eyes. "You know that I love you, too, JJ."

Her hand flew up to her mouth, and her eyes glistened. "You love me?" JJ's voice was a broken whisper. "But you walked out of the café, David. Why? What is there to think through if we both love each other?"

He cringed to hear her innocently call him David. He took hold of her hands and held tight. Hers were trembling. "You once told me that you never break your promises. Does that still hold?" He tried to smile, but the threat of losing her weighted his soul.

JJ nodded.

"Promise you'll hear me out. . .hear everything I have to say before you give me your verdict. There's so much I need to tell you."

"Verdict?" JJ licked her lips, and her face paled. "Is this going to turn out bad?"

"That's up to you, JJ. I hope not."

"Okay, you have my word. I'll hear you out."

Branson nodded and swallowed hard. "If I'd known I would meet you before I decided to play at the café, I never would've carried out this charade. But by the time I realized I was in love with you, it was too late to backpedal."

He slid his hands up her arms to her shoulders and looked directly into her puzzled eyes. "Do you remember how I told you about my father? How I was always trying to win his confidence?" Branson didn't wait for her response. "When

I graduated Harvard with a business degree, I figured that would earn me a modicum of respect in his eyes, but—"

"Harvard?" JJ whispered.

He disregarded her comment and pushed on. "After that, I went to work for my father's company and discovered that he called all the shots at the office—just as he'd done in my personal life. He refused to give me an executive position with the company unless I could come up with an idea for a new business venture and see it succeed."

JJ tilted her head in a show of sympathy. Apparently she hadn't gotten the picture yet.

He felt too choked up to go on. Branson drew a long breath and shook his head. "In order to wiggle out from under my father's thumb, I did come up with an idea to prove I could succeed on my own, JJ."

The look in her eyes turned to wariness. Branson brushed a wayward lock of her hair from her cheek. "Before I say anything else, you have to believe that I never meant to hurt you. I only meant to get honest feedback from the customers and staff. . .and I wanted to know how people would respond to me, minus my money and position."

JJ stared at him, mute. "No," she breathed.

"With that in mind, I didn't want to walk in here as—"

"Branson. . .Branson Smythe." JJ reeled back against the bookshelf. "All this time."

"I tried to tell you JJ, but I knew you hated Branson Smythe. I didn't want to lose you."

She removed her glasses. Her face was damp with tears. "Are you finished yet?"

"No." Branson pulled his handkerchief from his pocket and handed it to her. "I already asked the Lord to forgive me, and now I'm asking you. Will you give me another chance, JJ?" He cupped her chin in his hand. "I'm sorry. I know what it's like when someone you love betrays you. But I promise I never meant to hurt you. If you give me a chance, I'll explain everything and vow never to deceive you again. Over time, I think you'll come to see I'm not half as bad as you think I am. Please, won't you forgive me?"

She waved her hand. "Forgiveness is beside the point. As a Christian, I've no choice but to forgive you." JJ pressed the hankie to her face, shaking her head. Her gaze suddenly snapped to his. "You—you're the one who sent the anonymous check to the nursing home, aren't you?"

Branson nodded slowly. "I won't lie to you again. I'm guilty as charged."

"Oh." Fresh tears slipped down her face. "I don't know how I can ever repay you, but I promise I will."

"JJ, I don't want your money. The donation was a gift. No strings attached."

In his rush to comfort her, Branson pulled her into his arms. Without forethought, he lowered his head, pressed his lips to hers, and tasted the kiss he longed for.

"Pardon me!"

Branson's heart stopped at the sound of his father's voice.

JJ pulled back from Branson, her eyes wide.

"What's going on here, Son?" B. D. growled, his face crimson. "I suppose I've stumbled upon a classic case of 'when the cat's away, the mice will play,' hmm? I should have known you'd far exceed the bounds of professionalism in my absence."

Branson stepped in front of JJ, trying to block her from his father's line of fire. "We'll talk about this later, sir."

"There's nothing to talk about, except for you to offer me an apology for betraying the faith I'd placed in you. . . ." B. D. stepped around him.

"And you!" With narrowed eyes, B. D. pointed a shaking finger at JJ. "Have you no workplace ethics whatsoever? Shamelessly falling all over my son with your disgusting public display of affection—" The elder Mr. Smythe looked as though he might self-combust. "You're fired, you little gold digger. Now get yourself out of my store."

Branson's fists clenched. "If you weren't my father. . ." He turned from B. D.

"JJ, please come back."

Branson sat with Mike at a window table in the health club's restaurant. He shot another glance at the boutique across the street, as if by sheer willpower he could make JJ return to the shop. "I've got to find a way to contact JJ."

Mike shook his head. "You've tried everything, Smythe. If you leave JJ any more phone messages, she's likely to charge you with harassment."

"It's been four days. Where is she?" Branson took another swig of his vegetable drink and shuddered. "I went over to the nursing home this morning. I asked around, but nobody there has seen JJ either. She no longer lives at the apartment we list as her last known address in her file. Kara says she forgot to update the records when JJ moved last summer."

Mike groaned. "Make that harassment *and* stalking." He held his breath and downed his second carrot and greens drink. "Sorry, I'm only kidding you."

"I know, but what am I supposed to do?" Branson returned his attention to the pedestrians navigating the slushy sidewalks. He found himself looking for JJ in every passing face. "My father left JJ jobless." Though he'd slipped a note of apology into the envelope with her severance check before Kara mailed it to JJ's home address, he expected it to come back any day marked UNDELIVERABLE—NO FORWARDING ADDRESS.

"Firing JJ was a rotten thing to do, Branson. But you know B. D. It's his way or the highway."

Branson stood to his feet. "Not this time. I've proven myself with Camden Coffee's success, and the company is mine. Ol' dad is going to have to accept my business decisions—and my decisions in matters of love—like 'em or not. He's the one who let the company's best employee go, and I plan to rectify his mistake."

Mike nodded. "When you find her."

"When I find her," Branson said and reached for his chiming cell phone. "Hello."

"Hi, Branson, it's Kara." Her rushed words kicked his pulse rate up a notch.

"Have you heard from JJ?"

"Yes," Kara said. "She's coming into the store to get her things."

"When?" Branson swiped his suit jacket off the chair back. "What time?" He nodded at Mike, and his friend gave him a thumbs-up.

"She said she'd be here in about half an hour."

"I'll be right there." Branson snapped his cell closed and shrugged into his jacket. "I'll catch you later."

"Right." Mike clapped him on the back and smiled. "You've got it bad, bud."

Branson nodded. Nobody had to alert him to that fact. Four days without JJ and he knew he couldn't live without her in his life.

He exited the health club and crossed the street to Camden's underground garage. He stopped dead in his tracks at the sight of B. D. standing with the head honcho of Peterman Financing. All he needed was to be detained now. But Rich Peterman was not a client he could afford to ignore.

Branson stood in the shadows, barely breathing. B. D. turned as if he sensed his presence and looked straight at him.

"Branson!" His father waved him over. "I was looking for you."

Branson approached the two. He shook Peterman's outstretched hand. "Good to see you again, Rich."

"Same here," Rich said. "So let's do lunch. Steak's on me."

B. D. nodded and opened the car door.

The passing seconds felt like an eternity as Branson stood his ground, forming a polite refusal in his mind. "I appreciate that," he directed to Rich. "But I've got to make haste right now or I'll be late for a meeting."

Rich gave him a mock salute. "No problem, maybe next time."

Branson watched his father's face turn a boiling shade of red. "Nonsense!" B. D. grumbled. "Cancel it."

Rich got into the front passenger seat. B. D. held open the rear door and jerked his head, a silent order to get in.

"I'm not going with you, Dad." With a final nod, Branson headed for his car. He stopped and looked over his shoulder just in time to see his father's incredulous stare. "I'm off to see JJ, and then I'm going to beg her forgiveness."

As he neared his vehicle, he heard B. D. utter, "Fool."

Branson couldn't keep a laugh from escaping. Yeah, he'd been a fool all right. A fool for not standing up to his father long ago. His mutiny over JJ's firing brought such a sense of freedom, he wished he had done it long before now.

JJ walked into the bookstore on cat's feet. She hoped to make it to the inventory room undetected by her coworkers. After being publicly humiliated by B. D., she could only imagine what they thought of her.

"JJ!" Kara screeched. She bounded over, arms open wide.

A smile came to JJ's face as she returned Kara's hug. She had no idea how much she would miss her quirky coworkers.

Minnie called to her from behind the café counter. "Great to see you, girl, are you back?"

JJ's eyes stung. She shook her head. "Just getting. . .my things."

Kara draped her arm over her shoulders. "Come on, I'll walk you."

In the inventory room, JJ grabbed an empty carton, then went straight to her locker. "You don't have to wait around for me, Kara."

Kara responded by dropping into a chair beside the packing table. "Oh, JJ, I'm so sorry this all happened." She laid a gentle hand on JJ's arm. "I have no doubt you'll end up with an awesome job."

"Yeah, right." JJ opened her locker. A lavender-colored bag snagged her attention. "Oh, somebody must've put this in here by mistake." She pulled it out of her locker and showed it to Kara.

Kara stood, peeked into the gift bag, and retrieved a box. "Well, your name's on the envelope."

"What?" JJ's heart pounded. Maybe Branson. . . She tore open the envelope, and Kara excused herself with a smile.

Please forgive me, was written on the front of the card. JJ flipped it open. *I know you admired this dress. I believe you admired me, too, once. If you would—if you could find it in your heart to forgive me, I shall forever be grateful. Love always, Branson.*

"Oh," JJ whispered and pressed the card to her heart. She looked at the box, set down the card, and lifted the lid. Her breath caught. "How did he know?" She took the silky red garment from the box, and the tears she had tried to restrain burned her eyes.

"JJ?"

Still holding the dress, she froze at the sound of his familiar voice. He must not see her crying. She needed all her strength to resist him.

She'd done a lot of thinking over the past several days. She faced the loss of every longing of her heart, yet she could not, did not, hold Branson responsible. Looking back, she realized the awkward predicament in which he'd found himself.

In a way, she even felt sorry for him, despite his wealth. She'd witnessed firsthand the power Branson's father held over his son, recognized Branson's desperate need to earn his father's admiration and prove himself capable. She knew all too well the lengths one would go to for independence and a measure of self-respect. Such goals seemed next to impossible for Branson in light of the interchange she'd observed between father and son.

"Branson," she managed, her back to him: "The dress is beautiful, but I can't accept such an extravagant farewell gift."

She may have suffered the brunt of B. D.'s wrath in this one exchange, but Branson faced a lifetime of such battles if he didn't find the strength to confront his dad. As much as she loved him, as much as the thought of living without him drove a stake in her heart, if Branson couldn't speak for himself or stand up to his father in matters of love, she wasn't meant to be the right woman for him.

She heard his footfall as he closed the distance between them. His hand on her shoulder sent a cascade of tingles down her arm. She steeled herself against the compulsion to throw herself into his arms. She refused to give in. There was no future for the two of them. This was good-bye.

"I didn't give you the dress as a farewell gift—"

His breath warmed her neck as he spoke, and she closed her eyes, frantic to contain her emotions.

"And it's really more than a peace offering." He tugged gently on her shoulder, urging her to turn toward him. With a sigh, she gave in to his nudges. She opened her eyes to meet his gaze, his lips within kissing distance from hers.

"Please, I wish you'd reconsider accepting the dress. I dream of seeing you in it when you make your grand entrance at the party I'm throwing—"

A party? What kind of party is he throwing? JJ's mind swirled with a thousand possibilities.

"A party to announce my new marketing VP of Camden Coffees." Light danced in Branson's eyes. He smiled. "I'll be playing a new song I wrote just for the occasion. You have to be there, even if you don't want the dress."

JJ jerked away from his grasp, shoved the dress into his chest, and took two steps back. A flash fire of anger burned her ears, choked off her air supply. How could he be so cruel as to invite her to a party to flaunt the fact that he'd given her dream job to another? She'd allowed love to temporarily blind her from the truth—Branson Smythe must be every bit his father's son after all.

At last, she managed to tame the fire in her throat and find her voice. "How could you? Why would you want to hurt me, humiliate me in front of my peers? Are you so easily swayed by your father's opinions that you've turned against me already? Isn't it enough that I'm stripped of my job. . .my income. . .my hopes for a future. . .my one true love?" She buried her head in her hands and spun on her heels.

"JJ, wait! You've misunderstood." Branson stepped in front of her and blocked her retreat, dropping the dress into the open gift box. "I've bungled everything by trying to be clever. Please let me explain." He pulled gently at her wrists until she lowered her hands, then crooked his finger under her chin and tipped her face toward his. "I'm here to rectify my father's sins. . . ." He closed the distance between them so that he once more stood a mere breath away. "The new Camden Coffees marketing vice president I'm hoping to introduce is *you*. You've got all the skills and talent I'm looking for in my marketing VP. . . ."

She swallowed hard and shook her head, unable to comprehend just what he was trying to say. Was he pushing to new depths of cruelty? Could he possibly be sincere? He seemed to be serious, but she'd been deceived by his performances before. *Oh, please, Lord. Dare I hope that my wildest dreams are coming true?*

He stroked her cheek with his thumb.

Through her tears, she saw love in his eyes—a love not even Branson could stage.

"There's a lot about me you don't know, JJ. And there's a lot I still don't know about you. I can't think of a better way to rectify the situation than to work side-by-side, day in and day out." He paused just long enough to brush his lips across her forehead and then pulled back, his gaze suddenly serious. "I have to warn you, though, I'm seeing this position as a steppingstone to an equal partnership on down the road—a union we'll contract before God and in the presence of witnesses. One sealed not with a handshake but a kiss."

JJ threw her arms around Branson's neck, accepting his offer and ceasing all further negotiations by meeting her lips to his.

SUSAN K. DOWNS

Susan lives and writes in Canton, Ohio. When she isn't writing, Susan works as a freelance fiction copy editor. She and her minister-husband have five children, now grown, and are enjoying their new roles as grandparents to their grandson and granddaughter. Read more about Susan's writing/editing ministry at her Web site: www.susankdowns.com.

the perfect blend

by Anita Higman

Dedication

To DiAnn Mills, one of those treasured finds. . .
God tools the heart of a willing soul
and creates a gift refined,
a most welcomed friend—the purest gold,
a brilliant and treasured find.
A. H.

Many waters cannot quench love;
rivers cannot wash it away.
SONG OF SONGS 8:7 NIV

"For stony limits cannot hold love out."
SHAKESPEARE

Chapter 1

An emotional power surge. Kasey Morland felt like she was in the middle of one. She rarely indulged in self-pity or maudlin thoughts, but something had definitely zapped her. Hormones? She was too old for puberty. Too young for menopause. She shoved some loose strands of hair back into submission. It was at least one thing she could still control.

Kasey noticed Jacques, the owner of the Café Rose, lumbering toward her. He eased his portly frame down in the seat across from her. The wooden chair made a woeful creak. She set her *Wall Street Journal* aside.

"So, little one, what is it you're thinking? It looks like a fitful daydream to me. You can tell Jacques. Yes?"

Kasey mustered a smile for her older friend. "You know, I've always believed I was gifted at business. I was born to make this happen. But why do I keep losing my focus? And why do my businesses go belly-up?"

"Hmm. That's a question as weighty as my pastry chef, Raoul." Two fingers lighted on his cheek as if to organize his thoughts.

"I'm not an expert, but I think one thing that helps is to know something about the businesses you're buying. What I mean is, do you truly know and care about running a megafireworks store? Or what was the last one you bought? A drive-through kitty pet resort? What is that? I thought you had a cat phobia."

"No, I just can't breathe when I'm around them." Kasey touched her throat and winced just thinking about it. "Anyway, the kitty resort was priced right. And the fireworks warehouse had *great* potential."

"Yes, *great* potential to send you to heaven a little early," Jacques replied.

"Well, how could I have known my new hire was a pyromaniac?"

"Yes. I know. It wasn't your fault."

"Don't worry," Kasey said. "I intend to keep to the simple life from now on. No more explosions. Now for a new subject. Well, sort of. I went to a wedding planner today."

Jacques studied her as he twiddled one of his bushy eyebrows. "And are you about to tell me that nuptials are in your near future?"

"No." Kasey gave him a wry grin. "I looked into buying her business. But I'm afraid it didn't work out very well. I got maybe a little too honest, and she—"

"Bolted like a spooked coyote, eh?" Jacques threw his head back in a chuckle.

"How did you know? Don't answer that. Anyway, by the time I'd finished telling her about her dry cake and bitter brew she. . ." Kasey noticed Jacques' gaze assessing her. "But the wedding planner asked me point-blank, and I had to be up-front with her. Didn't I?" Kasey shoved her heavy black glasses up the ridge of her nose and waited for Jacques' response.

"Well, the answer to that is as hard as the crust on my bread. Truth is the only way. Yes? But there are ways to coax fish into a net without hooking them in the mouth. I also have to be careful with being too candid with some people. It can be overwhelming, like the taste of too much nutmeg when it was meant to be like a sweet perfume. I'm glad *we* can 'tell it like it is' with each other though. You put up with my fatherly chastisements well. And that is to your credit."

Kasey reached out and tugged on her friend's sleeve affectionately. "I want you to always be that way with me. I need honesty, and I want it. Even if sometimes I act like I'm rejecting it. Do you know what I mean?"

"Well, in that case, I'd like to know something honestly." Jacques cleared his throat. "Little one, where does God fit into all of these businesses you buy?"

Kasey's gaze drifted to a baby whimpering nearby. "I don't want to bother Him with all the little stuff, like a nagging child. It all seems so trite compared to famine and war and world affairs. I'll leave the more important issues to Him and hope He gave me enough common sense to make a living."

"If He counts the hairs on your head, little one, He surely expects you to inquire about the rest of your life, too. Don't you think?" Jacques patted her hand.

"Even though you're almost always right, I have trouble acting on other people's wisdom. It's my Achilles' heel." Kasey took another long sip of her coffee and grinned up at her dear friend who always made her life road a little easier to walk.

"Well, we all possess one." Jacques leaned toward her. "You're a very gifted young woman, Kasey. Never forget that. All things are possible. But I do wish you'd have a long talk with your Abba. I think you'll be surprised how much more you'll be able to celebrate life. . .rather than wrestle with it."

Kasey noticed more people filtering into the café for lunch. "Your rush time is coming. I don't want to keep you." Kasey rubbed the sudden stiffness in her neck. "And it's hard for me to say, Jacques. . .but thank you."

"Anytime." Jacques pointed to her dessert as he rose. "I see you selected the pear flan. Excellent flavors and texture. Paradise for the pallet. Myra made it. I hope you'll try a few bites."

Kasey watched Jacques charge off like a locomotive to greet his new arrivals. She fingered the smooth ball of her earring as she went right back to chewing on the problem at hand. Yes, her last business opportunity had bitten the dust. She would have to find the right business soon or start one from the ground up. Otherwise, she'd need to make longer-term investments with her inheritance money and get a job, working for somebody else. As a business graduate, she chose not to concentrate on that last thought. At thirty, she knew she still had time to get her act together, but not *that* much time.

Was good old teddy bear Jacques right, or was he just a sweet aging chef who loved to dole out advice with his quiche? Maybe she *did* have the gift, but it would take lots more work, learning even more about the business up front. Hard work had never frightened her, only failure. And as far as asking for God's advice, her heart cried out for Him, but something still held her back.

Wrapping up her bout of whining, Kasey snapped her *Wall Street Journal* back open. *I might as well have another go at this nebulous thing called business.*

Hamilton Wakefield's morning had shaped up nicely as usual. His private banker shook his hand as if priming a pump and then waved good-bye with equal enthusiasm.

Hamilton's polished wing tips met the cool black granite as he smoothed his Armani jacket. He grinned one of those slow and satisfying grins that says to the world, *I've got a good day here. I've had a lot of those lately.*

Today held an even greater air of celebration, marking the time he finally had enough money from his stock dealings and investments to buy the business of his dreams. It was just a matter of finding the business, and that part would be more fun than hard work.

The door gave way to his touch, and Hamilton hit the streets of Houston with a vigorous stride. Even in the steamy heat of August, all elements of his day seemed to greet him like a silver tray of gifts. Without warning, a level of the sidewalk seemed to rise up to greet him, too, and he tripped into a man near the curb.

"Wow. Hey, I'm sorry. Did I hurt you?" Hamilton tried to regain his composure.

The stranger, who was dressed in tattered clothes, grabbed Hamilton's arm. "No, but *you* look shaken up, son."

The old man seemed to peer into his soul with a searching gaze. *Who is he, and why did he call me "son"?* Before Hamilton could say another word, the old man released him and disappeared into the crowd. He stood still, as confusion and shock washed over him.

Hamilton's day unraveled in that one piercing look. The stranger who'd seized his arm had looked like an older version of himself. How could that be? And the vacant stare. The utter sadness in his eyes. He would remember that look for the rest of his life. But why? Did he somehow feel connected to the stranger? *Boy, that sounds a little wacko.*

"I'm fine," Hamilton mumbled to no one at all. He whirled around awkwardly and slammed into a light pole. A burst of pain engulfed him.

Chapter 2

Hamilton groaned inwardly. He forced himself not to yell out and make a scene. He felt his nose. Nothing broken. Only a few drops of blood. He'd survive, but he did feel a little wobbly as if the street sounds were on a merry-go-round. Glancing around, he did think it odd the way people barely slowed down to see if he was all right. Had people always been so robotic and thoughtless? He tried to regain his momentum, but his limbs felt like they belonged to someone else. What was happening to him? He yanked out a handkerchief and dabbed his nose.

Had seeing that old man messed up his mind? His imagination was certainly working double-time. He shook off the sense of what? Dread? No. He refused to be the worrying type. He told himself it was just one of those quirky moments in time. Nothing more.

Hamilton beeped his blue sedan open and slid down into the soft leather. Ah. It already made him feel better. He jerked the rearview mirror down to see himself. He looked a little funky with a red nose along with his green eyes. Oh well. Wait a minute. There seemed to be more gray hairs among the brown ones. And at almost thirty-five, was his hairline now betraying him, too? He knew some guys went totally bald before they got a chance to go totally gray. What a thought. *Get a grip, man.*

With a roar of his engine, he tore out of the parking space knowing exactly where he was headed. The Café Rose. Jacques' chicken with herbs, a crisply folded *Wall Street Journal*, and French roast coffee. Three cups would do it. It always did. Relief was only a short distance away!

Ten minutes later, Hamilton threw open the door of his favorite café and breathed deeply. Walking into the Café Rose was like taking a trip without having to fly anywhere. The ambiance felt European. Wooden floors, a brick oven, classical music, and the hideaway nooks offered an atmosphere of pleasure and pause, not the eyeblinking feel of fluorescent and frantic. Then there was the aroma of freshly baked bread, pastries, and coffee. Oh, the coffee. It tasted good enough to make you want to hang around all day and do nothing but drink it in.

Hamilton caught Jacques barreling toward him with purpose in his eye.

"I've seen you in here for years, but not with *that* expression. You'd better tell old Jacques. What is it that's troubling you?"

Hamilton tried to smile convincingly but wondered if his expression looked more like a boy who'd been caught cheating at marbles. "Nothing is the matter."

Jacques exploded with laughter.

"I'm just hungrier than usual."

"Yes, my friend. Hungry for a good wife," Jacques said.

"I was thinking more of your chicken right now. I could

smell it when I walked in. By the way, when are you going to tell me all the herbs you use in that? Two of them are basil and thyme. Right?"

"Look. You've had a strange day. I can tell," Jacques replied. "But what you really need is the right woman to marry."

"You're never going to tell me what you put on that chicken, are you?"

Jacques folded his burly arms and stared at Hamilton with one of his concerned looks.

"Okay. You know I want to marry a nice, sweet woman one day. I'm just not in the mood *today*. But go ahead. If you send over a really great woman, I'll go over my mental checklist, and then I might ask her out."

Jacques clicked his tongue. " 'A woman would run through fire and water for such a kind heart.' "

"Shakespeare again, right?" Hamilton shook his finger at him. "You're good, Jacques. Very, very good. But hey, don't be too hard on me. I'm just trying to find the *right* woman."

"I just hope this checklist of yours doesn't include assessing her teeth like a horse. I can see we have a lot of work to do here." Jacques sniffed some spices and then tasted a patisserie. "Women's desires remind me of my two soups. They want the surprise, the romance, and the mystery of my soup du jour. But they also need the stability and security of what they know is always on the menu, which is my tomato basil. It's always here, and it's always good." Jacques raised his eyebrows as he rubbed his graying beard. "And as far as the right woman, ask God. He'll tell you. I've heard He's very good at giving advice."

"Hey, I ask Him all the time for advice. That's how

I've made all my money, and how I can afford to eat here." Hamilton grinned with renewed confidence.

"That is good news, my friend," Jacques said. "By the way, God is blessing you again today in yet another way. The woman I've wanted you to meet is here. She's perfect for you. You both are slices from the same cheesecake. And I'm not just referring to good looks. Anyway, you tell her I ordered you to sit there with her. She's hogging a big table, enough for four people. She knows the rules here about sharing when it's crowded. And it's the truth, because since we have been talking, every last table has been taken." Like fireworks, Jacques burst into laughter again.

Hamilton paid for his meal. "If you've picked her, I'm sure she's wonderful, Jacques. Right?"

"Your mademoiselle is at table number nine, directly under the arch." The sound of crashing dishes and an argument in French erupted from the kitchen. Jacques' smile went weak as he fled down the hallway. "By the way, her name is Kasey Morland. And—may God be with you."

"What did you say?" Hamilton asked over the noisy crowd. But it was too late. Jacques had already bulldozed into the tempest raging in the kitchen. Hamilton's nose still throbbed, and he wondered if he still looked like Santa's sidekick. Oh well, he thought, the woman Jacques was forcing him to meet probably had some imperfections, too. He just wondered what sort of deficiency it might be.

Balancing his tray of food, Hamilton reached into the community newspaper caddy for his favorite paper. He found plenty of local papers, but someone had taken the last *Wall*

Street Journal. Now his day really nose-dived. Mumbling to himself, he glanced at Jacques' table number nine, directly under the arch. He couldn't see the woman's face because she was buried behind a paper. His eyelid twitched. There on the table she'd spread out her gargantuan lunch and boldly sported his *Wall Street Journal.* Hamilton stood still long enough to calm himself. He deliberately softened his smile, and with only minor traces of indignation, he charged to table number nine.

Chapter 3

Hamilton shuffled his feet as he stood in front of the woman buried behind the newspaper. No response. Not even a rattle. He cleared his throat. Still nothing. "Excuse me," Hamilton said, trying to keep his temper on a leash.

Finally a face slowly emerged from the top of the paper. Hamilton discovered it wasn't just any face. She had creamy skin like those white peaches he'd bought at the store recently, and her brown eyes lit up with gold. The effect was mesmerizing. He fought the urge to touch the softness of her face.

Those magical eyes stared at him with interest. Or was it merely curiosity? Except for those black-rimmed glasses, she was a beauty. He was truly in the company of a celestial creature. His thoughts strayed a little, nearly forgetting how his day had come to a screeching halt and why he'd been so distressed.

Then the vision behind the paper spoke. "May I help you?"

"Yes, as a matter—"

"Oh, I'll bet you're one of those single guys Jacques sends over under the pretense of having run out of tables. I don't want to be rude to Jacques, so I guess we're stuck with each other."

Even with her angelic attractiveness, Hamilton thought *"stuck with each other" was not the best choice of words.* "But there really *are* no more tables," he said in defense.

The angel-woman glanced around. "I'm sorry. I hadn't even noticed. Please sit down since I have a table for four. I'm not shopping for a husband, so you're safe with me. By the way, I'm Kasey Morland."

"Hamilton Wakefield. It's good to meet you."

"Please make yourself at home, like Jacques always says." She lifted the newspaper back up like a paper wall.

Hamilton noticed Kasey didn't talk like other females. Many women were somewhat shy at first in revealing their inner thoughts. *She apparently serves it to you straight.* Hamilton wasn't sure if that trait annoyed or excited him. He also noticed Ms. Kasey Morland made no effort to move her wide array of dishes, so he shoved some of her semiempty plates over to her side of the table. It looked like she'd sampled everything in the café. For someone so trim, he wondered where she put it all.

Hamilton eased himself down on the small wooden chair and organized his space. Chatty bliss and laughter seemed to flit and swoop around them like mocking parrots. To break the awkward silence at their table, Hamilton let out a noisy puff of air. "So, I see you're interested in business. What do you do?"

"Right now. . .I'm afraid. . .nothing," she replied from behind her paper defense.

"Oh. Independently wealthy?" Hamilton suddenly felt a little playful.

"No. You'll have to guess again." Kasey took a slow sip of

her coffee and let out a tiny satisfied moan.

"This is an interesting riddle. You do nothing, but you're not rich. That means you are either in between jobs, or you're a bum. You're much too well-groomed to be a bum, so I'm going to assume you are in between jobs." Hamilton slid a piece of chicken into his mouth and sighed at the aroma and taste. "Wow, this is so right. I wish I could re-create this chicken at home." Hamilton continued to make noises of pleasure over Jacques' chicken.

Kasey lowered her paper again with a loud crinkling noise. "It's very simple, actually. You buy a jar of his herbs and then analyze them at home. I'm sorry. Who did you say you were?"

"Hamilton Wakefield, a friend of Jacques' who needed a place to sit down." Hamilton noticed his lovely table partner seemed to stare as if she were trying to read his thoughts. Or was that attraction in her eyes?

"And also looking for someone to marry?" Kasey added as an eyebrow arched upward.

"Maybe. *If* you're my type." Hamilton offered her his best smile. The one that always seemed to do wonders with the ladies at his singles group at church.

Kasey chuckled. "If I'm *your* type? Are you trying to win some kind of award for saying all the wrong things? I have to tell you. That prize usually goes to me."

For the first time, Hamilton saw her smile. Her whole face lit up like the break of dawn. Beautiful. "In answer to your question, no, I was just trying to make a potentially uncomfortable situation a little friendlier." Along with her smile, Hamilton noticed she wore a man's tie and trousers. Unusual. But he also took note that with her delicate blouse the outfit was unusually alluring.

"Friendlier. . .so you can marry me?" Kasey asked plainly but with a hint of a smile.

"Why do you keep saying that?" Hamilton asked, becoming even more intrigued.

Kasey fingered her earlobe. "Because I want you and Jacques to admit your sneaky behavior. He sent you over here to hook us up."

"Well, there are those things called talking, dating, love, and then engagement if all the other points of interest work out. But yes, Jacques just feels sorry for—"

"Sorry for whom?" Kasey folded up her paper. The gold in her eyes glimmered with fire.

Hamilton thought maybe the brown-haired angel sitting before him was now growing a very dainty set of horns. He squelched a grin, put down his chicken leg, and asked, "Are you finished with that paper? I wanted to check out something in there. *If* you don't mind."

Kasey put the paper down with a little slap, crossed her legs like a man, and poked her fork into her cold salmon. "I'm about finished with it anyway. . .Mr. Wakefield."

Was she grinning or frowning? He couldn't tell. Nevertheless, Hamilton sensed it was time to hide behind the news to let her unruffle her feathers a bit. Besides, he was not only wanting to check up on a few stocks, but he needed to ponder the swift decline of his manly cool. Any silver-tongued smoothness he'd ever possessed was looking as inviting as moldy bread. He wondered if he'd hit his head along with his nose, because this table session was turning into some kind of verbal kamikaze mission. But on the other hand Hamilton thought it might turn out to be even more delicious than Jacques' chicken. He spotted some red markings inside the paper and commented, "I see what you've circled here. I'll bet I can guess your riddle. You're searching to buy a business."

"Yes."

Hamilton lowered the paper. "Hey, I'm only trying to lend a hand. I'm in the process of finding a business to buy also. They say I have the golden touch. Just thought I could help."

"I might be able to use some help. Maybe," Kasey replied without looking up.

"Have you ever run a business?" Hamilton felt energized and inquisitive.

"Yes. I have." Kasey's voice rose again.

"And where are those businesses today, if you don't mind me asking?"

"Even the most brilliant business people lose to the fickle public and to a bad economy. I am merely a victim, and I intend to succeed. It's just a matter of time," Kasey said with confidence.

"I assume you mean that the businesses failed. I'm truly sorry to hear that. It's pretty rough out there," Hamilton said. "Maybe what you need is passion."

"I know you're going to tell me what you mean by that."

"Passion in your *business*. You have to love it, pray it, breathe it, dream it, or you won't make it." Hamilton stuffed a scoop of Jacques' wild rice into his mouth.

"I think you can force a round peg into a square hole if you force it hard enough."

He swallowed a little more loudly than he intended to. "But won't life be miserable if you try to work at a business you weren't created for?" Hamilton's cell phone rang. He looked at the number and shut it off. Why was Jacques calling him from the kitchen? To give him pointers?

Kasey fingered her earlobe and earring. "I don't know how to answer you. To be honest, I'm not used to people questioning me about my decisions. That is, except for Jacques."

Hamilton handed the paper back to her. "You know, there was a time I was too proud to admit I needed help. And I suffered for it. . .greatly." *Oh, brother.* What made that come out of his mouth?

"Is that what you think? That I'm too proud? But you don't even know me."

"You're right. I don't." *But I'd certainly like to.*

On the surface their conversation felt like nibbling on cayenne pepper, but underneath, he had to admit, there was something else cooking. What was it? Could it be the fusion of two perfect ingredients, like cutting butter into flour? And why did that earlobe and the curve of her neck suddenly look so enticing? Before he could reason out its full consequences, Hamilton lowered his lid in an old-fashioned wink. He noticed the sudden jaw-quivering countenance on his table partner and thought she might either lean over to kiss him or whack him soundly with her newspaper. Yes, he thought, he had definitely lost control of his day.

All Kasey could think of was this man had actually winked at her. Was he trying to be obnoxious or seductive? And *why*

did she feel so odd? It was the same unsettling sensation she experienced right before she got her annual flu shot.

Not really knowing what else to do, Kasey began gobbling her pear flan ferociously, hoping to signal a real end to the conversation. How could Jacques send this guy over on such a bad day? What was he thinking? Where was Jacques anyway? Probably hiding in the kitchen. It could be worse, she reminded herself. This Hamilton guy had a pink nose, but he wasn't a total fright to look at. Tall, sort of muscular without being too burly, and a face that radiated confidence. Oh. And eyes with a hint of surprise. Why was she even bothering about his looks?

Kasey let the last of her flan slide down as she looked back up at Hamilton. He'd apparently watched her pig out on the whole dessert! Suddenly all the silly emotional behavior she despised in other people flowed out of her mouth like a flooded river. Kasey folded her arms. "Okay. You want to talk *pride.* No self-respecting man would parade around with a nose that looks like it's been in a back alley brawl." That comment was by far the most infantile and witless thing she'd ever said in her life. Her bluntness had blossomed into meanness. She had long ago missed her cue for an exit. Jacques would be so displeased with her. To soften the blow of her cruelty, Kasey decided to give him an exaggerated wink back.

Before she could rise to go, Hamilton raised a finger. "By the way, how can you even *see* my nose through those night goggles you're wearing? And while I'm on a roll here, may I also say a mouth like yours should come with a cute little *warning* label."

Is he laughing? Kasey accidentally let out a chuckle. Their encounter felt so utterly crazy and unexpected, it was funny. She closed her mouth and blinked back a smirk. "Tell me something. Do you always insult women you don't even know?"

Hamilton gladly fell under her spell, but he still couldn't quite get an apologetic word to his lips. Noticing people were staring at them like primates at the zoo, Hamilton lifted his chin. "Only when I find it necessary to," he replied. For that last statement he would suffer tonight with no sleep, wondering what buffoonish thing had come over him. The rest of the night he'd ponder what it would have felt like to silence that incredible mouth of hers with his own lips.

Chapter 4

"If you'll excuse me." Kasey rose with a jerk and gestured with her hand, giving flight to her cup of coffee. The amber liquid made an impressive landing on Hamilton's Armani jacket.

Hamilton frowned but decided to go with the flow. He pointed to the other side of his jacket. "Could you make one to match right over here?"

Kasey yanked out a twenty-dollar bill as if her pocketbook were on fire. "I'm sorry. I'm not usually so clumsy. This should take care of the cleaning." She turned to go and then hesitated. "But I hope you're not planning on eating breakfast here, too. If you are, it might be better. . .less. . .hazardous for you if we sit. . .at two different tables." Kasey said good-bye several times and then tromped out.

Hamilton watched her go. What had just happened? Had she consumed too much caffeine, or did her excitement fall into some other category? He glanced around. The interested couples who'd been staring at them had gone back to their munching. A playful smile crept across his face. He knew just where he'd eat his breakfast every morning and wondered what a woman named Kasey Morland would do about it.

Through the window he saw her make a hasty exit. She climbed into a blue sedan. Interesting. Same blue sedan as his. Same make. Same model. Hmm. He shoveled another round of food into his mouth, but without Kasey, what had been delectable before now seemed to lose its flavor.

Kasey sped a little too fast to her apartment on Houston's northwest side. She gave herself a much-needed pep phrase. *You are a coolheaded survivor, Kasey Morland, not a wimp.* But a familiar thought kept spreading in Kasey's mind like the ugly stain she'd made on Hamilton's jacket. Yes. She'd made one more human being fall madly in *hate* with her. But this time it felt more. . .complicated.

Later at home Kasey decided to make some dessert to unwind. She lifted down a copper pan from the rack on her ceiling to make the ganache for some petit fours. She brought the cream to a boil and added the chocolate and the other ingredients. Kasey slid a piece of the delicate chocolate into her mouth. Instead of just eating it, she let it linger on her tongue, truly tasting it. Sweet. Dreamy. Inspiring. Wow. Women and chocolate. *Would men ever truly understand this relationship?*

Fingering through the mail, she dropped her smile again. Yet another singles dating brochure. Good-looking people with their heads together, laughing as if to say, "We're having fun. You're not. Buy a life." It made her feel they were in this little circle of light and happiness, and everyone else shivered outside in the cold, pressing their noses against the window.

What was that funny smell? Oh no. She gasped when she saw what had happened to her sweet mixture. The bubbling confection now coated the pan with blackened pits like the darkened Planet X. Quickly, she turned off the gas burner, but the offensive odor filled her apartment. Kasey plopped down on the overstuffed couch wondering if she had lost a piece of her mind today as well as her pride.

The phone rang, and she jumped. *Who can that be?* She rarely got calls. Kasey picked up the phone. "Hello. . . Oh, hi, Aunt Lila. . . I'm fine. . . . Yeah, I've been cooking. . .well. . .burning. . . . Yeah. . . What? You're kidding! A double wedding? I didn't think anybody had those anymore. . . . Well, tell them both I'm very happy for them. . . . I guess I need to start buying wedding gifts in wholesale bulk for my cousins. . . . No, I was just kidding. . . . Yeah. . . I'm doing okay. . . . No wedding bells for me to announce. . . . Yeah. You're right. I guess I did let myself drift away from everybody. I'll try to make that right. . . . Love you, too. . . . Bye." The phone suddenly felt a little heavier.

Kasey heard megaphone-type laughter booming just outside her door, but when she peered out around the corner, they'd already disappeared. She pulled a sign off her door and read the huge black print:

To Kasey Morland,

We'd love for you to come to our Get-to-Know-Your-Neighbor party Saturday night at 7:00. We know you don't get out much but hope you can make it!

Mr. and Mrs. Morgan, next door

Kasey groaned. Apparently *that's* why people were cackling. She might as well wear a banner declaring it as her reigning motto: Kasey Morland is single, and she doesn't get out much. She could wave to the crowds from her Lonely Hearts float like a spinster queen and watch the throngs throw sad looks and orthopedic shoes at her.

Kasey licked the last of the chocolate from her lips. Too tired to have her calves hold up her body, she slid to the floor. Her apartment looked different from that perspective, making her feel childish and insignificant. Not at all like how she'd felt even a few days ago. Things could change so quickly. Feelings once locked away now seemed vulnerable, like a gate left open. And confidence thought to be shatterproof could indeed be broken.

In the utter stillness she could almost hear a rock tumbling to the floor. Then another. Kasey knew the world she'd created was crumbling. She couldn't guarantee anything for herself, just as she couldn't guarantee her parents' safety years ago. She promised them if they drove down from Oklahoma she'd show them the best of Houston. And one spring morning they drove down. That same fine day a train crashed into their car. Her promises had been replaced with a funeral and a hole in her heart. No guarantees. She could accept what happened. But lately everything seemed up for grabs. Kasey swiped at the tears trickling down her cheek.

When would it be time to let go of all the quick fixes and bother the Great I Am with her problems? Kasey sighed knowing she still liked to stand in front of the cosmic control buttons. The driver's seat held danger, but at least it felt familiar. Kasey tapped her cheeks lightly. Maybe she really just needed some thyroid pills. She made a mental note to call her doctor. And as far as Hamilton at the Café Rose, he would have to find his own table from now on.

Too much emotional ping-pong. She rubbed her head and went back to her mail. That singles dating brochure still haunted Kasey like a hated song that played all day in her brain. She flipped the brochure over. *Unbelievable.* The photo on the back was a guy she'd dated a couple of years ago. *What was his name? Oh yeah. Lloyd Ludlow.* How could she forget *that* name? They'd had nothing in common, and he'd agreed with everything she'd said. It'd driven her to utter boredom.

Putting emotions aside, Lloyd's dating service intrigued her. From the fancy brochure, he must be doing well. She could always call and ask him. Very professional-like. She grabbed her address book and pushed in all the right buttons.

She heard his machine pick up and then left a message. A Christian dating service. Hmm. She knew nothing about it, but the learning process could start with a lot of good solid questions this time. An idea to sleep on.

The next morning Kasey plugged in her pep-talk video and stepped on her treadmill with thuglike steps. Suddenly the thought of buying a dating service seemed certifiably insane. Oh well. When Lloyd called, she'd just wish him well and move on.

The treadmill proved boring again, but it kept her healthy and happy. Was she happy? She didn't need a man to be content, yet something seemed awry. Could the red-nosed man with the green eyes be some puzzle piece? *He's a piece of work, all right. Focus, Kasey.* She tapped her face. Her mind-droppings were getting out of control.

She glanced in the wall mirror, frowned, and picked out a few gray hairs. Kasey tossed her eyeglasses across the room. Time to dig out her contacts. And maybe color her hair again. No sense in looking as awkward as she felt.

Kasey peeked in the window of the Café Rose, wondering what she would encounter. Her breath fogged up the glass as she spotted Hamilton in line for breakfast. Yes, he was like the static cling you couldn't spray away. Kasey quietly got in line behind him.

As if Hamilton could sense her presence, he turned around and smiled.

"Didn't you get enough of me yesterday?" she asked without thinking.

"I don't know. Why don't we have breakfast together, and we'll find out if I can stand any more of you." Hamilton chuckled warmly.

Kasey ignored his remark. "By the way. . .about yesterday. Things got kind of. . .unexpectedly. . .well. . .I'm sorry."

"Me, too," Hamilton said, sounding sincere.

"Tell you what, as a humanitarian gesture, I'll give you permission to eat here this morning." Kasey smiled. "But don't let it happen again."

Hamilton laughed. "Thank you. Do I need that in writing?"

She'd forgotten how much his voice reminded her of chocolate syrup. Smooth and irresistible. And he must *really* be working out. She'd noticed he was tall and trim, but today's clingier shirt revealed his muscular arms and chest. She blinked hard and then looked away. "But I still think separate tables would be. . .safer."

"Alone can be good," Hamilton said a little too sweetly. "It's a good, solid word. You know, solitary. Lonesome. Detached."

Kasey rose to his banter. "How about exclusive? Pure? Indivisible?"

Hamilton seemed impressed and nodded. "Not bad."

"Thanks. But I still think separate tables would be. . .less dangerous for us."

"Okay. Have your way. . .Ms. Morland." Hamilton headed toward the coffee bar.

Kasey slid down into her usual chair at her favorite table, which rested directly under the arch. Jacques always called it the Love Arch, but Kasey liked it best because of the view of the little courtyard. Lush tropicals. Flowing water. It was a patch of serenity.

Hamilton walked right by her. Kasey heard the chair *thump* and knew without looking he'd taken the table behind her. So much for focus. *That certainly is negative.* She'd just been pumped up by one of the greatest business tycoons of all time, and yet the puffed-up feeling had popped like a balloon at a kid's party.

Hamilton sat quietly, probably reading the same business magazine she pretended to study. Other noises crowded in her space: clinking dishes, yak of every kind, and shuffling feet. She tapped her fingers. Was she sinking lower in her wicker-bottom chair, or was it her imagination?

Hamilton made little sound, except for answering his cell phone a few times. All business calls. She grinned with satisfaction. Quiet again.

Strangely annoyed, Kasey ruffled her magazine shut and got up to get some coffee. When she came back, he appeared to be busy reading. Yeah, it was the old I'm-going-to-ignore-her trick. What nonsense. Like kids playing checkers with two sets of rules. But hadn't she asked to be alone?

Kasey looked around for Jacques. He seemed to be lost in the kitchen. Oh well. She needed to get on with her day. Maybe as she continued her search for a business, she could make an appointment with an investment company. Keep all her options open.

When no one, including the green-eyed monster, had said a word, she guzzled down the rest of her coffee and got up to go. Just as she passed through the door, she looked up at the table behind the arch. Hamilton lounged on a chair while gazing up at her. What was the look on his face? Smug? Yes. Most definitely. Hamilton was coated in smug like one too many splashes of bad cologne.

Chapter 5

Yes, indeed. Hamilton had played with her like a fox does an unsuspecting rabbit. Well, she was no helpless hare. Kasey tossed her newly dyed hair back in a huff and bolted toward her car.

After a wrangling session with her banker as well as an investment company, Kasey headed home. She flipped her shoes across the room, nearly breaking a lamp. She slumped into the middle of her couch and didn't move a muscle. The sofa swallowed her up whole. It had always felt like a couch created for the sole purpose of giving a chiropractor some good business. But right now, she thought it felt more like a warm hug.

Kasey knew clearly what ailed her and why she needed a cozy feeling after her day. Heavy decisions had to be made. And then there was this guy with green eyes who no longer seemed to have a red nose and kept attracting her attention. Well, it's not like he could force her to fall in love. She was safe and just as stubborn as he obviously was.

The next day Hamilton fell in line at the Café Rose and

breathed in another good morning. He usually planned a *great* morning, but something had softened his edge. He knew the female name of that "sandblaster of the psyche," but he couldn't seem to do much about it.

He'd certainly done his part when he'd asked Kasey to have breakfast with him. But she plainly refused yesterday. He didn't enjoy punishing himself, but he seemed to be kind of snagged up on the way he felt when she handed him one of those luring lines. The ones that sounded so cute and maddening all at the same time. And he never knew what unexpected things might come out of his mouth when he was around her. It was bewildering in a delicious way. She made him feel like when you flick on the Christmas lights for the first time. There's the gasp of wonder. *Oh, brother.* He'd definitely been watching too many chick flicks lately.

He glanced at the door again. Kasey bounced in just then as if she owned the place. She looked glorious. And her hair. She'd been doing something else to it. Nice. And day two without those night goggles! He could really get into her eyes now. He stopped his staring and grabbed a grapefruit juice and a cup for his coffee.

She smiled at him, so he decided to hurt himself again by talking to her. "Hi, there."

"Hi." Kasey pulled out a tray and began to order.

He noticed she'd suddenly donned the same closed expression from the day before. He'd be willing to throw himself in harm's way again if she would just toss one more inviting smile his direction. Not wanting to use the tidal wave method, Hamilton said no more. He paid for his meal and sat at the table next to the arch.

He held up his news magazine but couldn't read a word. Her spicy perfume left him drifting off like a kite without a string. Or was it a musky scent? He had no idea, except it made him goofy in the head. He suddenly focused on his magazine, which had been upside down. Quickly he folded it up. Too late.

Kasey laughed. "Do you get more out of it reading it upside down?"

He grinned. "Sometimes these analysts are so full of verbiage it makes more sense this way." He knew he couldn't talk himself out of it. He'd been caught, and everyone who mattered knew it.

"I see you always have Jacques' coffee. It's the best, isn't it?" Kasey sat down at a table near Hamilton.

"Yes, it's almost legendary. Are you a connoisseur?" Hamilton asked.

"I am of sorts."

"Tell me then, do you know your arabica beans?"

"Of course I do." She almost sounded offended. "They grow their best at altitudes above three thousand feet. Let's see. They make up 80 percent of the world's coffee business. And they have superior flavor and aroma. So put *that* in your cup and drink it."

"An impressive start," Hamilton said.

"Okay. What do *you* have?"

Hamilton turned toward Kasey, giving her his full attention. "Well, coffee tasters are into checking acidity, flavor. . . aroma. . . and body." He paused, taking a drink of his coffee, then licking his lips. "Mmm. It's so good. You see, there's the feeling in your mouth. . .that coffee gives you. I'm sure you know what I mean. Heaviness. . .richness, etc." He took another slow sip. "Anyway, that's the body part of judging a really *satisfying* cup of coffee." Hamilton grinned at her. "Was there something else you wanted to know?"

Kasey's eyes widened and her lips parted slightly. He caught her fanning herself with her small notepad, but she didn't seem to notice.

Hamilton felt drawn to her as if there were an unseen force winding around them, pulling them together. The urge to throw down his cup and pull her into his arms overpowered him. "I'm going to. . .ask you something."

Kasey turned toward him, gripping her chair.

Suddenly a stranger appeared from nowhere and stood before Kasey. "I thought I'd find you here." The man sat down across from her as if he knew her well. Too well.

Who is this varmint? Talk about breaking his flow. Hamilton suddenly wondered what his tomato omelet would look like artfully smeared into the guy's crisp white canvas of a shirt. It could be an expressionistic painting.

"What are you doing here?" Kasey asked. She turned toward Hamilton's table, looking flustered. "Uh, excuse me, Hamilton, this is Lloyd Ludlow." She sort of mumbled the rest of the introduction.

Oh, this is great. Hamilton shook Lloyd's hand. Cold. Sticky. And solid as a jellyfish. He tried to say something non-threatening. "You must be an *old* boyfriend." The guy had too much gel on his bleached spikes, too much billboard flash, and way too much smile directed at Kasey.

"Yes," Lloyd said. "But I'm hoping the word *old* will change to something more current sounding."

Chapter 6

Hamilton didn't care for Lloyd's smile. The man wiggled too much, and he acted all nestled into her life. So Hamilton fumed while visions of bloodsucking parasites danced in his head. He stared at Kasey's unreadable expression.

"I think this conversation should continue right outside," Kasey said after an eternal pause.

"Yes, you're right, dear. I've never liked the Café Rose anyway. Too *European*. Let's find a more quiet place to talk about *us*," Lloyd said.

Hamilton smashed his finger against his eye to make it stop twitching. He had a powerful need to spout some very hot words. He would have to turn down the temp on his agitation, or it would singe the guy's hair. *What little hair that's left on his pointy little head, that is.* Hamilton suddenly brightened with an idea. Ah, reverse psychology. "Yes, Kasey, why *can't* you go with him?"

Hamilton felt the white-hot blast of her gaze on him. Adorable, but sizzling. He at least knew the truth about Lloyd now. The man appeared to be a glorified mule at best. And obviously Kasey thought so, too; otherwise she'd want to go with him to a quieter place. Now for the bad news. In the process of unearthing the truth, he'd gotten Kasey all steamed at him again. It would take days to unruffle her now.

"See, even Harrison here thinks we should go." Lloyd, the unwanted load, rose from his chair with confidence. "Besides, we're creating a scene here."

"Hamilton is the name. On second thought, I'd rather you not take Kasey anywhere. We kind of have a *thing* going here."

Lloyd stared at him with an odd expression. "A *thing*? What are you talking about? Kasey, explain to me what this thing is. You're not even sitting at the same table with him."

Kasey shook her head as if she were trying to wake up from something. "This is nonsense. Unless I'm in someone else's body, I don't have a *thing* going with anyone."

Lloyd sat back down like a lost puppy and nodded. "I understand. But then why did you call me the other night?"

Hamilton knew he was going a step too far, but he wanted to know. "Yes, why *did* you call Lloyd?"

Kasey faced Lloyd. "I thought I'd made myself perfectly clear in my message."

"My machine hasn't been working too well. I only caught your voice at the end." Lloyd sighed.

Kasey rubbed her temples and turned to Hamilton. "And what did you mean 'we have a *thing*'? We haven't even been out on a date."

"It would be a date if your chair was over at my table," Hamilton said.

Yes. Another dim-witted thing had flown out of his mouth, buzzed around his head, and called him idiot. His cell phone suddenly vibrated, and he had the urge to hammer it into tiny unrecognizable pieces. Instead he glanced at the number. His private banker. He'd have to catch him later.

Kasey rubbed her temples again. "I'm sorry. I have to go."

The man named Lloyd just sighed. Then he got in line to eat breakfast with no argument.

Who *was* this creep? Hamilton would have chased after Kasey had she been his love. He would have even slain a couple of dragons. This Lloyd guy must be a milksop type. Certainly *he* wouldn't climb any castle walls.

Hamilton slapped his newspaper down as if he were squashing a bug. He couldn't eat another bite, and he certainly had no plans to watch boy Lloyd slobber all over his breakfast. How could something so fine go so wrong? And what did he mean when he said they had a *thing*? Most of his life he'd said a lot of right things, but Kasey had this way of making him come out looking like a fool.

As Hamilton stalked away, he spotted a brochure on the floor next to Lloyd's chair. Out of curiosity, he picked it up. A Christian dating service. This was too much. That guy would really need one. He turned it over and discovered from the photo this Lloyd character actually owned the company. Was that weird or just funny? Not sure.

Hamilton looked back to make sure Lloyd still stood in the breakfast line. He flipped through the brochure. On the inside he saw someone very familiar. Kasey. A really good photo of Kasey. What was she doing in there looking beautiful and looking for a date? The blurb next to her photo mentioned some of her finer qualities. Had she paid big bucks to be in this thing?

Wait a minute. None of this made sense. This Lloyd's an old boyfriend. Then he features Kasey in his brochure to sell her off. *Now* he wants her back? Sounded like a soap opera. He crunched up the brochure and jammed it into his pocket. Later he would take it back out and tear it into little pieces.

The next day, Jacques leaned out the kitchen door searching for a sighting of Hamilton or Kasey. No sign of them. What a disaster he'd witnessed the day before between those two. He couldn't hear what they were saying, but he could tell from their scrunched-up faces that whatever happened wasn't good. He wondered who that guy had been who popped in to spoil the soup. Whoever he was, the man actually tore his croissant into tiny pieces and dipped them into the little jam pots. Certainly no bon vivant. The man couldn't be Kasey's type at all.

All at once, Hamilton tripped in, looking a little lopsided. Ten seconds later Kasey crept in, nearly knocking over a display table. *Yes,* Jacques thought, *they're both as loopy as tipsy toads today. It's got to be love.* He stroked his beard. "They just need a little more wind in their sails," he whispered to himself.

Myra, Jacques' assistant chef, patted him on the shoulder. "Snooping again?"

"No, just a little *overseeing,*" Jacques said. "I do love my customers. Yes?"

"I know. But is it your job to marry them *all* off?" Myra asked.

He looked into her sea blue eyes and wanted her to understand. "You see, sometimes I get these. . .promptings. That I could ease a lonely heart or two."

"All I know is that you've got the *biggest* heart I know." She sighed like a contented child and scurried off.

Jacques mused, *If I weren't so old for Myra, I'd take care of my own lonely heart.* He focused his attention back on Kasey and Hamilton. Jacques noticed the two were now at opposite ends of the café. Kasey had even abandoned her favorite table under the Love Arch just to avoid Hamilton. *Not good.* He then looked around the café and noticed two other couples he'd tried to get together, and they were sitting apart, too. Didn't anyone see the stirring hand of Providence anymore? But he couldn't force people to fall in love. He could only set the stage.

Suddenly, Sally, one of his waitresses, ambled over to him and handed him a note. "Here's one of those love notes again. I know you always like to deliver them. I think we serve more love notes around here than food." She trotted off before he could ask her more about it.

Doesn't matter. He'd just take a look at the name on the envelope. Somebody had jam on his hands, and the signature was smeared a tiny bit. But it certainly looked like "Kasey." He smiled, knowing that his dearest friends were getting closer to taking the plunge. Jacques danced a jig over to Kasey's table.

She lit up when she saw Jacques coming. "Morning! I haven't seen you in so long. Where have you been hiding?"

"Oh. Watching. . .out for my customers. Look. I brought you a note, little one. Hope you enjoy your breakfast." As he dashed off to the kitchen he called back, *"Bon appetite!"*

"Wait a minute. Jacques?" Kasey said.

He didn't answer her but walked briskly back into the kitchen. With a mischievous expression, Jacques removed the classical CD and replaced it with some romantic piano jazz. He listened for a moment and sighed. *Ah. Just right for romance.*

Myra handed Jacques a cinnamon scone from the oven and chuckled. "I know God's watching out for the sparrow, but the rest of the time I think He's trying to keep *you* out of trouble."

Her cooing laughter sounded like an enchanted flute to him, and he remembered her lovely name, Myra, was Old French, and that it meant "quiet song." He'd looked it up one evening in a book and thought how saying the name always brightened his day.

Jacques saw something in Myra's eyes just then. *Could that sparkle be for me?*

Kasey sat there with her note, which was obviously from Hamilton. She still wasn't going to converse with him. He would have to suffer a bit. She tapped the note against the table in time to the music. *Jazz? Since when did Jacques play jazz in here for breakfast?* She took another bite of the gooey apple filling in her crepe. Intoxicating. Was that nutmeg?

Her shoulders softened along with her heart as she opened the note and read the contents:

> *Since I've met you I've had a little trouble concentrating on my work.*

Actually, I've had trouble concentrating. . .period.
I find you irresistible.
I would love another chance to share a table with you.

Kasey read it again, gingerly folded it back up, and slid the note into her purse. Irresistible, huh? What a line. *He's probably got a whole drawer full of these little goobers. Maybe on slow days he drops gooey notes from airplanes all over the city like war propaganda. He must leave the ladies swooning.* But she'd never been one to swoon. Instead, she drummed her fingers and narrowed her eyes.

Kasey suddenly remembered her neighbors' comment on the party invitation attached to her door. She pounded her fist, accidentally upsetting a tiny vat of marmalade. Sticky sweetness attached itself to every part of her arm and sleeve. Quickly she tried to clean up, dabbing a wet napkin here and there, but making an even bigger mess of her clothes.

In frustration, she gave up the scrubbing process as she remembered Hamilton's note. Could he be genuine? Maybe on a good day they might have a chance, but they hadn't had any good days yet.

Kasey took a long whiff of the fresh pink rose at her table and another bite of the crepe. The food was obviously tainted with something to make her confused, because she felt her legs get up almost against her will and walk over to Hamilton. Kasey held her arm to cover a bit of the stain as she looked down at him. She tapped her shoe waiting for a response. Still waiting. Now what was she supposed to do? Grovel?

Chapter 7

Slowly Hamilton lowered his newspaper and looked up at Kasey.

For a guy who thought her irresistible, he didn't look enraptured. In fact he looked startled, like the proverbial deer in the headlights. Perhaps he thought she wouldn't come over. *I guess he wants me to say something.* "Something." Kasey cringed at her faux pas. "I mean, hello." Had he turned into carved marble? How embarrassing.

"Hi," Hamilton replied without offering any obvious warmth.

Well, that's better than nothing, Kasey thought.

"Do you want to sit down?" His tone sounded cautious.

"Sure. Okay." She eased down across from him.

Hamilton's cell phone rang, and he answered it. Kasey got up to leave, and he motioned for her to stay. He wrapped up the call quickly and turned back to her.

Hamilton seemed to eyeball the stains on her clothes. "Tell me. Is your coffee having trouble staying in its cup again?"

Kasey laughed. "No. It was marmalade this time. It's sort

of like sweet glue. By the way, I hope your jacket recovered."

Hamilton offered a slow smile. "It did."

After a squirming pause, she said, "Yesterday was kind of. . .uncomfortable."

"Old boyfriend troubles?" Hamilton asked.

"It was a misunderstanding. I merely wanted to ask him some questions about his dating service," Kasey said.

"Dating service? I thought you weren't looking for marriage. Remember?"

"No. I wasn't asking Lloyd about signing up with his dating service. I was just curious about the business side of it. He seems successful from his publicity materials and Web site. Investmentwise, I simply thought—"

"You would *actually* want to invest in *his* company?"

"Well, no," Kasey said. "I suppose I just wondered what it would be like to own one."

"You were *actually* thinking of starting up a dating service?" His tone got a little more animated.

"Do you have to keep using the word *actually*?" Kasey felt flustered again, but knew she didn't want to walk away.

"Sorry."

Kasey wondered if it was their fate to always make a scene wherever they went. She lowered her voice. "Look. Maybe I should just go back to my corner again. At least we can have a rest before we duke it out in round two." She tried not to but couldn't help breaking into a grin.

Hamilton's smile weakened. "Cute. But not as cute as this photo of you." He opened the crumpled dating brochure to Kasey's photo and then shoved it across the table to her as if it were Exhibit A in a courtroom.

"Where did you get this? And why is it so crinkled? It looks like it's been through a garbage disposal."

"It had crossed my mind," Hamilton said.

Kasey mashed out the brochure. "Wait a minute. This photo inside. It almost looks like me."

"It *is* you."

"Well, I never signed anything or even talked about this with Lloyd. He never got my permission to do this. In fact, he is in so deep here. I'll have to ask him to take me off their list immediately or face my attorney. I wish I *had* an attorney." Kasey stormed around in her brain wondering what this all meant. Would she get weird phone calls at home from strange men? Why would Lloyd do such a thing to her?

"Looks like Lloyd is in trouble." He took a sip of his coffee, obviously trying to look innocent.

"Okay, Mr. Wakefield. You can wipe that gloating expression off your face right now."

"Tell me, do you always exude such warmth, or do I bring out that gold flame in your eyes?"

Hamilton's last statement knocked her out of her rhythm. Kasey crossed her arms and wondered why in the world she'd come over to this quirky mess of a man called Hamilton. She knew why deep down, and it worried her even more. "You're jealous because you thought I wanted to be in that goofy dating brochure. But you have no reason to be. You barely know me." Then she added, "Oh, I almost forgot. You find me *irresistible*."

"I do?"

"Yes. . .you do." Kasey frowned. "Don't you?" She wondered

what game he was playing now.

Hamilton leaned in. "Why do you think I've been eating breakfast here every morning?"

"Probably because I forbade you to eat breakfast here every morning."

Hamilton seemed to touch her face with his gaze. "All I know is I'd like to get to know you better. . .that is if we can stop this verbal jousting thing for a few minutes."

"All right. I'll tell you something about myself," Kasey said. "I love eating Jacques' cooking and then trying to re-create it at home. And I love Jacques, too. He's a dear man. There. How's that?"

"That was good." Hamilton said. "Yeah. Everybody loves Jacques." He leaned closer to her. "He's been almost like a father to me since my own dad passed away a few years ago."

"My father died some years ago, too."

"I'm sorry. It's hard, isn't it?" Hamilton's face echoed his compassion.

"Yeah. It is. Lately it's been even harder. I think I'm just now grieving for both my parents after three years of sort of. . . holding my breath. Do you still have your mom?"

"No. I wish I did," Hamilton said.

He said no more about his mother, so Kasey let a thoughtful silence settle between them.

"So you like to cook?" he finally asked.

"I love it," Kasey replied. "I've even been entering contests."

"Won any?"

"No. But I will."

"I like your confidence. I'll bet you'll win," Hamilton said.

"I haven't gone that direction. But I do have enough original stuff for a cookbook."

"Except for Jacques, I've never met a man who loves to cook."

"Well, you've never met me before."

Kasey had trouble focusing when he used his deep radio voice. Was he doing that deliberately? What was he saying? "Excuse me?" Kasey asked.

"I was saying maybe we could go for a walk. Rose Park is across the street, and I think there are still a few uncooked flowers in this heat."

"Don't you think it's too warm for a walk?"

"We'll catch it before it gets too hot. . .won't we?" Hamilton asked.

Kasey caught herself twirling her hair like a young girl. Hamilton must have paid Jacques to drug her crepe.

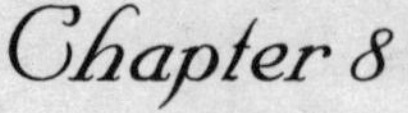

Chapter 8

She'd never acted this way before, not even in high school. Perhaps she was suddenly making up for lost time. His green eyes were doing marvelous things to her. . .or was it the whole package? "Okay," she said.

Hamilton offered his hand to help her up. "Shall we?"

Kasey rose to the touch of his fingers on her arm. Warm. Confident. Inviting. "I don't think I've ever taken a walk in that park. . .or any park. I never take the time." The rest of the story was she'd never known anyone interesting enough to bother taking a walk with. Until now.

Just as they were leaving, Jacques hurried over to them almost out of breath. "I need a favor. A big one."

Kasey reached out to Jacques. "Are you all right?"

"What can we do?" Hamilton asked.

"A lot of my help is sick today, and I have to leave for a slight emergency. I will only be gone one hour. You both are gifted in the kitchen. Do you think you could lend a hand in there until I get back?"

Kasey glanced at Hamilton who also had a startled expression. "Sure."

"You bet," Hamilton said.

Jacques patted Hamilton on the back. "Myra is in the kitchen. She'll show you both what to do. I have never asked my customers to do this in my life. . .but then you both are more than customers to me. You know that. I will make it up to you. You will see."

"We'll be okay," Kasey said. "Now get going."

With a grateful expression consuming his round face, Jacques sped toward the front door.

"Hope everything's okay with Jacques." Kasey frowned, rubbing her forehead.

"Me, too." Hamilton stared after Jacques until he was out of sight. "Let's go see what Myra needs us to do."

Myra looked up as they came into the kitchen. "Oh, good. You both will save the day. Don't worry. I'll give you something easy to do. We need another large bowl of fruit salad. Maybe you both could work at this table cutting the fruits.

Hamilton and Kasey washed their hands and began to work on the tray of melons, strawberries, and grapes. As they sliced, Kasey stole a glance up at Hamilton. He seemed amazingly at peace, as if he truly belonged here. And then she realized even in the midst of the clattering and noise, she liked it, too. A lot. Of course, it was only a tiny taste of the business, and yet she somehow felt at home.

Hamilton smiled at her. A really great smile that warmed her all the way through.

"Having fun?" he asked.

"Yes. I think I am." Kasey poured her cut fruit into a large ceramic bowl. "You know, when I was a little girl, I used to really enjoy making cookies with my mom. I loved it so much, she showed me how to make homemade breads, too. And then sauces and meats. In the summertime when the other kids were busy taking swimming lessons, I was learning how to make shrimp scampi and baked Alaska." Kasey looked up. "Where did you get your love for cooking?"

"My uncle. He owned a café. Kind of a hole in the wall, really. But he used to have a lot of customers drive from all around the county just to eat his catfish and hush puppies. Sometimes he'd let me come into the kitchen and watch. It was a small operation, but it looked like a big magic show to me. I was fascinated by it all. His name was Charles. I miss him. He was a good cook and a good man."

Kasey didn't know what to say. She just grinned at him. In fact, Kasey did so much grinning at Hamilton she nearly cut her finger.

The time slipped away, and before she even wondered about Jacques, he slammed through the kitchen door. "False alarm! My sister just had false labor pains. Sorry." He raised his eyebrows at Hamilton and Kasey. "You had a good time. Yes? But I really am so grateful for your help. Go now, and have some fun somewhere. Shoo. . .shoo."

They all said their friendly good-byes, and Kasey and Hamilton headed out the kitchen door.

"Rose Park is still waiting for us," Hamilton said.

"You're right. It is." Once outside, she looked up at the sky. "The clouds look kind of like angry bulls, don't they?"

"I don't think they're ready to charge just yet. Let's take a chance."

Their brisk walk turned into a run as they raced across the street to Rose Park.

Kasey knew she should be doing something useful, but she'd spent so little time doing pleasurable things that the sensation fascinated her. She'd had dates, but they always seemed more like work than pleasure. As they strolled along the path, Hamilton turned his green-eyed gaze on her.

"Are you trying to read my thoughts?" she asked.

Hamilton chuckled. "Tell me. Are you always so blunt?"

"Most of the time. I really do hate lies. They cause nothing but trouble. I watched a friend of mine years ago have endless problems because of one lie that got out of control. It destroyed her in the end. So I guess I have a real zeal for the truth. But I tend to forget the gentle part. Sometimes I think I use honesty as a weapon. I load up in the morning and then shoot my way through the day."

"I think you're really like a toasted marshmallow. You like people to see the crusty outside, but inside, there's all this sweet mush."

"I never thought of myself quite like that." Kasey picked up a pinecone and twirled it around in her hand. As she became very aware of its sharp points, she couldn't help wondering if that's what it felt like to be at the receiving end of her barbs.

"I think your honesty is one of the reasons I'm attracted to you." Hamilton added, "*That* and your smile. . .among other things."

"I'm not going to ask what the other things are."

"You can. . .I wouldn't embarrass you."

"If you're so enthralled with me, why do you want to argue

with me at every possible opportunity?" Kasey asked.

"Funny, I wondered the same thing about you."

They both stared at each other and then burst into laughter.

Kasey relaxed her shoulders. "I'm sure you know attraction has its consequences."

"I hope we can make them all good ones." Hamilton touched her back to guide her around a clump of lower tree branches. "Now. How about you tell me your life's story, and then I'll tell you mine?"

"I wouldn't know where to begin," Kasey said. "No one has ever asked me that before."

"Tell me what you were like when you were little. Did you give your parents a lot of trouble?"

"No, I most certainly did *not*. I was like a cherub. In fact, that was my nickname."

Hamilton led Kasey to a gazebo near a willow-lined pond. Mallard ducks moved across the water, making arrow-shaped trails in the still water. The ducks murmured as if they were chatting quietly. Suddenly a child near the bank hurled a piece of bread out into the water, causing one of the mallards to release a greedy squawk. They watched the drama as the one duck waggled past his friends, speeding after the morsel until he consumed it in one big gulp.

"Reminds me of my stockbroker," Hamilton said.

Kasey chuckled.

They sat down on a wooden bench inside the gazebo. Hamilton looked relaxed and in a very good mood. He seemed to be waiting patiently for her to speak.

Kasey looked up to see a canopy of pink roses above her

swaying in the breeze. *How beautiful.* She breathed deeply of the perfumed air and thought of a story to share from her youth. She told Hamilton of the rocking horse her father had made for her when she was three. And how it had brought her so much delight, she'd saved it all these years. As the morning unfolded, Kasey took notice of the way Hamilton drew out almost forgotten memories, as well as her dreams for the future.

She asked about his life and passions, and discovered he loved many of the things she did: Jacques' coffee, classical music, Italian and French cuisine, and most of all, he loved the Lord. The minutes glided by like the petals floating on the pond. "I can't believe it." Kasey looked at her watch. "We've talked for almost three hours. But this has been nice. I feel as if. . ."

"As if what?" Hamilton asked gently.

"I think you already know what I'm going to say." A cluster of the blousy roses bowed down to her face in the gust. She welcomed their baby soft petals playing on her cheek. Their intense and exquisite fragrance held her in a spell for a moment as she recalled her mother's description of the scent. . .the perfume of angels. Kasey wanted to pick one but decided instead to buy some roses for her patio. Lots of them to remind her of this day.

She glanced back at Hamilton. He'd been watching her in her reverie. A shiver went through her in spite of the heat. "Hamilton. . .what's happening. . .between us?" Even though it seemed like a reasonable question, Kasey could feel the moisture building up on her skin. She tugged on the collar of her shirt to give herself some air.

"I don't know what's happening. . .yet. But I know I'm not

going to walk away from it. Are you?"

She shook her head. "I don't think so."

"By the way, I have another good idea," Hamilton said.

"You do?"

"How about you scoot over here so I can tell you what it is."

Kasey cocked her head. "That's the oldest trick in the book. And what makes you think I want to do that?"

"Because even your eyes can't tell a lie."

Kasey hesitated and then slid over next to him. "Okay. So what's your idea? But for the record, that's not why you had me come over here. Is it?"

Hamilton brushed away a strand of hair on Kasey's cheek. It seemed an innocent gesture, but it didn't feel that way inside her. With his finger he traced down to her chin and then up to the soft lobe of her ear. He seemed to study the dangling bobble on her earring. A flurry of air loosened Kasey's scarf until it unraveled.

Hamilton took the silky material in his hands. "Looks like you've come undone." He slowly retied it.

Kasey became hypersensitive to his touch. She drifted into a sweet agony. The breeze made her hair float up around her face. She searched his eyes. Did he notice her erratic breathing? More and more air. Maybe she would pass out from hyperventilation. It reminded her of the time in high school when she had to give a speech. Too much air. Would she pass out this time, too? She bit her lip. Her mind answered no to her query. Because this time she didn't want to miss a thing!

Hamilton finished tying her scarf and then leaned down

to her face, just missing her lips. Kasey straightened, hoping for a closer encounter. She could feel his breath on her cheek. Thinking Hamilton was about to kiss her, she closed her eyes, waiting for him to pull back and cover her mouth with his. Instead, Hamilton whispered in her ear, "What did you think I was going to do?"

Startled out of her dreamy state like the sharp slam of a door, Kasey opened her eyes. She forced herself not to sound disappointed. "I thought you were going to kiss me."

"My goodness." Hamilton shook his head. "Kasey, we've not even been on a real date yet." His smile appeared just a little too sporting for her liking.

"You ought to be hog-tied and whipped within an inch of your life." Kasey tried hard not to laugh, but it was no use.

Chapter 9

"You have the spiciest mouth I've ever heard. I wonder if it tastes the same way."

Kasey scooted away from his touch. "Well, I guess you won't know now."

"Go out with me tonight. I know a place on the Buffalo Bayou I think you'd love. Northern Italian cuisine."

"Oaks Lodge?" Kasey tried to calm down from their intimacy.

"How did you know?"

"I've been there," Kasey said. "It's beautiful."

"So did you go to Oaks Lodge with Lloyd, the lovesick lump? Sorry. I couldn't help myself."

Kasey chuckled at the funny way he revealed his feelings. "You know, it's silly to be jealous of him. My relationship with him was like. . .like a goofy limerick with no rhyme or reason."

"Good simile. I feel better now." Hamilton's brows flickered a little. "I just hope that's not how you describe our date tonight."

Kasey shook her head at him as a flash of merriment crossed her face.

"I'll take that as a yes." Hamilton glanced upward at the clouds. "Come on. I think those bulls are ready to charge now. Let's run."

The sky released a spattering of enormous drops. Kasey couldn't help but laugh along with Hamilton as they raced back down the garden path, trying to avoid getting soaked. They hurriedly made their plans for the evening, tucked themselves into their sedans, and then sped off in different directions.

Kasey snapped on the radio. She caught herself tapping out a tune with her fingers. But too country and way too whiny. What were they singing about anyway? Impossible love that went down the drain or that drove someone insane? That one didn't fit. She pushed another button. Classical. But too operatic. The last note felt like it gave her a face-lift.

Kasey's car suddenly hit a large speed bump. Her whole body felt the stunning jolt. She flicked off the music and gripped the wheel. *Kasey Morland. What are you doing?* Then she groaned, remembering the miserable business at home. Lloyd and his brochure. She was looking forward to that confrontation like a double root canal.

At her apartment, she noted thirty-two messages. *Oh no.* She pushed the button and waited. "Howdy, little lady. My name is H. D. Kimball. The H. D. stands for 'Handsome Dog.' " The caller paused to "hee-hee" a bit. "I picked you out of this here dating service. You sure are a purdy thing. Give me a ring. I'm itching to meet ya."

By the time the cowboy had left his phone number, Kasey felt a headache coming on. She popped a ginger ale from the fridge while she listened to the next message.

"Hey, what's going down? I'm Zee," caller number two said. "Everybody just calls me 'the Zee man.' I read your groovy bio thing from this dating place. I can dig it. You seem to jive with where my head's at these days, so thought maybe we could hang out and rap for a while. Oh, I'll have to give you a friend's phone number cause my phone is out. . .since. . .well, I got evicted from my pad 'cause I lost my gig at the music store. Bummer, right? So, okay, catch you later. . .babe."

Do people like him still exist? An overdose of life started pounding in Kasey's head. Luckily it drowned out Zee's phone number. She stared at her answering machine as if it were something coming back to life in a horror flick. Wait a minute. Why was she being so dramatic? She never resorted to theatrics. It was a waste of valuable time. In spite of her reprimand, Kasey smashed the stop button with her fist, hoping the machine might break. Even her ginger ale couldn't help her now, so she downed an aspirin and eased onto the couch with an ice pack.

She knew clearly all of those thirty-two calls were about Lloyd and his finagling with her life. What did Lloyd mean by doing this without her permission? That's not how legitimate dating services worked anyway. Wouldn't she see the photos of the guys, too, and then agree to the calls? She'd even known of some people at church who'd successfully used dating services. Obviously the problem was Lloyd. Perhaps he plotted some kind of revenge for their breakup. "Well, I intend to put a stop to this," she said out loud to strengthen her resolve.

Kasey eased up from the couch and punched in Lloyd's number. One ring. She drummed her fingers on the counter. Too many rings. Not at home. Or did he notice who popped up on the Caller ID and he got too chicken-livered to answer the phone. Kasey decided to leave a sharp message for Lloyd on his machine, so there would be no future misunderstandings about how she felt about what he'd done.

Now back to the couch and maybe some soft chamber music to calm her sputtering nerves. She glanced at her watch. "Seven," she whispered. The number of hours before liftoff with the guy who'd propelled his way into her life. Hamilton.

Kasey recalled today's "almost kiss." It had indeed been heady, but all the new sensations lately certainly would make life complicated. *I don't do mess.* And emotions that rode like a roller coaster were more than distracting. They could actually keep a person from being successful. Already two men had kept her from her daily planner. Hamilton and Lloyd. She took another sip of her ginger ale and vowed all her distractions would have to be reevaluated and possibly eliminated. But lately all her determination and personal pledges never seemed to amount to much.

She felt a gentle tug in her spirit but didn't know how to label it or how to respond. While God was busy handling the globe, was He trying to impress upon her that He was paying close attention to her world, as well? Certainly something to ponder when she could schedule it in.

Hamilton glanced at the number near the door and pushed the doorbell for the second time. He shuffled a little wondering if Kasey had changed her mind about going out with him. If she did, he could live with it. Well, no, he couldn't. He was already neck deep, which unfortunately included his heart. Just as he started to sweat it, she opened the door.

Kasey stood there drenched in the word *female.* She wore a pink dress with some kind of shimmery thing around her that fortunately didn't do a very thorough job of covering her almost-bare shoulders. Even her cheeks glowed like the inside of those seashells he'd picked up in Galveston. *Well, well. She's certainly getting in touch with her softer side.* He knew she'd be lovely tonight, but the Kasey in his imagination couldn't come close to the real-life version. And he wanted to do something about it. Just for starters he'd like to sweep her into his arms and kiss her soundly. Right this second, in fact. But he chose to manage the more aggressive side of his manhood. . .for now. He adjusted his tie and voted for a more controlled reaction. "You look like a peach."

"Thanks. But I hope you don't mean round and fuzzy," Kasey said.

"No. Soft and. . .sweet." With a warm smile, he whisked her off to Oaks Lodge.

Later, the evening unfolded flawlessly. Candlelight. Vivaldi. Great conversation. Great food. And a truly great companion. Perfection. All except one thing. Kasey seemed a little distant during the meal. Why? Probably second thoughts about their sudden relationship. But the lodge had a lit path along the bayou, and he thought a stroll by the water might work its magic to reel her back in.

As they finished up their coffee and gelato, Hamilton decided the time had arrived. "You know an evening at the Oaks isn't complete without a walk along the bayou." He settled back in his soft leather chair, trying to look confident. "And look, there's a full moon."

Kasey sat stroking her strand of pearls. "Maybe a. . .short stroll."

Hamilton helped her with her chair and then placed his hand at her elbow as they walked through the door and down the outdoor staircase. He felt a tremor run through her, and the lamplight revealed goose bumps on her arm even though the night air felt warm. Was she hiding something? Perhaps she suffered within the same state of amorous delirium as he did. He certainly hoped so. With renewed determination, he decided he would find out just how unraveled she was. In fact, he wondered if he could have her safely in his arms and moving toward a kiss within fifteen minutes.

Once near the water, Hamilton steered her to the right. "Let's go this way. It will take us to something I think you'll like."

"The infamous Gazebo of Rhapsody?"

"You really *do* know this place." He couldn't help but wonder how many men had brought her to the Oaks. Hamilton decided to use Kasey's straightforward approach. "You've had second thoughts about us, haven't you?"

Kasey pulled back in surprise. "I think you already know me too well."

"You're a serious-minded woman. Maybe you're concerned that what's developing is frivolous like some teenage infatuation. And *possibly* even a waste of your time. But what if God wants us to be together? Ever thought of that?"

"And what if you're—"

"We are both dipped out of the same pot of stew. That's

what Jacques would say, wouldn't he?"

"You *are* amazing."

"I know," Hamilton said.

"*And* an egotistical maniac."

"I'm going to ignore that last arrow." Hamilton made an exaggerated flourish of his hand and bowed low to her. "Madam, your chariot awaits."

Kasey chuckled as she stepped into the gazebo of lattice and wisteria.

Hamilton pointed to the tall grasses below. "Look, fireflies."

"Where?"

Hamilton gently took hold of her shoulders and pointed her in the right direction. A cooling chill ran over him. What was that perfume she was wearing? *My, my.* She wore it well. Whatever the scent was, he was surprised it was legal.

"They look so pretty down there by the water. . .like fairies dancing," Kasey said. "You know, when I was a kid, I always wanted to catch them. Sometimes I actually did. . .catch a couple."

"And what happened?" With reluctance Hamilton released her so she could see the fireflies more closely.

"Oh, well, they glowed a little after that, but I could tell they didn't like the confines of my jar. I think the fireflies really needed to be free to glow their brightest."

Hamilton didn't like the way the firefly chat was going. . .at all. New subject. He pressed the light button on his watch and glanced down briefly.

"Do you need to be somewhere? We can go."

"No," Hamilton said too quickly. "Sorry." *What a blunder.*

He'd need to be more careful, or she'd disappear like the fireflies. "So, what do you think? Is this romantic?"

"Well, there's soft lighting. A winding path along the water. And piano jazz piped out here. They're the perfect ingredients to make people swoon with giddy heads. . .and do things they might regret later."

Chapter 10

Giddy heads? Hamilton almost groaned out loud. What was happening? Just when he thought he'd made headway, he was forced to take two moves backward like on a board game. "Kasey, don't hold back here. Tell me what you're really thinking."

Kasey laughed. "I thought you could read my mind."

"Not all the time. I really want to know."

"Why do you care so much?" Kasey seemed puzzled and concerned.

"I don't know for sure. . .yet. I mean why are people attracted in the first place? It's a mystery. Why are some people brilliant at math and others at music? Why does God bother to love any of us? Why did He place only one moon up there? The world is full of mysteries. And here's one right now between us I intend to thank Him for without too many questions. How about you?"

"You certainly have a way with words, Mr. Wakefield."

"I think you bring it out in me." Hamilton noticed something soften in her lovely eyes. Maybe the right words were finally flowing out of his mouth. "*And* you certainly have a way of looking at me that makes me want to take you into my arms."

"That sounds like a rehearsed line, but you say it so convincingly."

A slow and inviting piece of jazz drifted out over the bayou. Hamilton wasted no time in moving toward her. He wrapped one hand around her waist and the other he intertwined with her fingers. Kasey looked up into his eyes. His longing to kiss her turned into an ache. He drifted with her to the rhythm of the night until his whole being told him the time felt ripe for a kiss.

Kasey looked up at him. "Are you going to tease me again like you did earlier today? Pretend you're going to kiss me and then pull away."

"I have no intention of *ever* doing that again. It drove me half crazy."

"Well, you know, girls don't like to be teased," Kasey said lightly.

Hamilton laughed. "You are. . .a delight."

"In between being a pill?"

"Well, you're a pill I don't mind taking."

Kasey let her arms fall back limply like a rag doll. "I'm duped. I'm lost to whatever game you're playing. I surrender. Now kiss me."

Hamilton studied her. "Wait a minute here. I'm desperate to do that very thing, but not like this." He let go of her waist. "I don't want you to think it's a game. It's not. Okay?"

"Who are you trying to convince here?" Kasey seemed a little startled. "Okay. I believe you. Hamilton?"

"Let me see it in your eyes."

Kasey stepped into the light. "Are you convinced now?"

"Maybe. If I do kiss you, you're not going to disappear like the fireflies are you?"

Kasey removed her shoes and then set them down next to her. "There. I can't run very fast without my shoes. Now will you kiss me?"

Since he'd suffered some, he thought he'd give her a taste of the torture of waiting. "Say please."

Kasey put her hands on her hips.

Hamilton knew he was on dangerous ground now. Fortunately she had nothing in her hands to throw at him. But he wouldn't make either of them wait one more second. The distance dissolved between them as he pulled her into a sound embrace. Hamilton saw Kasey's satisfied grin as she seemed to sink down with him in that wonderfully weightless feeling that comes in the anticipation of a truly meaningful kiss.

As Hamilton feathered her lips with kisses, the word *melt* came to mind. What a very good word. In the distance somewhere cars blared their horns, people chatted, the world spun busily around, but there in the midst of it all, Hamilton and Kasey were sweetly melting together. And it felt so right. How many kisses had he enjoyed through the years? It didn't matter. None had even come close to this.

He finally came up for air. "Darling, you almost taste like. . . nutmeg again. You had that scent at lunch. Jacques must have fixed you some apple crepes." Hamilton sprinkled kisses across her cheek. Were those people passing by? *Who cares?*

"What did you just call me?" Kasey asked in a wispy voice.

"I called you *darling*."

"No one has ever called me that before."

"Do you want me to say it again?" Hamilton asked.

"I think so. Yes. It's such *sweet* talk. . .like chocolate mousse. I think I'm getting hungry again."

Hamilton laughed softly. "Maybe I'll make you some mousse tomorrow. And feed it to you. Would you like me to do that?" He brushed a kiss just below her earlobe. "Darling?"

Kasey looked a little blurry-eyed. "Now I forgot what I was going to say."

"Does it really matter?"

"Oh, I remember. The note. I haven't thanked you properly, yet."

"I'd love a thank you." Hamilton wondered what sweet pleasure was in store for him.

Before he could say another word, Kasey suddenly took his face in her hands, kissed him soundly, and then released him. She left him nearly gasping for breath. "Well, that was by far the best thank-you gift I've *ever* received." He placed her fingers on his wrist. "Take my pulse."

Kasey obeyed. "My goodness. Did I do that?"

Hamilton nodded as he pulled her close again. "Now what did you say that kiss was for?"

"The note," Kasey said. "You sent it to me this morning at the café. Right?"

"Note? *I* sent a note?" Hamilton noticed the flame turned itself down a notch.

"Yes. It said some lovely things." Kasey continued with a slight edge in her tone. "No. I guess you don't know what I'm talking about." She reached down in her evening bag for the note.

"You keep it with you?"

Kasey looked a little shy. "Well, yes. It's what started all this between us."

"No. The second we met is what started this between us." Hamilton tried to hurry himself out of his haze to deal with this odd turn of events.

Kasey handed Hamilton the note as if it were a treasure.

He slid the note out of the envelope and studied it for a moment. All he could think of was how much trouble he must be in. But why? "Okay. This is what I *would* have written had I thought to do it." Hamilton held the envelope up to a nearby lantern. "Wait a minute. Look at this on the envelope. The name isn't Kasey, it's. . . Haley. Look. The *H* is smudged, and the top of the *l* got rubbed off."

Kasey stared at the name in the light. "I see it now. I wonder how Jacques made the mistake. Although I know notes get passed around in that place like it's math class in high school." She sighed. "Jacques started that tradition years ago."

Hamilton could hear the disappointment in her voice, and it tore at him. "Jacques is after all. . .an incurable romantic."

"And you're not?" Kasey asked as she slipped her shoes back on.

"Well, what do you really want? I thought we were bottom-line people first."

"Sort of. But it means this whole evening wouldn't have happened without this note. And this note is nothing more than a. . .lie."

"No. Not a lie. I am sure it was an honest mistake. And you can ask Jacques all about it tomorrow morning." Hamilton moved toward her again, but she backed away into the shadow.

"Sorry. The music has stopped, and I think the magic is wearing off."

"I think we'd better start this one over again." Before he could figure out what to do next, a vivacious-looking redhead strode toward them. *Oh no. Not Alex!*

"Hamilton? Is that you?" Alex shrieked. "It's so good to see you here. Uh-oh. I see you have a guest. Let's see who we have here." She peeked into the gazebo. "Hmm."

Hamilton wondered why the moon had turned on him. Everything had glowed so warmly. All of life seemed to move in rhythm like one celestial slow dance. And now disaster hit him at every turn. What next? An alligator attack? An abduction by aliens? Well, that last one might be a positive at this point. Since it was clear Alex wasn't going anywhere soon, he thought he'd better speak up. "Kasey, this is an old friend of mine, Alex Warren. Alex, this is Kasey Morland," he said as quickly as he could without being rude.

"Former *fiancé*, that is," Alex said. She managed a sashay even though she was standing still.

Hamilton noticed Alex had tried on her sweetest smile. *It still doesn't fit her.* He suddenly took note of the poor slob standing out on the pathway. Obviously Alex's date. So sad. The guy had a pathetic dying-animal look in his eyes.

Alex turned to Kasey. "Hon, if you plan to marry him, know that in the end, it will always be about business. You will help him meet his goals. Won't that be fun? Think of the upside. You both will always have *lots* of money. I'll leave the downside for you to think about." She broke the air with a giggle. "Good to meet you, Kasey. Good-bye, Hamilton." She scrunched up her nose at them, showed her red talons, and then dashed off with her now embarrassed escort.

"Great speech, Alex. Thanks for stopping by," Hamilton said loudly even though Alex had already gone. He saw the fear in Kasey's eyes and realized how apropos the word *good-bye* was going to be.

Chapter 11

"Well, that was exceptionally strange." Kasey edged toward the opening of the gazebo.

"Yes. It was. I'm going to say she is just jealous of you. But you're not going to believe me. I can already see it in your eyes. But it's true, because I'm the one who broke off the engagement."

"*You* broke off an engagement? And you never mentioned it to me even though we've told each other all the important highlights of our lives?"

"It seemed insignificant at the time," Hamilton replied.

"An engagement may be insignificant to you, but not to the rest of the known world."

"That's not what I meant. What I was—"

"It was like a lie," Kasey said.

"I didn't lie. It just never came up." Hamilton felt a coiling ache in his stomach. It pained him to see the mist in her eyes. He wanted to wrap his arms around her to take away the hurt and misunderstanding.

"And what this Alex woman said was a quite an indictment

of your character. Shouldn't I be a little concerned here?" Kasey's voice shook.

Hamilton realized there was no right way to answer her question.

"I want to go home."

"I'll take you home, but I won't let this go until I have a chance to explain myself." Hamilton turned to reach for her hands, but she folded her arms tightly.

"I think I've had enough explaining for one night. Please excuse me. I'm taking a taxi home." Kasey put her hands up in the air to stop him from following.

"There's no need for this," Hamilton called after her as she nearly ran up the path.

"Please be careful," he said at full volume but knowing she was no longer listening.

Kasey didn't even glance back. Anger rushed through him. *Alex. She certainly finished off the evening with her little announcement.* But he felt much angrier at himself for letting Kasey get away. "I'll talk to you tomorrow," he whispered as a promise to himself. He would have chased after her, but something told him she needed the space and some time to calm down. Was that God talking to him? Or just his brain shaking words around like a baby's rattle? So much for slaying dragons. Just then a firefly lighted on his arm. He stayed still, just watching it, not bothering to capture it. Didn't matter. He knew he would just have to let it go anyway.

Hamilton frowned, remembering Kasey's smile and warm hands on his face. He gritted his teeth. He would win at this. *Win at what?* He'd almost finished his thought with the word *game*. Surely he didn't mean it. Games and goals and winning at all expense? He had always loved a good challenge, but did it spill over into all of his life? Suddenly his cell phone rang in his jacket, and he realized he hadn't even turned it off for their first real date. Had Alex's indictment been right? Maybe he really didn't deserve Kasey.

In a moment of fury, Hamilton hurled the ringing telephone out toward the bayou. It sailed through the night air. Seconds later, he heard a splash and pondered how good it felt to cut off what had become like an appendage to his body. Then he remembered the old man on the street who he'd run into recently. *What had he said?* For some reason it seemed important now.

Kasey hammered the alarm clock for the zillionth time. She winced at the light streaming in the window. She'd only had about an hour's sleep, but she tried to sit up anyway. *What a miserable situation. That's what love does.* Did she say the *L* word? She threw herself back on the bed. How did this nonsense happen? She'd commanded herself to be in control.

She touched her lip, remembering the thank-you kiss she'd given Hamilton the night before. Kasey knew clearly though that what she felt for him was more than physical. It spilled over into the heart, and there was nothing she could do about it.

She knew it would be easy to make excuses for her emotional state. She'd probably even want to defend Hamilton. But it did remain true that Alex could have been lying, and it really wasn't Hamilton's fault about the note. But on the other hand, too many events seemed to point to a relationship built on lies, which she could not tolerate. Ever.

And hadn't she determined relationships were a distraction? But a distraction from what? She'd failed at her businesses. She'd also been good at ruining some of her relationships. She didn't even have any close female friends. Only one or two she could call for lunch. Jacques was her closest friend. How odd not to have built more caring people into her life. Maybe she really was a loner and a loser. She heard the birds chirping outside and pounded her fist on the alarm again.

The clock showed lunchtime, but for once food didn't entice Kasey. *I can't ignore the whole day.* She heaved the down comforter over to one side as if it were made of lead instead of feathers. Her tired feet stuffed themselves into her new bunny slippers. *Ah. Well, at least not everything in this life is painful.* But every part of her still wanted to climb back into her womblike bed and disappear. *Wow. This is really not like me.*

Distraught, Kasey climbed into some jeans, took a quick brush through her hair, and stumbled out the front door. She lumbered in circles around the neighborhood as if to wear off the pain. She felt more of her rock wall tumble down, and somehow it felt good this time.

Suffering, but wanting relief, Kasey finally gave in to her heart and walked up to a nearby chapel. *Here and now, Kasey. It's time to hand it over.* She stared upward. The church and its steeple seemed to rise above the street like an ancient testament to those who were lovers of the faith. Even though the building appeared rugged, she felt it welcome her. She'd been searching for guarantees. Perhaps this one was all she ever needed.

Once inside the chapel, Kasey sat down on one of the

wooden benches. How could she begin? She knew how to pray, sort of, and yet it had been so long since she'd *really* talked to God. She bowed her head and remained quiet for a while. Nothing yet. Minutes later, the words and tears began to flow. The anger over her parents' tragic deaths, the disconnect from people, the whys of all her failures, and the need to control all her comings and goings. It all poured out, draining her and filling her at the same time. After about forty-five minutes of visiting with God, she sensed it was time to finally give permission to let her Lord really *be* her Lord.

Hamilton fumbled with his keys, not wanting to get out of his car. But he'd driven downtown with a purpose in mind, so he knew he'd have to follow through. He gazed out the windshield and noticed the same homeless man he'd seen days before. The old man sat on a bench not far from his car.

Resigned to his decision, Hamilton got out of his sedan and strolled over to the man. "Hi. Do you mind if I sit here?"

"Nope. Don't mind at all," the old man replied with a friendly gesture.

The man was humming something. Some unfamiliar tune. Was that a *Wall Street Journal* he held? Amazingly the man appeared freshly shaven and was dressed in a suit. An old but clean suit. Hamilton sat down. "I don't think you'll remember me, but—"

"I remember you, son."

"How?" Hamilton asked with surprise and mild concern.

"Well, I run into your types all the time, but I remember

you." He folded up his paper.

Hamilton wondered what that meant. Was the old guy trying to insult him? "Types like me?"

"I used to be that type some years ago. . .until I got greedy." The man chuckled.

Hamilton paused, not wanting to seem too pushy. "What do you mean?"

"Well. . .I made myself a fortune in the stock market. Made some wise investments. But I always had to have more. And I did make more. That's okay, but there's a men's shelter downtown here for the homeless. They came to me for help. They really needed me. And I refused them."

"Why?" Hamilton asked, almost scared to hear the answer.

The color seemed to drain from the old man's face. "Because I didn't want to share the blessing."

"Do you mind if I ask what happened? How did you lose your money?" Hamilton could feel the intensity in his own voice, and it unnerved him.

"I made one too many wrong decisions. The kind of big moves that can either break you or make you some truly serious money."

"And it broke you?"

The man nodded slowly. "As easily as snapping a piece of peanut brittle in two. And the hardest part of it was that in the end I had to go to the same men's shelter and ask for help." A bus stopped in front of them, creating an earful of squeaking brakes, but the old man didn't seem to notice. "I wish I'd been more generous with my money. . .*and* my heart. I wasn't with either. And I lost my wife, too."

Hamilton felt bad for the old guy. What would it feel like? To lose everything? Even the woman you loved? "Do you think you'll ever make a comeback?"

"The men's shelter is helping me get back on my feet, but I promised God I'd never be a self-serving lunatic again."

Hamilton left a thoughtful pause between them. "Thanks for telling me. . .your story."

"You're welcome." Suddenly a sparrow perched itself on the old man's shoulder.

Hamilton stared, wondering why the bird wasn't afraid. He then noticed all the people zooming around them, almost in a blur. All in a hurry to get somewhere else. Someone within the blur shouted, and the tiny bird flitted away. Hamilton cleared his throat, not sure what to say next. "Do you need some money. . .or some help?"

"No, but that's a good start, son." The old guy winked and smiled.

He shook the man's aging but strong hand. Once Hamilton made it back to his car, he glanced back. The old man had already gone. . .somewhere.

Kasey looked up into the sunshine. She wiped the tears from her face and walked down the chapel steps. She had some direction in her life now and the peace to pull it off. But most of all, it felt really good to be on speaking terms with God again.

Once back at her apartment, Kasey saw all the phone messages. She laughed this time, knowing Lloyd had taken care of the problem and soon the calls would end. She listened to the first five. Each man sounded unique and scary in his own way. The more she listened the more she realized how Hamilton would be a great loss. Suddenly Hamilton's voice sprang up on the machine. "Hi. You're probably still angry. But if you can bear it, I'd like a chance to explain myself." Kasey smiled. She would indeed give him a chance to tell his side of the story.

The next voice startled Kasey. "Hello. My name is Alex Warren. I talked to you at Oaks Lodge last night. I guess I need to apologize. What I said was only partially true. Hamilton does have a *lot* of goals, but he's a good guy. He could love someone." She paused. "He just didn't love me. I tried to force it, but I learned you can't. . .make someone love you. Anyway, we were only engaged for about three weeks. And it was a year and a half ago. I'm sorry if I messed something up between you guys. Oh, and Hamilton doesn't know I called. It just feels good to do the right thing for a change. Bye."

Kasey heard an awful noise outside and stopped the machine. She ran upstairs and looked out the window. *What in the world?* There by the pond below was the handsome Hamilton bellowing off-key and holding a humongous bouquet of pink roses. In fact, roses of every kind filled her lower patio like a lush garden. She yanked the window open to hear him. It was some sort of love song. She still couldn't hear well but noticed he'd certainly attracted quite an audience of ducks. People passed by on the sidewalk, but he didn't seem to care. He just kept rolling at full volume. Something about "melodies of the heart and too painful to be apart."

Kasey waved for him to come up. In minutes the doorbell rang. She threw open the door. "Now what is this all about?"

"So are we talking now?" Hamilton asked.

"Yes. We are."

"These are for you."

Kasey took the roses in her arms and breathed in their wonderful fragrance.

They both spoke at once as Kasey offered him a seat.

"You go first." Hamilton sat down on the couch, and Kasey followed.

She looked down and then around the room, not knowing what to say. *Am I actually having a demure moment here?* "Well, I guess you could say. . .I had kind of. . .an epiphany today. For one thing. . .I think God would like me to hear what you have to say."

"Okay, that's good news."

"And I think He's telling me the right business is out there. I just need to have a little more patience." Kasey sighed. "I also found out it's easy to point at other people who I think have lied, but I know now I've been lying to myself for years. I'd denied the fact I needed to be more open in friendship and. . .love. I sort of shut people out after my parents died." Kasey took in a deep breath. "And I discovered I need the Lord for every part of my life. . .that it's a relationship. . .that's meant to last forever."

Hamilton smiled back. "I like what you said. All of it."

"Thanks. Now what were you going to say?" Kasey asked.

Hamilton got up. He shoved his hands into his pockets. "Listen. I'm glad Alex came by last night. It forced me to look at myself. Some things about me. . .weren't so good. I've been too single-minded with my business dealings. Too many goals. . .and not enough heart." He raked his hair back and looked intently at Kasey. "I don't want you to be something on a checklist. I want to care about you for all the *right* reasons." Hamilton sat back down next to her.

"Alex called me and explained some things. You're sort of off the hook, but Hamilton. . .I think she still loves you."

"I'm sorry, but I can't marry someone I don't love. Would you want me to?"

"No," Kasey said. "But. . .well. . .maybe you two didn't know each other well enough. Was that it?"

Hamilton shook his head. "Alex and I have known each other a long time. We grew up together. She and I got engaged because it was. . .very comfortable to do so. But that's not how it works. . .comfort is not enough. I know it now. You have to have some compatibility. . .commitment. . .love." Hamilton raised his eyebrows. "And a little attraction helps, too."

"Oh? Is that so?"

Hamilton traced his finger along Kasey's cheek and down the curve of her neck, making her immediately aware of what he was referring to. She looked at him thinking she must look flushed.

"See? We have *that*, too. You don't have to be embarrassed about what we're feeling. Haven't you read Song of Solomon?"

"Yes." She laughed.

"It's how we're created. That's how people fulfilled the command of multiplying and subduing the earth."

Kasey studied his eyes. "Well, mankind was always pretty faithful with *that* one." She arched a brow at him.

"By the way, since we're on the subject, I hope you like

kids." He squeezed her hand. "What do you think about a baby or two?"

"Maybe. But not with just anybody." Kasey grinned.

"Good!" Hamilton chuckled. "By the way, I have something else to say before I kiss you on this miserably overstuffed couch." He cleared his throat and moved more than an arm's length away from her. "I've enough money to not only buy a house and a business, but I have some extra cash to help our church build another men's shelter downtown. They really need it, and it's something I want to do."

"I like your idea. . .a lot."

"Good. By the way, I think there's something you'll like that's hidden in the roses." He moved closer to her. "At least I *hope* you'll feel that way."

Like a kid on her birthday, Kasey searched through the huge mound of flowers. "What am I looking for?" She found an envelope tied to one of the roses. "Oh. . .a note." She gently opened it to read:

Dearest Kasey,
This is not the original note,
but it comes with love enough to fill a boat.
Put me out of my misery at last.
Say yes, because I am falling hard and fast.
Love from
Your Hamilton

Kasey laced her arms around Hamilton's neck. "That is undoubtedly the worst poetry I've *ever* read. But it's as dear as any writing could ever be. It's even sweeter than Jacques' marmalade. But what am I saying *yes* to? It's a little too soon for a proposal. I mean, we've only had one real date."

"Well then, have lunch with me," he said.

"*And* coffee?"

Hamilton kissed her nose. "As long as you don't toss it on me."

She pulled away, laughing. "That was an accident!"

Hamilton pretended a frown. "I was never sure."

Kasey tugged his tie to gently admonish him, then decided the move was quite productive. She pulled him down to her mouth and savored the best taste she'd ever known. Even better than Jacques' French roast with homemade whipped cream.

"I just remembered something," Hamilton whispered in her ear. "I promised you a chocolate mousse."

After its creation in Kasey's kitchen, Hamilton spooned the mousse into crystal cups. Later, they fed the sweet concoction to each other between kisses and funny stories of recipes gone awry.

Three hours later Hamilton and Kasey burst into the kitchen of Café Rose, looking for Jacques and some explanation about a certain note.

Jacques winced at them. "I discovered that a young woman named Haley didn't receive her note. I'm afraid I should have asked Sally more questions when she handed me the note. I'm sorry for the mistake. Do you still love old Jacques, or have you come to throw him to the sharks?"

Kasey chuckled. "We've come to tell you we still love you."

"Yes, but do you love each *other*?" Jacques asked.

"But we've only had one real date!" Kasey said.

"The phrase 'love at first sight' is not just an airy soufflé. It's got some meat to it, kids. Come on. You can tell Jacques. Yes?"

Hamilton took Kasey's hand and gave it a squeeze.

"That's what I thought." Jacques nodded like a judge. "I've seen it two times before like that. Yes, all things are being made right. Now listen to me. I've been doing some serious talking to my friend, Jesus. And *that* is what you need to do a lot of—to run your business as well as your marriage. That is my best and only advice. Well, not my *only* advice." Jacques chuckled at his own joke.

Jacques put his hands on his hips, looking serious. "First, I expect you both to have your wedding reception here. . .at no charge. Second, I would love to be your child's godfather, but that's for a little later, of course. And maybe you could even name him Jacques. Just kidding." His grin became as wide as his éclairs.

Suddenly, Jacques pointed two fingers in the air. "*And* something else you might like to know. God has told me it's time to finally chase my second dream. I realize my sweet Café Rose won't die without me. . .and so. . .if you agree, I'm willing to sell it to you both at a very good price, because to cook with love is the gift God has given you both. I can retire knowing it will be in good hands."

Not waiting for their response, Jacques just waved his hands joyfully at them. "We can talk and pray about it later. But dear ones, I'm going to travel, too. A lot. But before *this* dream can come true, I want to finally acknowledge my gift from the Almighty. And that is. . .my *quiet song*. . .Myra. I'm going to propose to her. Do you think she'll have me?"

Myra looked up from her bread-making in surprise. "Me?"

"Who else, my love? You are my delight every day. Now you will be my delight at night, too."

Myra blushed. With her powdery hands she came over and planted a loud smooch on Jacques' mouth.

" 'So we grew together, like to a double cherry, seeming parted, but yet an union in partition; two lovely berries molded on one stem,' " Jacques quoted.

Myra giggled. "You have so much panache, my Jacques. How can I resist you and Shakespeare both?" She threw up her hands in the air. "Now I shall make you pear flan!"

"I think that was a yes," Hamilton said.

Kasey suddenly remembered something Jacques had said about celebrating life. She smiled, feeling those words to their fullest.

Hugs and congratulations spread through the kitchen like fresh pâté. Laughter and love continued to bubble up, and Kasey thought the merry sounds of it must be ringing like church bells all over the Café Rose. . .and all the way up to heaven.

ANITA HIGMAN

Award-winning author Anita Higman has been honored in the past as a Barnes & Noble "Author of the Month" for Houston. She has sixteen books published for both adults and children. She also has contributions in four anthologies with three more coming out. One of her coauthored books won two awards, including a Westerners International Book Award.

Anita has written for radio and television. She has won two awards for her contribution to literacy and has raised thousands of dollars for literacy with her book *I Can Be Anything*.

Ms. Higman has a B.A. in speech communication from Southern Nazarene University. She is a member of American Christian Fiction Writers. Anita lives with her family near Houston, Texas.

Anita would love for you to visit her Web site at www.anitahigman.com.

breaking new grounds

by DiAnn Mills

Dedication

To Melanie Stiles who helps me see life
in a unique perspective.

Satisfy us in the morning with your unfailing love,
that we may sing for joy and be glad all our days.
Psalm 90:14 niv

Chapter 1

Tuesday, October 18

Good coffee is like an old friend," Kae Alice said. She closed her eyes and inhaled the nutty aroma swirling through the steam in her cup. "It keeps you warm and always coming back for more."

"One day, I'm going to make a plaque for each one of your coffee sayings." Gene's clear brown eyes glistened beneath his thick white hair. "Then I'm going to peddle them to all the coffee shops and get rich."

"How much of a cut will I get?" Kae asked with a wry smile.

"Maybe as much as 25 percent."

"That's robbery. The quotes happen to be my originals. Better rethink your get-rich-quick scheme."

"But I'd be the brains of the outfit. I'd do the promotion and the marketing, pay for the ads, and approach the right people." Gene lifted a brow. "All right, 30 percent."

She frowned and took a sip of the dark, French roast brew.

Retro music sounded above the buzz of the café's lunch crowd, easing her out of her near irritation. "Do you remember when we couldn't get enough of Buddy Holly and Patsy Cline?"

Gene chuckled and emptied two packets of sugar into his coffee. "Yeah. I remember I used to sneak off to the high school dances and rock and roll my heart out. My parents never found out." He poured in a generous amount of Half-and-Half, stirred it, and lifted the cup to his lips. A wide grin spread across his wrinkled face. "Ah, that's a mighty fine cup of coffee."

"You always say that, but you ruin it with the stuff you put in it." Kae glanced around at the fifties-style setting, complete with stainless steel tables and turquoise-colored vinyl chairs. Even the waitresses wore poodle skirts, bobby socks, and black-and-white saddle shoes. One of the girls blew a bubble the size of her face—until it popped. "I love coming here, especially since the renovation to the fifties theme. Makes me feel like I'm in my twenties again. Although—" Her gaze swept across the Coffee Grind for another seasoned citizen. "We are the only ones here who actually lived this era."

The lines around Gene's eyes deepened with his hearty laugh. "Remember, I actually had a '57 Chevy, while all they have are pictures on the wall."

"And black-and-white photos of James Dean."

"I like the one of Marilyn Monroe."

"You would."

"I remember *I Love Lucy* and when bread was fifteen cents a loaf," he said.

"And I remember drying sheets on a clothesline."

He took another sip of his brew. "Times do change, Kae.

Imagine making three thousand dollars a year and still managing to save a little." His shoulders lifted. "I don't remember coffee this good, though. I do love the Coffee Grind's coffee bar. I even dream about it."

"That's probably because you've tasted every one of their coffee specials." She took a glimpse across the room at the espresso bar in the corner, the one item from the old Coffee Grind that the management hadn't changed. "Guess we wouldn't have been coming here for five years if we didn't like it."

"Their cherry Cokes don't taste near as good as the ones I remember, but they do whip up a mean chocolate malt."

Kae leaned across the table. "We're getting old, Gene. Our taste buds aren't the same anymore. Also, the older we get, the better sweet things taste. At least that's what I read in a health magazine." She sat up straight and paused for a moment. "As well as I can remember, you hated chocolate malts. Always ordered strawberry."

He frowned and opened his mouth to say something, but the perky waitress, complete with a ponytail and a pink sweater tied around her shoulders, stood ready for their order. Her name tag read BETTY LOU. She chomped away on a piece of bubble gum, reminding Kae of a cow. Her real name was probably Ashley, Jenna, Lindsay, or something cute and twenty-first century. Betty Lou pulled a pencil from behind her ear and leaned on one foot. *This girl plays the part to the hilt. Next she'll be jumping on the table and doing the hand-jive.*

Swallowing a giggle, Kae peered across the table at Gene. "What are you having today?"

"Cheeseburger and onion rings." He tossed a challenging

look Kae's way. "And a triple-thick chocolate malt."

Kae shook her head. "Old man, you are clogging your arteries with that sugar and grease. If you don't watch your diet, I'll be visiting you in the hospital and pushing you around in a wheelchair."

He made a face, then glanced back up at the waitress. "And I'll have a big slice of that double-fudge chocolate pie for dessert."

Double heart attack material, if you ask me.

Betty Lou crossed her arms over her chest and shook her head. "I don't believe this. You are amazing. The fudge pie is awesome, and my favorite." She turned to Kae. "And what would you like?" She popped a bubble that flattened against her whole mouth. Kae might have to give the waitresses a lesson on bubble popping. Once Betty Lou pulled off the pieces of gum and had the remains in her mouth again, she stood poised to take Kae's order.

"A bowl of vegetable soup and a side order of cottage cheese." Kae tossed Gene a smug look.

He chuckled. "You won't ever have any fun eating the boring stuff. Seriously Kae, you've lost enough weight lately."

She ignored him. Maybe she'd try a white chocolate chip macadamia nut cookie later. "And I'll have a refill on my coffee, please."

"Decaf and black?" Betty Lou asked.

"Yes, thank you." She waited to hear Gene give her a bad time about drinking unleaded coffee. Luckily he hadn't heard the last of her order. . .must not have had his hearing aid turned up.

Alias Betty Lou disappeared with a twist of her poodle skirt. The song changed to "Blue Suede Shoes."

Gene sang a few verses. "Now, where were we?" he asked.

"Reminiscing about the past." Kae folded her hands on the table and studied his face. How that man could still have the prettiest white teeth with his age still wowed her. No wonder the waitress flirted with him.

"I've never figured out why my mind says yes to all the things I used to do and my body says no." He lifted his cup to his lips, closed his eyes, and then smiled as broadly as Cary Grant used to do on the movie screen. "Do you remember when air-conditioning here in Alabama was a luxury? Why, we just stuck a fan in the window when it got too hot. Most of the time it didn't matter."

"We used to sleep on the porch. I remember listening to the mosquitoes buzzing in my ears and pulling a sheet over my head to drown them out." Kae laughed. "Now we worry about a little standing water breeding more of those dreadful things and fret about dying of more weird diseases than I could ever imagine."

Gene took a long slurp of his coffee. *Someday I have to tell him how annoying that is.*

"I quit worrying about what's going to do me in," he said. "Can't stop age anyway."

"True. Sure wish some of them old, old people we carry back and forth to the doctor had that attitude."

Gene sputtered. Laughter took over until he wiped his eyes with his napkin. "Do you realize that we're older than some of those folks we cart to the doctor and bring meals-on-wheels to?"

Kae wiggled her shoulders and feigned annoyance. Why did he always have to be so right? "We're being good role models." She took a quick peek at her purple and pink watch. "You'll end up with heartburn by the time you get to eat your cheeseburger. We have thirty minutes until we have to pick up Ethel and Pete for their weekly checkup."

Gene groaned. "At least we can take our coffee to go."

"Sure." Kae wiggled a finger at his face. "But you absolutely cannot drive, drink coffee, sing along to the fifties radio station, and talk on the cell phone. You're going to kill us."

"This is the age of technology. I'm as spry and alert as I was at eighteen."

Betty Lou waltzed over with their lunches. She set the soup and cottage cheese in front of Kae, then turned to Gene. "Here you are, honey. You look like a man who would love a big old cheeseburger." She flashed him a big grin and winked.

Kae thought his mouth was going to hit the floor.

A few hours later, Gene closed the newspaper right after the obituary page. He removed his bifocals and slipped them into his shirt pocket. No point advertising to the whole world he needed them. Lately he found himself reading through the obituaries to see if there was anyone he knew. Stupid thing to obsesses about—as his nephew said—but when he did find a familiar name, he followed up with contact to the family. *It's my Christian duty,* he told himself. Really, he wondered if the good Lord planned to call him home before he found the nerve to tell Kae how much he loved her.

"Here's the paper." He folded it and handed it to her. "I bet Ethel and Pete will be hobbling through those doors any minute."

Kae laid the paper on her lap. "Probably so. They aren't doing well, Gene."

"I know, and I've been praying for them. What amazes me is their age—just five years older than we are."

She nodded. "But we've always been active, ate right. Well, one of us eats healthy." She patted his arm. "We live to help others, and God has blessed us with good health."

Kae made sense, but then she usually did—even if he didn't always agree. He took one of those special moments to peer into her sweet face. A few lines creased around her eyes, but her skin still had the look of a much younger woman. That was his Kae. She'd always been into health foods, vitamins, and staying out of the sun. And her hair was the same pale blond as the first time he laid eyes on her when they were fifteen years old. Naturally he assumed the bottle took care of what age had denied. Her green gaze met his. His heart turned a somersault, and he quickly glanced away before he reddened.

The doctor's office door slowly swung open, and Pete and Ethel shuffled out. "There they are," Gene said. He and Kae helped them from the doctor's office, on out of the building, and into Gene's van. A few moments later, the van headed toward the assisted living center in the same complex where Kae and Gene enjoyed the retirement condos.

"Thank you," Pete said in between breaths. When he breathed, he sounded like a freight train, a condition that resulted from years of smoking.

"You're welcome," Gene said.

"We'd be lost without you two every week." Ethel sighed. She looked fine, but rumors were of another problem—pancreatic cancer.

"Oh, we enjoy giving you a ride," Kae said. "Gives us time to visit."

"How long have you two been married?" Pete asked. "We're going on sixty-two years now—five children, eleven grandchildren, and three great-grandchildren."

"Congratulations." Gene took a sideways look at Kae. No emotion creased her face. "We aren't married."

"But don't you two have the same last name—Richards?" Ethel asked.

Gene cleared his throat. "Miss Kae was married to my brother, Paul. He passed on about twenty years ago."

"Well, I thought for sure you two were mister and missus," Ethel said. "Seems like you're always together."

"Oh, we're the best of friends." Kae shifted to face the couple in the backseat. "We've known each other since we were kids. We help folks with rides to the doctor and running errands. Plus we volunteer for meals-on-wheels. That's why you always see us together."

But I would like to be married to you. Gene's thoughts raced away, just as they had for the past fifty-five years. Some days, like today, he wondered if he'd go to his grave with this love swelling in his heart. A long time ago, she chose his brother, Paul, over him. The pain in his heart had never eased up. *Kae, my pretty lady, I'd love to slip a ring on your finger and have you be Mrs. Gene Richards.* But she wasn't the least bit interested. He'd have seen something in her actions to encourage him over the years since Paul died. In fact, he'd looked for a sign. Nothing. But he'd vowed that Kae wouldn't ever need a single thing. Most folks referred to his dedication as responsibility, but he called his feelings a much deeper emotion. Carrying his love for Kae to the grave seemed sad and empty.

"Gene, you forgot to finish your coffee." Kae picked up the insulated cup from the cup holder between the seats. "It's been hours, most likely too cold for anything but dumping it out."

He forced a smile. If only she knew.

Chapter 2

Kae finished pulling the weeds from her impatiens. She snipped off the leggy ones so the flowers would grow back bushier. Her yellow mums bloomed in vivid yellow and spread all over her flower bed. They reminded her of children who wiggled out of their seats at school. She giggled. Overexuberant mums were easier to manage than children. She should know after raising two boys and two girls.

With fall in the air, the temps had dropped from ninety to seventy degrees. She'd never minded the heat anyway. A little sweat helped clean out the pores. Kae lifted a bottle of water and drank deeply, then mentally calculated that this was glass number seven for the day, and it wasn't even midafternoon. Got to get in at least eight cups of water to stay healthy.

Kae surveyed the small garden area along the brick fence lining the back of her condo. Nice and neat the way she liked it. Just enough flowers to give a splash of color to the green bushes. If only she could find a way to keep all the pine needles away. The tall, spindly trees offered no shade, only tons of needles and pinecones for her to gather and stuff into a trash bag. Glancing down, Kae noted how full the bag at her feet had become. She gave it a tug, but it was entirely too heavy. Rather than bother Gene or anyone else, she divided up the lawn clippings into another bag, then dragged it to the pickup area.

Her yardman had offered to keep the beds weeded, but she enjoyed getting her fingers in the soil. The job gave her time to think, and if a problem plagued her, she and the Lord seemed closer when she was on her hands and knees in the dirt.

Today had been one of those days when she needed the Lord's guidance. She and Gene weren't getting any younger. Years ago he retired from the phone company, and she retired from teaching high school math. The longer she waited to confess her love for him, the more foolish the thought. Sitting back on the grass, Kae allowed her thoughts to wander back in time to when she and Gene were best friends, and Paul was the boy of her dreams. She had no idea Paul wanted to pursue her any more than she realized Gene had a crush on her, too. So sad for Gene; she never meant to hurt him. Paul stole her heart, and she had loved him fiercely. Long after he died in a car accident, she grieved. Then one day about seventeen years ago, she sensed her feelings had shifted toward Gene. Her best friend had moved into her heart right beside his brother. The thought shocked her. She even wondered if it were wrong. After a few days it frightened her. Now she kept it to herself for fear Gene might want to marry her out of duty or responsibility.

She yawned. Perhaps a short nap might be in order later. Sadness crept over Kae. Granted, she had dear Jesus and her precious family, but her heart ached for Gene. Oh, he had his faults. So did she. Had all the years she'd kept quiet about her feelings for him turned her into a selfish old woman by wanting him with her every minute of the day?

"Are you okay?"

Kae swung her attention to the right where Melanie Shepherd, her dear neighbor, studied her from the brick fence.

"Absolutely." Kae tossed her best smile, the one she used to cover up any display of melancholy. "I'm simply enjoying my weeded flower beds."

"Your yard always looks wonderful."

"Thanks." Kae placed one hand on the ground and rose to her feet. "I sure could use a fresh pot of coffee. How about you?"

"Umm. I'd love it."

"Good. I have some heavenly-flavored decaf beans. One is blueberry cream and the other is raspberry chocolate. What's your poison?"

"Blueberry." Melanie nodded, her brilliant carrot-colored curls bobbing up and down like corkscrews. "Can I tempt you with some Sara Lee?"

"No, ma'am. I'm still waiting on that knight in shining armor to cruise by in a white Cadillac and carry me off to his castle."

"Honey, at our age, what's a few pounds?"

Kae wiggled her shoulders. "The next time I get married, I intend to be carried over the threshold, not toted across in a wheelbarrow."

Melanie laughed. "I'm on my way over."

A few minutes later, Kae opened the door to Melanie—her dear friend who gave a whole new meaning to *eccentricity*. Some days she wore prints, plaids, and stripes that looked more like an interior decorator's nightmare than a grown woman, and other days she looked like she stepped off a model's runway. Today was not a model day.

"The coffee smells wonderful." Melanie presented a partial box of cinnamon rolls with rather crusty-looking frosting. "I bought these over a week ago, and I'm afraid they'll go bad if not eaten soon."

Kae inwardly cringed. "I don't want to disappoint you, but these are probably stale."

"You think so?" Melanie peered into the box. "Aren't they made with preservatives?" She picked it up to view the ingredients. "Rats, I left my glasses at home. What does it say?"

Kae cleared her throat to keep from laughing. The writing on the box looked fuzzy. The laser surgery on her eyes must not have lasted, but then the doctor had said she might need glasses for reading. "Not sure, Melanie. The print's small."

"Let's just nuke 'em. I'm sure they're fine."

Help me out of this, Lord. "I'm not hungry, but I love cinnamon rolls. I'd be glad to take them off your hands." *And trash these rock-hard babies as soon as you leave.*

Melanie clapped her hands. "Wonderful. You are such a good friend. Don't know what I'd do without you. Too many times the residents here take my individuality as too different." She shrugged. "I'm a little on the left side of norm, but hey, I like it."

Kae felt conviction all the way to her toes for her condescending thoughts about Melanie. "Let's just have us some coffee. I have new lovely pink and purple cups that I'm dying to use."

"Pink is my favorite color." Melanie adjusted her hot pink

T-shirt with the words HOT BABE printed across the front.

Don't even go there, Kae. You'll only sink deeper.

On Friday morning, Gene met Kae at the Coffee Grind. By now they'd grown accustomed to their favorite coffee shop's new fifties look and menu. Along with their choice French roast blend, they ordered breakfast. Gene chose scrambled eggs, bacon, grits, and biscuits while Kae decided upon egg substitute and wheat toast. She was famished, but pride kept her from ordering pancakes to go with it.

"We don't have a single person to transport to the doctor today," he said. "We have all this free time until noon meal delivery."

"How about the library?" Kae tilted her head. A whole morning with Gene sounded wonderful. "Or a walk in the park since the weather's cooler. Hmm, we don't have time for the zoo or a museum. What were you thinking?"

"Volunteering in the Alzheimer's section," he said. "We could take a few of those folks into the sunshine and give the nurses and aids a break."

Conviction hit Kae again. Twice in two days she'd been heart-whacked for her selfishness. Why ever would she tell Gene how she felt about him? Selfish. Selfish. Selfish. "Sure. I could paint the ladies' nails and do their hair."

He offered a quick nod and a smile. "All right. Let's have our breakfast and do it."

Kae attempted to rouse enthusiasm for the morning, but fatigue swept through her. Lately the desire to sleep kept her from doing a lot of the things she normally did. She took vitamins and went through her healthy ritual just as she had done for the past forty or so years.

"Are you getting enough sleep?" Gene's voice held more concern than she deserved.

"Of course I am. But I've been frettin' over Ethel and Pete and their failing health." She paused. "For some reason I'm not being included in Hannah's activities—you know David and Tracie's daughter—and then Melanie joined me yesterday for coffee. The poor old girl doesn't have many friends, and she has a heart big enough to plant a rose garden."

"Frettin' doesn't help a thing, but we both know that. Anything I can do to help?"

Kae shook her head and swallowed hard. *Where is all this emotion coming from?*

"Why don't we stop at Melanie's to see if she wants to join us? And we could visit Ethel and Pete before heading to the Alzheimer's section."

Such love you have for God's people. "Perfect. Now I won't have an excuse for looking tired."

Kae captured his gaze, and for a moment she saw a glimpse of the old Gene, the one she knew years ago. She didn't dare read any more into his eyes than an old friend's concern. But she remembered the teenager who swore he'd love her to his dying day, even if she married his brother. Now she knew how he'd once felt. For certain, the comfortable relationship they enjoyed now suited them both. The only thing warm they shared was the French roast coffee every Tuesday lunch and Friday breakfast.

"I have a doctor's appointment tomorrow morning," Gene said.

She met his gaze. "On a Saturday? Everything okay?"

"Sure." He rested on his elbows. "The doc is a friend of mine, and it's strictly routine, a chance for the medical profession to earn a little money while writing me out a good health report."

"Will you let me know how it goes?"

"Of course. Don't know why I brought it up, except I have to fast in the morning. Skipping breakfast will kill me." He laughed, the deep sound that always reminded her of what an opera bass singer might sound like.

As soon as breakfast was over, the two stopped at Melanie's to invite her along. Pete and Ethel were off doing crafts.

"Thank you. Thank you. Thank you." Melanie clapped her hands. "Let me grab a sweater, scarf, and an extra pair of socks. Do I need to take my toothbrush?"

"You won't need them," Kae said. *Don't make fun of her. God knows your heart. He loves her just as much as He loves you.* "The temp is already seventy-one and rising. We'd love to have you with us."

Melanie beamed. It didn't matter a bit that her red corkscrew curls weren't combed or that she wore an orange turtleneck sweater and yellow sweatpants or that her gold earrings dangled to her shoulders. The smile of utter joy on Melanie's face was enough.

Once at the Alzheimer's section, Kae, Melanie, and Gene found most of the patients in a sitting area watching TV. The sky had clouded up and splatters of rain fell on the sidewalk.

"If I had a piano, I could entertain these folks," Gene said to a nurse.

"Sounds like a plan to me," the portly woman replied. "They will love it, and so will we."

Gene rolled in a piano from another room, and one of the staff members produced a bench. The change of pace created a hubbub of chatter. Humming an old Elvis tune, he ran his fingers across the piano keys. "Needs a bit of tuning up," he said. "But we'll make it work."

"Make it dance," Kae said. She loved to hear him play. "Do the 'Boogy Woogy.' "

He grinned, and in the next moment he was bouncing along on the piano bench in time to the music.

"Play it again," one man said. He slapped his knee and laughed.

"No, play something different. Do you know any gospel music?" a woman asked.

Gene turned to the man who wanted a repeat of the "Boogy Woogy." "I'll do the best I can with the requests, but I promise I'll not leave until I play that song again for you." His attention swung to the white-haired woman who asked for a gospel song. "What would you like to hear?"

"Anything about heaven and my Jesus."

Kae swallowed a lump in her throat. *These people may not have any concept of time or recognize their friends and family, but this precious lady knew what was important.*

Gene immediately went into a rendition of several old hymns in a lively beat, and the white-haired lady cried. Some of the others sang along.

"I'll fly away," echoed from the crowd.

This is real living. Kae smiled at Gene, then back at the residents who continued to cheer him on. One woman began to sway with the music. Melanie took the woman's arms and danced with her.

I wish I could be spontaneous. Kae began to clap. She could at least show more enthusiasm.

"Watch 'em go," another man said and clapped with her.

Kae eased down on a sofa beside a woman who smelled of lilac. The woman reached over and kissed Kae on the cheek. "Are you an angel?"

Kae whisked away a single tear. "No, ma'am, but I think you are." She took the woman's veined and parchment-thin hand and held it. "Thank you for allowing us to visit."

The woman smiled. "I hope you come back. My mother comes every day."

And Kae realized she'd be back again and again, every time she felt the "selfish-bug" picking at her heart.

"Didn't we have a great time this morning?" Gene asked as they headed to the food pickup area for meals-on-wheels. His spirit had reached cloud level. "And to think Melanie stayed with those folks over lunch."

"She may have found her niche."

Gene threw her a sideways glance. "Let's face it. She has a lot in common with them. Maybe I shouldn't have said that."

Kae giggled. "I've been keeping an eye on her. Frankly, I think she's simply eccentric and starved for companionship."

Gene nodded. "Do you ever feel like we parent all our friends?"

"Absolutely. Seems like I have this special antenna that picks up on who's sick or depressed."

"We're a team." Gene wanted to reach for her hand, but he'd felt like that for years. Maybe now was the time. His hand crept across the seat, reminding him of a crab making its way along the beach. There. He did it. Her soft fingers now touched his palm. What a wonderful, sweet feeling. "Do you mind?" His question sounded like a croak. He stole a look Kae's way, but her attention seemed focused on the road.

"I don't mind."

No emotion, but her inflamed cheeks bothered him—a lot. "Why are you blushing? Did I make you mad?"

Not a muscle moved. "I'm not mad."

"Then what's wrong?" At that moment the car in front of him came to a screeching halt.

Kae screamed. "Watch out!"

He slammed on the brakes and released her hand. "Where are your brake lights?" he shouted at the driver.

"They were on. You weren't paying attention." She stiffened her shoulders. No doubt about it, Kae was hopping mad. "If you'd been paying attention—"

"I was—"

"I said, if you'd been paying attention and not holding my hand—"

Gene's face warmed while anger treaded water in an ocean of emotions. "So reaching for your hand caused me not to be a safe driver?"

"Sure looks that way to me. You're always doing too many things while you're behind the wheel."

Was she throwing his efforts to be romantic back in his face? "Now, Kae, I'm sorry if this scared you, but I believe there's something else going on here. I think you're more upset that I reached for your hand than the car in front of us using its brakes."

"What are you talking about?" She seemed to hold her breath; her body language spoke a million words. "We could have been killed."

I'm right. She did enjoy it. "I think you liked me holding your hand, and you probably have wanted me to be nice and cozy for a long time."

"Gene Richards, where did you get such nonsense?"

"In your eyes."

She always did this funny little intake of breath when she didn't know what to say. If he waited long enough. . .

Kae gasped. "I've never heard such a ridiculous claim." She crossed her arms and expelled a heavy sigh. "We've been friends for over fifty years. And you've never been this forward."

"Better late than never."

"I was married to your brother."

"Don't remind me."

She lifted her chin. "I think while you're at the doctor's tomorrow, you need your head examined."

The building where they picked up the meals loomed ahead. He didn't want to upset her, not ever. "You were married to the greatest guy in the world. I never would have interfered. He loved you. You loved him, but you had to know

I was in love with you."

Kae sighed, her focus straight ahead. "I knew."

"I never stopped, Kae." His heart pounded hard while silence wafted through the air.

"I had no idea your feelings hadn't changed over the years. You've always been right there for me—helping me through the funeral, putting a life together without him, moving into the same retirement complex, enjoying meals together. . . ."

"I wanted to be near you. What about now? Could there be anything for me? I understand if you think of us as friends." He pulled the van into the parking area. Why ever had he brought this up when he needed to be tending to something else? He turned to see her still staring out the windshield. "I'd like for you to consider spending the rest of your life with me. I hate the idea of going to my grave and never having the opportunity to love you like I've dreamed about since we were fifteen years old."

Kae lowered her head and wept, not a few drops, but big old alligator tears. Rats, he'd gone and hurt her real bad. Why couldn't he have kept his mouth shut? She'd always loved Paul. He was a fool to think anyone else could take his place, except he didn't want to take Paul's spot in her heart, just sit beside him. A stab of reality shook Gene's senses. What if Kae decided not to see him again?

Chapter 3

Kae tried desperately to stop crying. She willed it. She prayed for it. And still a river of joy mixed with grief for the wasted years wove a salty path from her heart to her eyes. How foolish they'd been.

"Are you going to be all right?" Gene asked. Mercy. He sounded as though he might cry, too. She pulled a tissue packet from her purse and proceeded to pull one out and blow her nose, at first gently, then harder until she made a sound resembling a duck call. "Sorry. Never could blow my nose like a lady." She forced herself to look in his direction and managed a smile.

"We could go hunting instead of delivering food."

"Some hungry folks might not appreciate it." *Say something about what his words mean to you.*

"Kae."

"Gene." She took a deep breath. "Go ahead."

"I'm sorry to upset you."

"I'm not."

He startled.

"I'm glad you told me you still cared. I'm honored." Kae moistened her lips to keep from crying again. "I want to think about all of this and talk later."

His Adam's apple bobbed up and down. "Tell you what. When you're ready to talk about us, you let me know, 'cause I won't ever bring up the subject again. I can't stand to see you cry."

But these aren't sad tears. Kae forced air into her lungs in order to tell him she'd loved him for years, but the words refused to form. They sat in her throat like a stale, dry cracker. Finally she nodded and blew her nose again.

Gene had been poked and prodded enough for one year. Yesterday his heart had been wrenched from him by confessing his love for Kae, and now some overanxious technician wanted every last drop of his blood.

"You've taken three vials of blood," he said to the young lady who looked to be in her midthirties. "What all are you testing for?"

"Everything." She smiled; or rather, she flirted. Any other day, he'd have flirted back.

"You mean I'm old and there are more things to go wrong?"

She eased out the needle and stuck a cotton ball on the open vein. "Hold this in place and raise your arm." Once he obliged, she patted his shoulder as though he were near senility. "Your doctor requested a complete workup. This is the same blood work that he requested last year."

Gene could not bring himself to say he couldn't remember last year's exam. Why give the little lady something to talk about later? Odd, he remembered the color of his fourth grade teacher's eyes, but he'd forgotten what he ate last night for dinner. "I understand. When will the doctor have the results?"

"Probably Tuesday." She took a peek at his arm, then peeled and pressed a Band-Aid into place.

"Thanks." He didn't want to voice his frustration about the doctor's new mandate. For all he knew, the two could talk on a regular basis.

"You look fit to me," the doctor had said. "But I do want you to change one thing."

"What's that?"

"Give up the caffeine. Drink decaf coffee and noncaffeinated drinks. It's not good for your heart."

"I thought my heart was fine."

"It is, but at your age—and you do want to live until you're at least one hundred?"

Gene nodded.

"Then why risk any problems by overloading your heart?"

Unfortunately Gene agreed in theory. "I gave up smoking forty years ago. Quit cold turkey. So now I'll give up caffeine."

Now as Gene drove home, he wondered if decaf had half the flavor of his favorite coffee. He'd counted on the buzz to wake him up for the past fifty years. Kae drank decaf and never complained. Maybe living to one hundred wasn't all that great. Quality of life meant a lot, too.

Then he remembered he was supposed to call Kae about the doctor's visit. He'd promised her. Normally he'd have snatched up his cell phone and pressed in her number, but after his confession of love yesterday he hesitated. He should have kept his mouth shut. His heart sat on the fence between a cow patty of embarrassment and a cow patty of a fool. Neither one sounded like something he wanted to step in. Besides, he'd been single all these years. Having a woman around with all that responsibility might drive him crazy, even make an old man out of him.

His phone rang. A quick glimpse told him it was Kae. No point putting off talking to her any longer.

"I expected you to call by now," she said.

"I just got to my van."

"And?" She sounded anxious.

"I'm fine. I gave my token to the blood bank for some tests, and I won't know about them until Tuesday. Just routine stuff."

"What else?"

"What do you mean?"

"Gene Richards, I've known you long enough not to detect there's more."

He frowned. "Actually the doctor said I have to give up caffeine."

She giggled. "I'm sorry, but you make it sound like it's pure torture."

"I don't like somebody telling me what to do, especially when it's under the guise of 'what's best for me.' I can't imagine a caffeine-free environment."

"I think your pride is at stake here," she said.

"Well, it makes me feel old."

"We are old. Decaf is really okay. The flavor is still there. Wouldn't you like to get rid of the feeling that your heart's racing?"

That feeling comes from being around you. "I rather enjoy it. Keeps me in high gear."

"Tell you what. Want to meet me at the Coffee Grind, and I'll treat you to a cup of French roast decaf?"

Gene patted the steering wheel. "It's a deal. I might need a chocolate sundae to go with it."

She sighed. "Mercy me, Gene. Chocolate has caffeine, too."

"I'm not giving up everything. Some things in life are meant to be enjoyed."

"What if I baked you a nice angel food cake?"

"Angel food cake? No, thanks. I hate the stuff, remember? Reminds me of toothless old people on restricted diets."

She giggled. Oh, how he loved the sound of her laughter. "All right. I won't push any more healthy habits onto you until you have the caffeine licked."

Sunday afternoon found Kae midway through a romance novel. She wanted a nap, but the book refused to let her go. Naturally the couple involved looked like they'd never get their problems worked out, but she'd read enough romances to know the problems would work out, and God would bless the couple with true love.

If only real life held the same promises. When she thought about her and Gene—their ages, the awkwardness of her having been married to his brother, and the fact Gene had never been married at all—well, a relationship other than their two-decade-long friendship looked impossible.

Maybe I should take up writing romance books.

"Nothing's impossible with God." She'd quoted the same line to other folks all of her life, but until this very moment, she hadn't considered its validity in her own life.

Gene had taken a big step in telling her his feelings. She admired his courage, especially when she didn't have the guts to bring up such a sensitive subject or even make him feel better by responding with the truth.

"But I could reopen the discussion." Kae shivered. Talking to herself bordered on eccentric, but Melanie led the way on that trait. No point in going there.

Gene did say she needed to bring up the subject.

Can I? Do I dare? Why keep thinking about him all the time? She shut her book and marched into the kitchen for her cell phone. A few seconds later, Gene answered.

"I'm in the mood for a game of Ping-Pong. Are you in the mood to get beat?"

He chuckled. "As well as I recall, I'm the Ping-Pong champion."

"I challenge you to a rematch. Meet you at the activities building in twenty minutes." Kae disconnected the phone. *Lord, I'm going to need a lot of help here. I'm too old to act like a giddy schoolgirl and too young to spend the rest of my life alone.*

"You're losing," Gene said. "I've won two out of four games."

That's because I can't concentrate. "I felt sorry for you."

He raised a brow. "You've got to come up with a better excuse than that."

She swallowed the mountain of doubt in her throat. "How

about I'm trying to get up the nerve to talk about your marriage proposal?"

All of a sudden the hum of voices and laughter surrounding them grew silent. Had she spoken so loud the others had heard every word? Humiliation seeped through the pores of her skin. When her gaze flew to Gene, his pale face mirrored her fears. She cringed. If only a trapdoor would let her sink into oblivion.

"We could take a walk," Gene said.

"Good idea," she said.

"Can we come along?" a man asked. "Sounds like what you two have to say is more interesting than this chess game."

"Or this movie," a woman said by the TV.

Too many people laughed. Too many people offered advice.

Kae dropped her paddle on the Ping-Pong table. She snatched up her bottle of water and her keys and hurried to the door. All she needed to do now was trip and fall on her face.

"Wait up," Gene called.

Laughter roared behind her. She'd have to move up north and change her name to get over this one.

"Kae, forget about them. Who are those old people anyway?"

She couldn't turn around and face him. "The ones we have to live with every day for the rest of our lives."

"I want to talk about us, like you said."

"And I'm humiliated enough to go back to drinking leaded coffee." Honestly, if she'd been a drinking woman, the episode in the activities building might have done the trick. Anything to forget what just happened. Maybe she'd head to China and grow rice.

Gene made his way beside her. "Nah, you don't want to wreck your good health by getting addicted to caffeine again. Besides, the headaches are horrible."

Sympathy washed over her. "Oh, I'm sorry. Have you taken any Tylenol?"

"Yep, and for right now it's under control. Thanks for asking."

Do it, Kae. Speak your heart. "Am I supposed to lead the way about discussing. . .you know. . .what you said on Friday?"

"I said my piece. No point in me rehashing it. I should have planned it all better, but my heart stepped ahead of good sense."

"Okay, so the rest is up to me." She took a deep breath. "Gene, you've been my best friend ever since I can remember. I broke your heart and married Paul, but you were right beside us all the years we were married. Paul's been gone twenty years now. But about seventeen of them ago, I realized I loved you. I have a very special spot for Paul, always will, but I have another one for you." Kae wanted to see his reaction, but her gaze stayed glued on the sidewalk. In fact, she felt a little dizzy. "I never knew how to tell you, so I kept my feelings to myself. That's why I cried on Friday. Not because I didn't like what you said, but because I was so happy and sad, too, for keeping my love inside for so long."

"Happy?" The word crept out like a whisper.

"Yes. Happy. I couldn't stop boo-hooing long enough to make an intelligent response."

"And I thought I'd hurt you, messed up your memories of Paul."

Kae swung around. "I was relieved. All of this time I thought I'd have to always keep my love hidden and never tell you about it."

Gene's eyes moistened, and a tear slipped down onto his cheek. She hadn't seen him this emotional since Paul's funeral. "Can I hold you?" He swung a quick glance back at the activities building.

"I don't care if they are looking."

He smiled that wonderful, pearly white smile meant just for her. Gene opened his arms, and she stepped into his embrace—the embrace that felt as fresh and inviting as the new life they planned to share.

Chapter 4

Church seemed a little sweeter that night: the music a little brighter, the Word of God a little more illuminated. He liked that word—*illuminated.* It rolled off his tongue and settled on him real comfortable. Discovery and understanding about God. All these years he'd loved Kae from afar and kept it between him and God. Sitting there on the pew next to her with his heart nearly overflowing with love, he had to believe all these years had been training ground. They'd talked all afternoon and up until time for church.

Gene glanced at her and she smiled. To think all this time she'd loved him, too. Whoever said young love was foolish. Why, he and Kae were living proof that old folks could be in love and foolish, too.

"Too many wasted years," she'd said on the way to the evening service. "I never knew how to approach the subject. With Paul, I was a teenager infatuated with the best-looking guy around. He must have felt the same, because we fell in love. With you, we were best friends. I didn't want to tell you and spoil our friendship by bringing up something uncomfortable."

"I had resigned myself to being a confirmed bachelor until I couldn't wait any longer." He shifted in the van seat. "I don't want you to think I ever thought badly of Paul because he won you, and I didn't. He was a good brother, and I remember—" Gene shook his head.

"What is it?"

"I remember when he proposed, right before the Fourth of July fireworks. That afternoon he said if it bothered me too much to see the two of you together, then he'd bow out and give me a chance to win you." He swung Kae a faint smile. "I wouldn't have ever considered such a thing and told him so. We shook hands, then we hugged."

"And I was too inconsiderate to see how badly you were hurt." Kae swiped at a tear. "I'm sorry. I should have thanked you back then for your understanding."

"No need. It all happened the way God planned. I had a lot of growing up to do." He forced a chuckle. "It's a wonder I didn't kidnap you before the wedding." He rubbed his jaw. "Thought about it though."

"What a ghastly scandal that would have been." Kae slowly moved her hand across the van seat until he grasped it in his. "We may be old, but our hearts are young. I can't wait to tell the kids."

He lightly squeezed her hand. "I imagine they'll think we've lost our minds."

"Probably so." She sighed.

"I intend to get down on my knees tonight and propose." He laughed. "Might need help getting back up."

"No need to hurt yourself. You already know the answer."

"Are you kidding? Kae Alice, I've waited a lot of years to ask you to marry me properlike, and I'm not taking any shortcuts now."

She tilted her head. "You haven't called me Kae Alice since I fell in the lake while we were fishing. I think we were sixteen years old."

"You hit me over the head with your fishing pole for using your middle name. You wouldn't have fallen in the lake if you hadn't taken off after you hit me."

"You do remember the strangest things." She paused. "All of this happiness has me thirsty."

"I'll swing into a convenience store and get you a bottle of water."

"You've always put my needs first," she said. "Thank you, Gene. I'll make it up to you, I promise. Whatever time we have left on this earth, I'll love you with all my heart."

Gene thought he'd burst. *Thank You, Lord. I'm the luckiest man alive.*

"You're what? At your age?" Kae cringed at the disbelief in her eldest son's voice.

"I said I'm marrying Gene. I believe you heard me the first time. He asked me last night after church."

"Are you sure you want to do this?" David blew out a heavy breath. "Are you having financial problems?"

Kae imagined her dark-haired son taking notes while they spoke. "No, Son. My investments are doing quite nicely, as well as my financial picture. Thank you very much."

"Ah, it's the companion thing, isn't it? With you two living in the same retiree center, a marriage of convenience makes good sense."

"We love each other." Kae sensed her frustration level rising. "I'm not spending the years I have left with Gene because I'm depressed or lonely. Truth is I've been in love with him for a long time."

"Oh, brother, Mom. I'm not sure this is the best situation for you. Uncle Gene has never been married, and this could be a real stretch for him. A divorce at your age could be devastating."

"Those things will not happen. We've talked about the adjustment, and he feels it won't be that difficult." She clenched her fist, sensing David's probing was because he questioned her good judgment.

"One of you will have to downsize, especially if you plan to stay in the retiree center."

"I believe we both will need to evaluate our living arrangements."

"I'm just wanting to make sure you've thought this through. We could sit down and talk about it all. You know, work through different scenarios. I know you're in great health, but women live longer than men and—"

She closed her eyes. "Can't you congratulate me? I didn't call to ask your permission to marry Gene." Thank goodness she'd had the foresight to contact David after she'd phoned her other three children. Mr. Skeptic was still the bossy one. "My mind is fine, and I'm a long way from needing someone to make decisions for me."

"I didn't mean—"

"Of course you didn't. You're simply looking after your aging mother. Right?"

"I want what's best for you."

"Thank you, but in the case of my upcoming marriage, you can just give me your blessing." Silence reigned between them, but she refused to change her mind about Gene.

"I love you, Mom, and I want you to be happy."

"Wonderful. I am ecstatic. Your sisters and brother have marked the date on their calendar, and this wedding will be one big celebration."

"Ouch. I didn't even ask the date."

Kae laughed. "I know. Do you feel properly chastised?"

"Absolutely. When is the big day?"

"Saturday, December 10. Gene is going to ask Pastor Thomas from our church to perform the ceremony. Now you can congratulate me, then call your uncle Gene and do the same." She took a moment before plunging into another topic. "Hannah had her seventh birthday last week. How did she celebrate it?"

"Tracie had a party here with the little girls from her class."

"I could have helped."

"Tracie didn't want to bother you."

"I always have time for my family. I also read in the paper that she had a dance recital."

"Yes, about two weeks ago."

Did Kae dare say exactly what she thought about her daughter-in-law's lack of consideration? For that matter, did David support leaving his mother out of Hannah's parties and activities? "I would like to have seen my granddaughter dance, but I had no idea she was in a recital."

After several long moments, David cleared his throat. "I'm sorry, Mom. I didn't know."

How many times have you apologized for Tracie? "I have a gift for Hannah's birthday, and I'd like to take her to a movie."

"I'll check with Tracie."

Do I tell him I called last week with the same request, but Tracie said Hannah was too busy? "Please do so and get back with me. I don't want to be a pest, but little ones grow up so fast, and I want to be a part of her life. Have a good afternoon, and I love you."

Kae replaced the phone on the counter. She refused to interfere in David and Tracie's life any further. Maybe she'd already gone too far. Marriage these days had two strikes against it by the time the couple sliced the wedding cake. A meddling mother-in-law could be the third strike. But denying Kae the right to be a part of her granddaughter's life seemed grossly unfair. Most of the time, she bit her tongue to keep from saying exactly how she felt. Irritability seemed to attack her more and more these days, but she'd read that older people often became less patient with their surroundings.

Tracie grew up as an only child, and although Kae would never outright accuse her of being selfish, the thought had occurred on more than one occasion.

Lord, You've blessed me a lot here lately and I'm grateful, but once again I'm asking You to mend the situation with Tracie. I beg of You to shut my mouth when I start feeling sorry for myself about Hannah.

Gene should have been dancing a jig on the piano about marrying

Kae. His prayers had been answered, and he couldn't wait for her to be his wife. *Mrs. Gene Richards.* Sure had a nice ring to it, never mind that she'd carried the name of Richards for more than fifty years. He rubbed his hands together. How lucky could one man be? Yet fear had suddenly sunk its claws into his head and heart. What did he know about being a husband? Worse yet, whom could he turn to for a quick mentor? A man half his age? Or a man who'd laugh at him from now on until December 10? Certainly none of those old men who had laughed at his precious Kae yesterday, except her loud statement had been so uncharacteristic. Love. . .sure was grand.

Marriage and the idea of spooning up next to Kae while they slept sounded wonderful in one breath, and in the next he wondered if he could even sleep in those arrangements. He might pull the blankets off her, and then she'd catch cold. And sharing a bathroom worried him, too. She'd have her own toothbrush and all those women lotions and makeup stuff. The smell might give him a headache. Would there be room for the two of them? They'd already decided a move to a bigger condo might be in order. He'd developed a lot of quirky habits over the years, and she might have problems with them. If he thought about it long enough, he might have problems with some of her ways of doing things.

Gene tossed a load of towels into the dryer. Would he and Kae do this kind of thing together? In the next breath, he practiced introducing her.

"And this is my wife. Kae. We have four children and six grandchildren." *Is that proper?* Could he claim Paul's kids as his? There ought to be someone he could ask about that. And counseling. . .their pastor would be a good source.

Kae's kids were a good bunch, and he didn't anticipate any hard feelings or resentment there. But what if one of them objected? Like David. That man reminded Gene of a walking ulcer. He always needed to know all the details and expected to be consulted on all matters concerning the family. *Was I supposed to ask David for his permission?* Gene cringed. Little late now. No doubt he knew about the wedding and had fired a zillion questions at Kae. Should he call David, take him to lunch, and discuss the wedding plans? Gene would rather have a root canal.

His stomach fluttered every time he thought about getting married. But he loved Kae, and he cherished everything about her. God had placed them together, and He'd make sure any little troublesome situations were worked out. Frettin' over it made no sense at all.

Chapter 5

Kae stared at the portion of foot-long sub left on her plate. Normally she barely ate a six-inch veggie on wheat, but her appetite had suddenly soared since Gene proposed. She picked up the sandwich and bit into it hungrily.

"You're going to gain weight if you keep eating like this," Melanie said. "I thought people lost their appetite when they were in love."

Kae hurriedly chewed and swallowed her food, savoring a tender avocado and tomato drenched in mayonnaise. "But I've been in love with Gene for the past seventeen years. I must be eating out of relief."

"Maybe so, or it could be a bad case of nerves. I only want to remind you of what you said the other day, about wanting to be carried over the threshold."

Kae set the sandwich back onto the plate. "You're right. I need to take good care of myself. I'll take the rest of this home for lunch tomorrow."

"Good idea. I see I'm going to have to watch you like a

mama bear over her cubs. Your cheeks could use a little filling out, but not an extra fifty pounds."

Melanie was enjoying this marriage talk entirely too much.

"Tell me about the wedding plans," Melanie said. "I want to hear every word."

"Oh, my." Kae startled. "All we've done is set the date. I have no idea where or how big a ceremony or a reception or any of those things." A mixture of excitement and anticipation whipped through her. "I don't want a big affair, just family and friends. We did decide on asking Pastor Thomas. Guess I need to talk to Gene about these other things."

"December 10 will be here before you know it." Melanie pulled a pen from her purse and grabbed an extra paper napkin. "Let's make a list before we forget it." She smiled, and with her bright orange shirt, she looked quite like a carved pumpkin.

Kae loved her quirky friend, and right now she'd appease her. Although she'd sit down with Gene tonight and go over every item on the list.

"Who will marry you is the first item, but you have that taken care of." Melanie scribbled the question on the napkin. "Where to have the ceremony is number two. Number three is how big do you want the ceremony, and number four is how many guests."

"You are a real wedding planner." Kae struggled to conceal her amusement.

"I love to plan parties. Let's see. . .a matron of honor for you and a best man for him," Melanie said.

Another matter Kae hadn't considered. Who in the world could they ask?

"Establish the time of day for the wedding. If you're to have a reception, then—"

Kae released a pent-up sigh. Suddenly she was exhausted.

Melanie wagged the pen in Kae's face. "Don't you even consider not having a reception. That's a must even if all you have is cake, nuts, and punch. So the next item is to decide where to have the reception and what kind of food." She closed her eyes. "I can see it now, a huge tiered cake with lots of pink roses. And a groom's cake for Gene, probably chocolate."

"Absolutely. That's his favorite." Kae laughed. "The bride and groom figurines have to be old, bent over, and leaning on canes."

"And the most important question of all," Melanie said.

Kae peered into Melanie's face.

"You know." Melanie frowned. "What you're going to wear."

"I have a beautiful ice blue suit with lovely pearls."

"Has to be new. None of the outfits you've worn before. We'll go shopping together. New dress. New shoes. Your pearls will be fine. And flowers, can't forget flowers."

This wedding had the makings of an expensive event. Kae remembered her daughters' weddings. No, absolutely not would she spend that kind of money. Gene could slap a step stool next to her first-story window, and they'd elope. She wiggled her shoulders. Eloping had a romantic ring to it.

"Just remember," Melanie said. "If you two decide to get married and not let the rest of us here at the retiree center enjoy the festivities, we'll track you down and party hard when we find you."

Leave it to Melanie to think of everything.

While Kae shared lunch and the afternoon with Melanie, Gene awaited for a 2:00 appointment with Pastor Thomas at the church office. The doctor's office had given him a fine report, and he'd celebrated at noon with chicken-fried steak, garlic mashed potatoes, fried okra, cornbread, and chocolate cake.

He squirmed in the chair like a little boy. A case of doubts had seized him about marrying Kae until he wondered if being single was the easier route.

The aging pastor opened his door. Just like the rest of Gene's friends, the men were either white haired or bald. The top of Pastor Thomas's round head looked like a light bulb. Gene wondered if the glow was a sign of holiness or from the smooth-as-a-baby's-skin head.

"Come on in, Gene." They shook hands, and the pastor gestured to a sofa in front of his desk. "You said this was urgent."

Gene expelled a heavy sigh. "I should have explained my situation a little better. With my age, I suppose you thought I had found out some bad medical news."

"Well, it did cross my mind." He eased into a chair beside Gene. His knees cracked.

"The truth is, I'm getting married."

Pastor Thomas's eyes sparkled, and his mustache flipped up. Gene started to laugh; the man looked like a walrus—but a pleasant one. "Congratulations. Who's the lucky lady? Hmm. I think I already know."

"My best friend, Kae Richards."

Pastor Thomas's grin widened. "Thought so. Have you set a date?"

"December 10. We were wondering if you'd marry us."

"Let me check my calendar before I say yes." He turned around and reached for his Palm Pilot.

"I have one of those, but I had a hard time getting used to it. Once I had it all figured out, I kept better track of who got meals-on-wheels, who had a doctor's appointment, and where they needed to be transported."

Pastor Thomas glanced up. "You amaze me, Gene. Nothing gets past you."

"Not if I can help it. If it's new and out there, then I want to know how it works. I've been taking computer courses at the college. Thinking about another degree in computer science."

"I might need you to give me a hand here. The church just updated their system, and I'm lost." He pointed to his Palm Pilot. "Looks like a clear Saturday on the tenth. What time?"

"I have no idea. I'll need to get back with you."

"Sure. I'll schedule the whole day until you call." He tapped in the information with the stylus. "Is this what you wanted to talk to me about?"

"Oh, there's more." All of Gene's carefully formed words seemed to vanish from his memory bank. Another problem with getting old. "I. . .I don't know how to say this."

Gene focused his attention on the pastor. "Is it possible for a man my age to have cold feet?"

"Did you have cold feet the first time you were married?"

"Never been. This *is* my first."

Pastor Thomas's eyes widened. "Now I see. This is serious business."

"I waited for the right woman. Can you help me work through this? I've been praying for a little peace."

"Sure can."

"How? Do I read a book? Take a class? I surely don't want to confess this to Kae."

"Hold on a minute. I'm a little puzzled here. Both of you have the same name."

"She was married to my brother. We've been friends for fifty-five years."

The pastor bit his lip, no doubt to keep from laughing. "Then you must know each other quite well." He paused and tilted his head. "We do have premarital classes—"

"For folks our age?" Gene could hear the laughter now.

"We don't have a stipulation on age. And many of the problems and situations are the same at any age. I think you and Kae have a lot to offer to a group of people contemplating marriage."

"Any of them seventy-five-year-old bachelors?"

The pastor covered his mouth, but Gene saw the smile. "Don't think so, but some of these guys need to know their fears are the same at any age. What about those stepping up to the plate who are taking on ready-made families?"

"I see what you mean." Gene felt this overwhelming urge to run. "I'm not sure about this. I was thinking more along the line of private counseling with you."

"We can do that, but I'd like for you to talk to Kae about the classes. They are ten weeks long and meet on Sunday mornings at nine before worship service. We have a class starting this week."

Gene wiggled his toes in his Nikes. "Okay, I'll talk to her about it."

"You love her, don't you?"

The question put all of his doubts into perspective. "Yes, I have for a long time."

"Are her children giving you a bad time?"

"One of them could. I've been praying about that, too."

"Would his objection stop you?"

"Nah, don't think so. The only problem I have is this jittery feeling in the pit of my stomach about filling the shoes of a husband and stepfather."

"Then, Gene, you're almost there. I believe after taking the classes, you'll get a leading from the Lord about getting married."

"Thanks, Pastor." The road ahead was sure like nothing he'd ever done before, but he wasn't getting any younger, and life without Kae meant a miserable existence.

The following morning Kae walked with Gene arm in arm along the hiking trail of the retiree complex. They'd spent the past thirty minutes discussing the wedding. The whole event sent shivers up and down her spine.

"I don't want a big wedding either," Gene said, "but I would like our friends to be there and a small reception afterwards."

Kae nodded. "How about checking on the activity center for the reception?"

"Sounds good. I was thinking of a wedding at five and a barbecue dinner afterwards. I bet we could get it catered pretty reasonable." He laughed. "We'll have to make sure the barbecue is good and tender so the old folks can chew it."

"When are you going to realize that *we* are old people?"

"Never! I'm a young man about to get married to the prettiest gal in Alabama."

For sure, life with Gene was not going to be boring. "Have you thought of a best man?"

He stopped for a moment and turned his attention to the right of him where ducks waddled on the bank of a pond; a couple toddled their way. "No bread today, fellas." He gave his attention to Kae. "Now back to your question. Honestly, I thought of asking David. He's all worried about us getting married, and this might help."

"What a sweet thought. Is Mr. Worrywart giving you a bad time?"

"He did call." Gene shook his head. "Guess he wondered if my intentions were honorable. I decided to take him to breakfast on Friday morning and ease his mind. I might ask him then, if you think that's all right."

"Oh, I think it's a wonderful idea. But do this for your reasons, not because he's my son." She paused. "Maybe I should ask Tracie to be my matron of honor."

"How's the situation there?" Gene said. "Have you ever figured out why she doesn't include you in Hannah's activities?"

Kae sighed and leaned closer on his arm. "I really don't know, and I'm afraid if I say much more, she and David will be fussing. He always seems clueless and very apologetic when I mention anything about Hannah. She's such a sweetheart, and when we do see each other, we have such a splendid time."

"You know I'm praying for you. Have you heard from them since you asked about Hannah's birthday?"

"No, and I'm not asking about it again. I can only pray David or Tracie will include me on the next special occasion." She patted his arm. "It doesn't have to be special. I'd be happy watching her play or sitting alongside her at the table and coloring."

"We'll wait patiently and see how God works this out."

Her heart seemed a little lighter with his words. "You always say the right things."

He grinned. "I'll remind you of that the next time my teasing gets under your skin."

Chapter 6

Gene dreaded the nine o'clock Sunday school class. All week, he'd looked for an excuse to get out of the session—even purchased a preparing-for-marriage book and workbook at the Christian bookstore in hopes Kae would think that was a better idea.

"Let's give Pastor Thomas's suggestion one try," she said. "If we walk away feeling like the brunt of a joke, then we'll try your books or visit Pastor Thomas."

Now as he and Kae stood outside the Sunday school classroom, a whole generation of young people crowded around them. Perspiration dripped down his face, and he longed for a cup of caffeine. He bent to whisper in Kae's ear. "If I make it through the next hour, we'll finish the sessions at Pastor Thomas's office."

She glanced around them. "This might not be so bad. In fact, we might learn something."

Before he could voice his doubts, a young man laid his hand on Gene's shoulder. "Cool," the young man said. "The pastor said we'd have mentors. Looks like we have a couple that must have been married fifty years."

Does he think I'm deaf? A few other remarks strayed across his mind, but before he could voice them, a young couple in their thirties grappled for everyone's attention.

"Come on in. We're ready to get started on the Pre-Wed class."

Kae tossed Gene a half smile. "This will be painless."

He scowled and gently guided her to the coffee and sweet rolls.

"Decaf," she said, barely loud enough for him to hear. "I imagine this is the power surge stuff."

Naturally she was right. Within a few minutes, each couple stood and introduced themselves along with how the couple met.

"My name is Troy and this is Wendy. We fell in love in college, and now that we've graduated and started our careers, we're planning to marry on Valentine's Day."

"Oohs" and "ahhs" followed. Gene thought he'd sink through the floor at the thought of standing before these people. What ever did he have in common with them? Finally it was his and Kae's turn. They stood. His knees shook like a crippled, hundred-year-old man's.

"My name is Kae Richards. I met Gene fifty-five years ago at a church picnic. He put a worm down my back."

Gene cringed at the giggles. "My name is Gene Richards, and Kae was married to my brother until he passed on some twenty years ago. We've always been good friends."

"How sweet," a young woman said. "So did your wife pass on, too?"

Gene took a deep breath. "No. I've never been married." If he had to say that one more time, he'd write it across his forehead. *Old and never been married.*

Luckily no one else asked any more questions. After the uneasiness of who's who faded, the facilitator of the class began the session.

"On your syllabus are biblical references to what we will be discussing. This week please read Ephesians 5:22–33. Since the Bible says a husband is to love his wife as Christ loves the church, does this change when there are children involved? Let's talk about that for a moment."

"Absolutely," a young woman said. "When children come along or if there are already children, the husband and wife love each other and the children equally."

Gene hadn't thought about that. He glanced at Kae who stared at him with no sign of her personal feelings about the matter. Praise God, Paul's kids were likable.

"What do the rest of you think?" the facilitator asked.

"She's wrong," a kid said, barely out of acne. "God says a husband puts his wife above the children, and she is to place her husband above the children."

"Which is it?" Gene whispered to Kae.

Her eyes grew large. "You don't know?"

"I think I do."

"Then pay attention." She smiled.

"You have the correct answer," the facilitator said to the young man. "Gene, with your age and subsequent wisdom, how do you view the relationship between spouse and children?"

His blood ran cold, or was it hot? "I. . .I don't have any

more to add to the subject than what that young man said. Just because I'm older doesn't mean I have any more wisdom than you. I've had wonderful years with the Lord but no experience with women. I haven't any children, but I'm about to have grandchildren. I'm lost."

The class roared. And for the first time, Gene understood why the Lord wanted him there. He had much to learn.

Kae woke from a long nap. For some reason she required more sleep lately. Must be from the stress of planning a wedding and working through the issues of her and Gene's upcoming life together. She had thoroughly enjoyed the first Pre-Wed class, and so did Gene.

She glanced around her bedroom. Yesterday after church, she and Gene had looked into a larger condo on the grounds and officially put their respective homes on the market. Not only did they have combined household and personal items, but they also needed a special spot for Gene's grand piano. Packing and moving was one aspect she'd easily delegate to a couple of volunteers.

"Won't take long to sell our condos," Gene had said. "Folks are on a list to get into the retiree center. We can count on a good price, too."

Still, it seemed strange to think about setting up housekeeping with Gene in a place of their own. *Almost like being a girl again.* She glanced down at the brown spots on her arm and the blue veins rising up from transparent skin. She thought about the lines around her eyes and giggled. Love sure had a way of making an old woman feel like dancing.

She scooted off the bed and folded up the blanket, then made her way to the kitchen for a bottle of water. Tonight the retiree center had the weekly Bible study, and she hadn't readied herself. Snatching up her Bible, she eased onto the sofa, when the phone rang.

"Hi, Grandma. This is Hannah."

Kae's heart quickened. Tears moistened her eyes. "Hi, sweetheart. How nice of you to call. Did Mommy or Daddy give you my number?"

The little girl giggled, and Kae envisioned her dimpled cheeks. "I got the number off Daddy's notepad in his study. That's where I am right now."

"Oh, I see. Honey, shouldn't you have Mommy or Daddy's permission to use the phone?"

"Hmm. Yes, ma'am, but I was afraid Mommy might say no. She doesn't want me answering it or calling people."

"Mommy has reasons for wanting to keep you safe. I love talking to you, but we need her permission. Why don't you lay the phone on Daddy's desk and go ask her? I'll be waiting when you get back."

"Okay. Don't hang up, because I want to talk. Grandma, I haven't seen you in a long time, and I miss you."

Kae bit back a sob. "I miss you, too. Now run along and hurry back."

The moments ticked by. Kae heard nothing, not even the sound of little feet skipping across the hardwood floor of David's office.

"Kae?" The familiar voice depressed Kae, but she refused to give in.

"Hi, Tracie. I do hope Hannah isn't in trouble."

"Of course not." Tracie sounded friendly, but she always did. "We simply have rules about the phone. And I appreciate your requesting she seek permission."

"Can she talk to me?"

"Oh, yes. I wanted to congratulate you on your upcoming marriage."

"Thank you." Kae laughed. "We're even taking premarital classes at our church."

"That's an excellent idea. Will it be a large wedding?"

"Not really, but we will have a barbecue dinner at the reception." Kae took a deep breath. "Could we have lunch one day this week?"

"I think that could be arranged. I'm available on Thursday." Tracie's voice sounded up, as though having lunch were commonplace.

"Let's meet at the Strawberry Patch around noon." Once the arrangements were confirmed, Kae realized how fast her heart raced. The conversation had gone better than she imagined, thanks to God.

With Hannah's sweet voice over the phone line, Kae closed her eyes and imagined spending time with David's family. It would happen. She simply needed faith.

"We have all the wedding arrangements made except the music." Gene grinned. Satisfaction always nudged him to celebrate.

"Yes. We are on top of it all," Kae said. "And at noon tomorrow I will have lunch with Tracie and ask her to be my matron of honor."

"Oh yeah, forgot about that. I'll handle my best man situation on Friday."

"Please pray that Tracie and I will draw closer. I have no idea where the problem originated. I simply want the relationship restored."

He reached for her hand across the table at their favorite coffee shop. "You bet. I see how it hurts you."

Unspoken feelings of love and compassion passed between them. Then the quiet background music switched to Elvis Presley crooning to "Jailhouse Rock" and changed the mood.

"What kind of music do you want during the ceremony?" Kae pulled her notepad and pen from her purse.

"You pick, honey. My mind draws a blank, except I'd like to hear 'The Lord's Prayer.' "

She jotted down his request. "I'll put some songs together, and we can go over them later." She wiggled her shoulders in the same cute little way that she'd done for years. "What about music for the reception? Do we want country since we're having barbecue, or do we want a mixture of things?"

"I'd like to hear some fifties tunes. . .and country-western. . . and even some big band. Guess I do have some ideas about the weddin'."

"I do agree with your choice of music. We probably ought to have a few new songs for the younger guests," Kae said. "I found a disc jockey who can play whatever we want."

"Go for it," Gene said. "I think the guests will like about

anything. I'll be dancing with my best girl and be just plain happy."

"Correction. Your best girl will then be your wife."

A smile tugged at his lips. "What a day we'll have. I'll remember it for the rest of my life."

Kae chuckled. "At our age, that won't be long."

He winked at her, then kissed her hand. Love sure made a fella act silly. "Did you read your scripture for our Pre-Wed class?"

"Yes, sir. Did you?" When he nodded, she eased back on the chair, almost as though she were tired, but this was breakfast. "I wondered how you felt about the submission aspect of marriage."

"No arguments from me. I grew up with my folks as role models for how husbands and wives were to respect and love each other. My dad always put Mama first. He fussed over her to take care of herself, and she fussed over him in return. Guess I should have told the class about them last week. Truthfully I was too nervous to think straight."

"I think you have more to offer those young people than you think. I remember how much your parents loved each other, and they were married a lot of years."

"When Dad died three months after Mama, I believed he willed himself to be with her. He told me he couldn't imagine life without her." Gene reflected a moment on how happy his parents had been. "I understood exactly how he felt. I loved you from afar—prayed for you and Paul—wanted your lives blessed with all the good things."

"You are such a caring man," Kae said. "I'm one lucky woman

to have known the love of two fine men."

Gene straightened. If he didn't change the subject soon, he'd be whimpering like a baby. "I need some more coffee," he said, "and another sticky bun."

"First topic after marriage," Kae said as she wrote. "Convince new, wonderful husband of importance of maintaining good health."

"And what else is on your list?"

"Number two: Encourage husband to drink decaf coffee. Number three: Watch sugar and grease intake. Number four: Have him eat more vegetables. Number five: Man does not live on grease and sugar alone. Number six: A kiss a day keeps the blahs away."

Oh, being married to Kae was going to be fun. She lifted her sweet face from the notepad. Something about her didn't look right.

Dear Lord, I pray this is my imagination.

Chapter 7

Kae sat in her little silver sports car in front of the Strawberry Patch and waited for the twelve o'clock hour. She reached for her bottle of water and drank long and hard. She'd prayed, made reflections, rehearsed her lines, and tried not to think about lunch with Tracie. Somewhere they'd gotten off on the wrong foot, and she was determined to change it. Communicating a good relationship stood forefront in her mind.

When she thought about it, Tracie had been standoffish from the moment David introduced her. For the past ten years, Kae believed the problem stemmed from Tracie being an only child, and with a tendency toward selfishness. But she was a good wife and an excellent mother to Hannah. Granted, she bordered on possessive when it came to her husband and daughter, especially at holidays. Tracie always insisted they be with her parents. She'd told Kae once that there were three other siblings to spend the holidays with Kae, and her folks only had Tracie. Now that was true, and Kae even invited Tracie's parents to her home on occasion. Always a refusal. Could it be because Tracie's parents were wealthy? Surely not. The problem had to be with Kae. So what had she done wrong? She didn't mind apologizing, if only she knew what for.

Kae glanced up. Her tall, slender daughter-in-law pulled up beside her in the parking lot. Kae waved and smiled. *Lord, I need all the help I can get.*

Gene left the Alzheimer's section with a skip in his walk. Nothing made him any happier than having folks enjoy his piano playing—especially those who were shut-in while life passed them by. Fortunately most of the residents in this retiree center had family and friends who visited regularly, whether the resident recognized the caller or not.

"God's called me to take care of folks who need help," he said to the head nurse this morning. "Whenever I wonder where I'm supposed to be volunteering, God lights the way for a new ministry."

"Thank you." The nurse handed him a cup of coffee—not decaf—but one cup wouldn't hurt. "As a Christian, I feel my work here is more of a ministry than a career. Some of the staff has a different view, that this is a job and nothing more." She hesitated as though pondering her words. "I think the residents deserve dignity and respect."

"So do I," Gene said. "We're here to help each other, and I want to do my part." He handed her back the cup before taking one delicious gulp. "I told the doctor I'd give up caffeine. I also promised my sweet wife-to-be."

With those words he realized that all the doubts

burdening him about taking on a wife were foolish because God had paved the way for him and Kae to be together. Granted, he'd lived a long time by himself, and he was so set in his ways that at times he wondered if Kae could live with him, but he also feared a short life with the woman he loved. The idea of calculating his age, health, and family history to find out approximately how many years he had left crossed his mind. He even had the Web site to figure it out. The truth settled on him like a sweet autumn breeze. He had no more years with Kae than God had orchestrated in the beginning. They'd take each day at a time and live it for God's purpose.

Gene made his way to the van. A couple of folks needed a ride to the doctor, and he didn't want to be late. He snatched up his cell and plugged in the hands-free. Kae had insisted he use it when driving.

"Mornin', Pastor. This is Gene Richards. I wanted to report in on last Sunday's Pre-Wed class."

"Did you enjoy it?" the pastor asked—with way too much humor.

"Now I'm interpreting your good mood to the fact that a seventy-five-year-old couple attended a class full of youngsters."

"Confession time."

"I suppose the facilitators gave a full report."

"A glowing one. They said you and Kae added a dimension they hadn't expected."

Gene laughed. "Yep. We gave a whole new meaning to *mature living*. Seriously, I'm looking forward to the next class. There's a lot for me to learn, and I think I might be able to help some of them, too."

"Wonderful. I took the liberty of telling the facilitators that you play a mean piano."

"I saw one in the corner. Tell you what, I'll show up a few minutes early to entertain them. They might like jazzed-up gospel."

"Perfect. Thanks, Gene."

He removed the earpiece and reached for his lukewarm coffee. Life couldn't get any better than this. Remembering Kae's lunch with Tracie, Gene sent a quick prayer heavenward. God had a way of working out all the most awkward circumstances.

Midway through a cup of roasted red pepper soup and a chicken salad sandwich, Kae fought for courage to ask Tracie a few questions. For some reason she was tired, or her desire for sleep came from dreading a possible nasty confrontation.

"I haven't eaten here in ages," Kae said. "The food is wonderful."

Tracie glanced up. Her shoulder-length hair framed her pretty oval face. "It's one of my favorite places. I love the different flavored teas, the garden decor, and the food is outstanding."

Kae grinned and pointed to a large table in the rear. "I see the Red Hat Ladies must enjoy it, too."

"Oh, Kae, they do everything here—showers, birthday parties, ladies Bible studies, book clubs. . . ."

"I'll keep that in mind. A group of ladies from the retiree center are always looking for a new place to have lunch." She took a deep breath. "Did David tell you any more about the wedding plans?"

"He sure did. Excuse me for not congratulating you in

person when I got here. Seems strange that Uncle Gene will now by Granddaddy Gene." Tracie set her spoon down. "I hope this marriage works out for you. David has his reservations."

David always has reservations. "I am very happy, and I'm kicking myself for not telling Gene seventeen years ago that I was in love with him."

Tracie's eyes widened. She actually looked amused. "Why did you wait so long?"

"Fear, mostly. We were such good friends, and I didn't want to spoil it." Kae giggled. "Imagine how I felt when he told me about his love."

"How utterly sweet. So tell me about the wedding."

Kae spent the next few minutes giving Tracie all the details, cluing her daughter-in-law in on all the plans. "As you can see, we're nearly ready. I do have one problem, though."

Tracie focused her gaze on her.

"I need a matron of honor. Would you do that for me?" There, she said it.

"Me?"

Kae nodded. A mixture of emotions swept over Tracie's face—surprise, concern, and a few Kae couldn't quite figure out.

"I. . .I don't know what to say. I haven't been a model daughter-in-law." She shrugged. "Betsy is a better choice."

Steve's wife was a peach. She and Kae spent lots of time together. "I wanted you."

"Is this a ploy to see Hannah more often? Or for David and me to spend a holiday with you?" Tracie stiffened.

Kae refused to allow the question to topple her resolve. "Not at all. I want a relationship with you, and I'm concerned that I set the pace for potential problems right from the start."

"You sure did."

Kae's confidence plummeted. "Would you tell me what I did wrong? I want to make amends." She placed her shaking hands in her lap. Fatigue threatened to take over, but she willed it away.

"You don't know? I can't believe this," Tracie said.

"I have no idea. I'm asking you to please help me make this right."

Long moments followed, and when Tracie reached for her purse, Kae feared her daughter-in-law would leave the tearoom.

"Do you remember the wedding shower my sorority sisters gave for me?" Tracie's eyes filled with tears.

"Yes. It was held at your parents' country club." An elaborate affair with nearly eighty ladies in attendance. The invitations even told the guests what to wear and the color. The same day Betsy gave birth to Jon-Mark.

"You left the shower before it was over."

Kae did her best to conceal her shock. She'd excused herself from the shower fifteen minutes before the scheduled event was over. "Betsy went into labor, and I hurried over there to take care of the twins."

"That was my day. Steve could have found someone else."

Lord, how do I handle this? Kae took a moment to regain her composure. "Tracie, I'm sorry about that day. I never intended to hurt you or take away from your shower. Please forgive me."

"It simply meant a lot to me for David's mom to be there. . . meet my friends. . .support me in my new life. . . This was a special occasion for me. All the gifts. Everything."

Lord, I want to shake her, but it is all about restoration, isn't it? "Can we get past this unfortunate situation and start fresh? I'd really like for us to be friends, and I do want you to be my matron of honor." Kae studied the young woman before her whose lips quivered and hands trembled.

"You mean forget the past ten years of hurt? Act like it never happened?"

"We could take it slow and—"

Tracie stood. "How dare you act like my pain could be discarded like an old rag? I can't wait to tell David about how once again his mother is so insensitive. I've spent countless hours with psychologists over this incident." She fled the tea-room in tears, not once looking back.

Kae considered going after her. Tracie shouldn't be driving until she calmed down. Without another thought, Kae hurried outside only to see Tracie speed backward from her parking spot and swerve the car around and onto the street.

David had lived with this neurotic woman for ten years? Should she call him and let him know the lunch had gone badly? No doubt Tracie would fill him in on the whole thing. How ever did he deal with her emotions? Had it always been this way? Kae bowed her head and prayed for Tracie. They needed God in a big way.

On the way home, her cell phone rang. She detested people who drove and talked on the phone at the same time, but a quick glimpse told her David was calling.

"Hi, David. Look, I'm sorry about—"

"No, Mom. I'm sorry. Tracie called me, and she was hysterical. She relayed what happened." He took a deep breath.

"We've had problems for years and spent a lot of time in counseling. Tracie needs to be on medication, but she doesn't like to take it."

"Oh, David. I don't know what to say." What a burden he must carry.

"It's all right. Hannah is my concern, and she does spend a tremendous amount of time at my in-laws. Tracie is a wonderful wife and mother when she takes her medicine. But she has to get a grip on this, or it will affect our daughter even more than it already has."

Now everything made sense. "Why didn't you tell me?"

"She didn't want you to know. We've tried to keep it from you all these years. For some reason holidays seem to be the worst. She wants to be superwife and supermom and believes that the medication isn't necessary."

"I wouldn't have loved her any less."

"I know that, but she's ashamed."

"Poor thing. Are you heading home to her?" Kae asked.

"Yeah. Pray for us, will you?"

"Sure. Call me if you need anything. I'd come over there, but I'm afraid I'd make matters worse."

"Thanks, Mom. I'll talk to you later."

Kae slid the phone across the seat. How horrible for Tracie and her precious family. She blinked back the tears. Some things were not what they seemed. Did Gene really want to become more involved in her family? He'd always been Uncle Gene, the lighthearted one who played piano, bounced the kids on his knees, and attended all the events involving family. But this had dysfunctional written all over it.

Chapter 8

Gene reached out and drew Kae to him. She'd cried her heart out over the situation with David's family. He'd wondered many times about his nephew's home life. The man looked unhappy. Now Gene knew why.

"We'll just keep that family at the top of our prayer list." He kissed her forehead and tightened his hug.

"Are you sure you want to get involved with all this?" she asked.

He stifled a laugh. "Honey, I've been in this since you and Paul said 'I do.' I've been reading this book about preparing for marriage, and one thing that stands out to me is a real man doesn't jump ship when the going gets rough. He simply paddles harder and lets God steer the ship."

"Thank you. I feel terrible that this has surfaced after you proposed." She stared up into his face.

"Well don't." He studied her for a moment. "You're tired again."

"I know. Must be the stress lately."

"When's the last time you had a physical?"

She shook her head. "Now there you are being overprotective. For your information I had a complete physical about a year ago."

"Would you do me a favor and have another one? I'd feel better knowing my best girl is in perfect health."

She snuggled into the crook of his arm. "If it makes you happy, I'll make an appointment today."

"Blood work and everything?"

"Absolutely."

A short while later she fell asleep against his chest. An empty bottle of water sat on the lamp table beside her. He sighed. A haunting suspicion crept across his mind, and he didn't like the implications. No, not at all.

Kae heard the nurse call out her name. She folded the day's newspaper and stuck it in her purse. Her physical was a month early, but she'd promised Gene. After the nurse greeted her, she led Kae to the scales.

"On board," the nurse said.

The computer-type scales registered ten pounds lighter than what she'd weighed for the past ten years.

"Nothing changes much with me, except my age."

"A lot of folks half your age could take lessons on how you stay healthy," the nurse said. "Although I don't think you needed to take off weight. Look at me. I'm nearly forty and forty pounds overweight. I have no excuse."

"Oh, it will happen when you're ready," Kae said. "It's not a diet. It's a lifestyle that focuses on good food choices and exercise."

"Yes, ma'am."

Kae laughed with the nurse. "Pardon my preaching. Comes with age."

Once inside the examination room, Kae learned her blood pressure and pulse were normal. If it wasn't for appeasing Gene, she'd thank the nurse and doctor, pay for her office visit, and head home. She'd given up breakfast and coffee at the Coffee Grind to fast for the blood work.

"Any problems?" the nurse asked.

"Not really. Seems like I'm a bit more tired lately, and a friend brought it to my attention that I drink a lot of water." Kae shrugged. "So I'm making sure everything is okay."

"Smart lady." The nurse jotted down Kae's answers and left her alone to wait for the doctor.

Patience was one of her finer attributes, but this morning she felt antsy, hungry, and thirsty. Pulling the newspaper from her purse, she let the time slip by with world news and the latest movies. By the time she'd decided none of the new releases were worth the effort, the doctor opened the door with her folder tucked under his arm.

"Morning, Miss Kae. Good to see you." He smiled and reached for her hand. "I understand you're wanting to see if a tune-up is in order."

"Right. And as I told the nurse, I want to make sure my tiredness is not due to some infection."

"I also see you're drinking a lot of water."

"I don't know that for sure. It was a friend's observation."

He laid her folder on the counter and eased onto a rolling stool. Scooting it next to her, his smile widened. "Let me ask you a few more questions before we do all the customary tests.

Are you having frequent urination?"

She considered his question for a moment. "Yes, but I drink a lot of water."

"Besides drinking a lot, what about extreme hunger?"

"I have been hungry more lately, but I've been on an emotional roller coaster since I accepted a wedding proposal."

The doctor smiled. "Love does make us react differently. Congratulations. Tell me about your tiredness."

"Not sure what you mean." Then it occurred to her exactly what the doctor was thinking. Her heart pounded a little faster.

"Are you more irritable?" he asked.

She nodded.

"Any problems with your eyesight?"

Kae remembered the blurred vision. She assumed she needed reading glasses, but now other things entered the picture. "I have classic symptoms of diabetes, don't I?"

The doctor paused. "Yes, you do. We'll simply take a few tests and eliminate that before moving on."

Dread washed over her. "Doctor, I take care of myself. Always have."

"That doesn't mean a thing. If we had a cause, we could develop a vaccine. Often diabetes goes undiagnosed because the symptoms can be explained away. If the tests are positive, we can begin treatment and avoid harmful complications."

"I see. Your office will call with the results?"

"Correction, *I* will call with the results."

She forced a smile. This wasn't how she'd planned her day.

Kae closed the browser window on her computer before

answering the door. Melanie wanted her to go shopping, and the time had come to leave. Frustrated at what she'd discovered about diabetes, she wished she had time to read more. Education about the unknown was supposed to calm the fears about certain medical conditions. At least that's what she'd read somewhere. Unfortunately, the more she read the more disgusted she became with herself. *I am probably overreacting.* Her mind couldn't seem to push the matter away. What ever did she think about before her doctor's visit?

Snatching up her keys and her purse, she hurried outside to meet Melanie. Kae had elected to drive; Melanie often got carried away with conversation and forgot to keep her eyes on the road.

"Are you ready for the mall?" Melanie asked as they walked to Kae's car. "I've clipped coupons."

"Ah, so we're armed and dangerous?" Kae asked. Right then she decided Melanie was the perfect antidote for her foul mood, a real answer to prayer.

"For sure. The professional shoppers had better look out today. Plus, this is the day two of the department stores give an extra 15 percent to senior citizens. We might not want to admit our age, but to save a little money, I'll swallow my pride."

Kae glanced at her friend's bright red and orange polka-dotted top with red pants. "Me, too. Can you imagine getting a senior citizen's discount in the bridal department?"

Melanie shook her head. "Let them laugh. We have wisdom and style. All those young gals have are cleavage and smooth skin."

Kae laughed until tears rolled down her cheeks. Yes, Melanie wrote the chapter on "How to Enjoy Life and Ignore the Tough Stuff."

Hours later, they returned with purchases bound to bedazzle any admirer. Kae held up a navy blue suit to the mirror: nice, good price, and a classic color. Except too dark and drab. She'd save it for the next funeral. She draped the plastic over the hanger and hung it in her closet. The second outfit had seized her attention from the moment she'd began searching through the dressy misses department—an ankle-length, deep rose dress with a matching jacket. Its elegance and design nearly took her breath away, as well as the price.

"You can wear it forever," Melanie had said.

"At our age, everything we wear is forever." She had turned in the three-sided mirror and sighed. "Sold to the old lady who plans to be a December bride."

Now, admiring the dress all over again, Kae could hardly wait to wear it. Then she remembered what she had to tell Gene. *I'd better keep the receipt. He may very well change his mind.*

The more she thought about the news, the more it sank her spirits. Tomorrow she'd return the dress. Tonight she'd break the engagement. Gene deserved more than a sickly wife.

Gene met Kae at the Coffee Grind Thursday evening for dinner. He believed they kept the place in business, but it made him feel young. He glanced at the lovely lady across from him and wondered why she'd insisted upon meeting him there instead of allowing him the honor of driving. She sounded strange on the phone. In fact she'd been acting a bit on edge. Best he get to the bottom of it. According to his preparing for marriage book, he should be upfront and ask her about things. He was now a take-charge man.

"Are you all right?" Gene asked.

She offered a faint smile and nodded, but the look in her eyes held another light.

"I have a strong feeling that either you aren't feeling well, or something has you upset." He hesitated. "Is it Tracie? Hmm, it's been four days since you went to the doctor. Have you gotten your test results?"

"Yes, I did." She lifted her chin.

Uh-oh. He recognized that stubborn stance. "What did the doctor say?"

"Nothing good."

His heart did a double-flip, and it was not the good kind. "Why don't you just tell me so we can talk about it?"

Her gaze flew to his—with a few sparks. "*We* aren't going to deal with any of it. I have diabetes, and I will need to watch my diet for the rest of my life. Hopefully I can avoid medication."

"Honey, you've watched your diet all of your life."

She swallowed hard. "I've decided that we have no business getting married. You've been saddled with me too long, and I'm. . .I'm breaking the engagement." She reached for her purse. "I need to go home."

She started to leave, but he reached for her hand. "Please talk to me, Kae. You're upset, and I understand this news is a little hard to take."

"Didn't you hear what I said? Diabetes. That means my vision will go, my heart could have problems, my feet could bother me."

"And I could walk out in front of a car and get hit. This is a part of life. I want you as you are."

Tears streamed down her face. "No, Gene. I refuse to put you through any unnecessary trauma. We'll simply have to go back to being friends."

He shook his head. "I can't go back there. We've come too far."

She jerked back her hand. "I'm leaving now. Please honor my feelings. We were a foolish old couple who thought we could gamble with age and disease."

The weekend dragged for Kae. Monday and Tuesday were worse. She felt as close to miserable as she'd been in years. She couldn't find joy in much of anything and even recognized a big case of feeling-sorry-for-me blues. Worst yet, she missed Gene, and the idea of resorting back to friendship when she loved him so much hurt more than she cared to think.

She hadn't told the kids about breaking off the engagement, or Melanie for that matter. Instead she'd stayed inside her condo and resorted to watching sitcoms—the absolute epitome of stupid things to do.

Logic told her to get on with life, return the beautiful rose-colored dress, tell her friends and family the truth, cancel the wedding plans, and see what she could do to help David with Tracie. The idea of helping out more with Hannah crossed her mind, but that looked like she was taking advantage of Tracie's mental condition.

All of her life, she'd looked down on folks who used depression as an excuse to crawl into a cave and stay there. She'd succeeded in being her own worst nightmare. And what else rattled at her nerves was that she had no desire to better herself—even prayer fell by the wayside.

Might as well let the diabetes do me in. I'm not good for God or anyone else.

Chapter 9

Kae had met her match on stubbornness. Gene had no intentions of letting her sink into self-pity about a little illness and cancel their wedding. He'd prayed and talked to Pastor Thomas about it, and right now he was paying a visit to David. Ever since the man had agreed to be Gene's best man, the two had talked every day, mostly about Tracie and family problems. This afternoon Gene had an idea, and he needed David's willingness to help him. At first he toyed with the fact that David had enough problems in his life without taking on another one. Then he realized that David took on diversion because of the problems with Tracie.

David opened the door to his accounting office. "Hey, Gene." They shook hands. "What brings you out my way?"

"Oh, I want to talk to you about your mother."

David's eyebrows lifted. "Serious?"

"Could be, if you and I don't come up with a way to help her."

David shook his head. "Let me get us some coffee. Decaf, right?"

"Unfortunately, yes. This old man has to be more careful."

David grinned. "By this time in the afternoon, I drink decaf. This old man can't tolerate the real stuff past noon. What is it with Mom?"

"For openers, she's learned she has diabetes—a mild case, but it has her pretty shook up. In fact she's called off the wedding because she thinks she's a burden to me. Utterly ridiculous, as I'm sure you'll agree."

"I'm sorry. What can I do to help?"

"I have an idea that I want to toss by you."

An hour later, Gene left David's office feeling once more on top of the world and with a sly secret that was sure to make Kae see his way about things. And if it didn't, he'd try Plan B.

The last thing Kae wanted to do was ride with David to the Coffee Grind on Sunday afternoon. Too many reminders of Gene. Over a week had passed, and she cried for him on a daily basis. How did David know she frequented the place? He was usually too busy to do much more than talk for a few minutes on the phone. Whatever his reason for spending an hour or so with her, she'd take advantage of it and tell him about the cancelled wedding.

A sad thought coursed through her. What if David was at his wit's end with Tracie? He might need help. How awful if he'd decided to end his marriage. Maybe the time had come for her to get out of this horrible mood. But life without Gene didn't hold that special lilt. *I have to stop thinking about myself. Now!*

As soon as David pulled up in front of the café, she saw it

was closed. "That's odd for a Sunday afternoon."

"Doesn't matter 'cause we're going inside anyway," David said.

Stunned, she tossed her eldest son a heavy dose of irritation. "I suppose you have a key?"

"I might." He pulled the key from the ignition and exited the car to open up her door. "You and I have an event to attend."

Confusion brought a slight chill to her arms. "What are you talking about?"

"My sweet mother and her fiancé deserve an engagement party at their favorite hangout."

Oh no. She should have told the kids. "David, we can't. I—I didn't tell you this, but I broke the engagement."

"Why?" His eyes narrowed. "Gene's a great guy, and you told me you've loved him for years."

Why had she waited to tell the truth? "It's not him, but me. I found out I have diabetes." She searched his face for a reaction.

"And I have high blood pressure. My wife has a chemical imbalance. Those don't stop us from loving each other and working through the tough times."

"But this may cause my death." He laughed, and fury raced through her.

"This may come as a surprise, but we all have been dying since the day we were born. All of us will die of something."

"You're making fun of me, and that's disrespectful."

His face softened, and he reached out and hugged her. She stiffened, then slowly she allowed his strong arms to comfort her. Tears dripped over her cheeks and onto his shirt.

"Mom, you've always been a fighter. Stand up and take this challenge. Gene loves you, and he doesn't care a bit about diabetes or anything else you might contract. Would you refuse to marry him if the diagnosis had been for him?"

"No, of course not."

"Then walk into the Coffee Grind, and let your family and friends know how much you want to be Mrs. Gene Richards."

David made sense, and suddenly realization about her selfishness brought on more tears. "I'm sorry, David. I can't stop crying. Yes, I love Gene and want to be his wife no matter how long we have together."

"That's better." He lifted her chin with his finger and kissed the top of her head. "Blink back those tears because I'm hungry."

At that moment the café's door opened, and Tracie stepped out. "Mom, we're waiting to party."

She's never called me Mom *before.* Kae's gaze flew to Tracie's face.

"I'd like to be your matron of honor. I'm sorry for the way I acted. I understand David told you about my problem, and I'm glad. No more pretending." She stepped toward Kae and wrapped her arms around Kae and David.

"I guess I have the best family in the world," Kae said.

"I'm sorry about Hannah," Tracie said. "The older she got, the more I feared she might tell you about my sickness."

"It wouldn't have mattered. I love you."

"I don't suppose you need a flower girl?" Tracie asked.

"Absolutely."

The door opened again. Gene stood there handsome as ever

with the biggest smile she'd ever seen. "Sure have lots of food in here." He focused his attention on her. "The jukebox is rolling. The coffee is brewing. My heart's pitter-pattering at the sight of you, and I have a big bowl of sugar free banana pudding with your name on it."

She took a deep breath. *Thank You, Lord, for getting through to a foolish old woman.* "Did you say banana? That's my favorite. We might have to serve that at the wedding."

Gene held out his hand, and she walked toward him. The future promised more joy than she ever imagined, and she didn't intend to waste a single day.

DIANN MILLS

DiAnn Mills believes her readers should "expect an adventure" when they read her books. She is the author of fourteen books, nine novellas, as well as nonfiction, numerous short stories, articles, devotions, and the contributor to several nonfiction compilations. Five additional books will be released in the next year.

She wrote from the time she could hold a pencil but not seriously until God made it clear that she should write for Him. Five of her anthologies have appeared on the CBA best-seller list. Two of her books have won the distinction of Best Historical of the Year by Heartsong Presents, and she is also a favorite author of Heartsong Presents' readers.

She is a founding board member for American Christian Romance Writers and a member of Inspirational Writers Alive and Advanced Speakers and Writers Association.

DiAnn and her husband are active members of Metropolitan Baptist Church in Houston, Texas.

Visit her Web site at www.diannmills.com.

coffee scoop

by Kathleen Miller Y'Barbo

Dedication

To Mary Knapp, attorney-at-law
and the best boss a writer could have.
Thank you for taking a chance on me.
May God bless you abundantly and above all measure.
And to Jodi Villarreal,
coffee connoisseur and precious friend.
May your cup of Café Americano always be full!

Better is one day in your courts than a thousand elsewhere;
I would rather be a doorkeeper in the house of my God
than dwell in the tents of the wicked.
PSALM 84:10 NIV

Chapter 1

"Now *this* is flying."

Carrie Collins snapped her seat belt into place and settled back into the broad, comfortable expanse of her first-class seat. The four-hour wait and the promise of flying home to Austin in style had almost been worth being bumped from her noon flight.

Wouldn't Millie be surprised when she heard? Tomorrow at work Carrie knew she would be giving her best friend all the details of her rare ride at the front of the plane. But then Millie lived for the details.

After all, she was a fact checker.

The book Carrie had begun in the airport beckoned, and she retrieved it from her carry-on. As she sipped her orange juice and prepared to be transported back to 1878 Texas, Carrie smiled. How often did a small-time reporter for the *Austin Times* end up in this sort of luxury?

Never, actually, but then she'd all but given up her dreams of the jet-set lifestyle of a real hard-news reporter. God obviously had other plans for her.

The fact that she'd been able to fly to California at all was a testament to the fact that God had some sort of plan for her life that involved writing. She'd never expected to get a scholarship to the prestigious Christian writer's retreat in the mountains north of San Jose. That in itself was a blessing, but when her boss told her she could consider the trip an assignment as long as she came back with an article for the religion section of the *Times*, she felt doubly blessed.

A girl with only one week of vacation didn't take that sort of concession lightly.

Carrie folded the book shut and stared out the window at the flurry of activity going on out on the tarmac. Above the fray, the brilliant orange sun touched the topmost peaks of the distant mountains, reminding her of the serene place she'd spent the past five days.

While at the retreat, she'd had time to think and pray about what God wanted from her, and she'd had time to gain a healthy respect for His sovereign control over her life. She came away refreshed, energized, and more importantly, knowing that she needed to do something big for God.

Something that would make a difference for Him.

Something like a becoming a serious writer whose feature stories were respected in both Christian and secular circles.

While Mr. Scott was kind enough to concede to the out-of-state assignment, Carrie knew he didn't believe she had the ability to break into feature writing. "That's okay," she whispered as she returned her attention to her novel. "I've got a plan."

The constant stream of passengers filing through the first-class cabin had become a mere trickle by the time Carrie finished the chapter. "Please stow your bag, ma'am."

Carrie looked up to see a fresh-faced flight attendant. "Yes, of course." She stuffed the book into the seat pocket, then tried to force the ever-so-trendy bag she'd brought aboard under the seat ahead of her. Two attempts later, the silver-haired businessman in the row ahead of her rose to give her a most ungentlemanly look.

"I'm terribly sorry for all the bumping," she said.

Rather than respond, he pointed to the storage bin over her head, then sank into his seat with a shake of his head. "All right. The overhead compartment it is." Unfortunately, the bag was stuck.

She tugged and pulled, all the while apologizing to the gentleman sitting above the battle. Finally she felt the bag come loose, just in time to send her reeling backward into her seat. The offending carry-on in hand, she stood.

Now to somehow lift the beast into the overhead compartment.

"May I help you, miss?"

A pair of arms covered in starched denim reached around her to easily place the bag in the last remaining spot in the overhead compartment. Carrie ducked beneath the arms to fall into her seat and get a better look at the man standing in the aisle.

He wore denim and khaki, and other than the interesting multicolored tie and the set of matching dimples, he might have been any other contemporary male at the local overpriced coffee shop. Dark hair cut in a fashionably messy style complemented tanned skin, giving him the look of a man who spent more time outdoors than in the boardroom.

The briefcase he held said otherwise, however.

It was black and made of leather, one of those expensive numbers that screamed quality and a high price tag. Just beneath the handle, two initials were discreetly placed in gold letters.

R.B.

"Ryan Baxter. 2-B."

"Excuse me?" She swung her gaze from the briefcase to its owner. "Oh, 2-B. I thought you were quoting Shakespeare. You know, 'To be or not to be'?" His blank stare told her he mostly likely thought her certifiable. "Never mind," she said as she snatched up her book and tried to find her place. Obviously the first-class crowd had a different sense of humor.

"So you're a fan of Shakespeare?"

"Yes, actually, I am." Carrie gave her companion a sideways glance. "Why?"

Mr. Baxter closed the overhead compartment and took his seat beside her. "Then maybe you can tell me which of Shakespeare's characters killed the most chickens and ducks."

Carrie laughed despite herself. "What?"

"Birds. You know. Chickens and ducks. Which character killed the most?" His face grew serious. "Does that mean you don't know the answer?"

She shook her head.

Casting a glance about the cabin, her seatmate leaned toward her. "Hamlet's uncle, Claudius."

"Hamlet's uncle?" She folded her book closed and turned in her seat to face him. "I don't understand."

" 'He did murder most foul'," he quoted in a perfect imitation of a British accent.

She groaned, then, as her gaze met his, burst into a fit of giggles. The flight attendant looked up from her recitation of the safety instructions to glare in their direction.

"Oh, that's terrible," Carrie whispered.

"It is, isn't it?" He snapped his seat belt closed and settled the briefcase into place, then thrust his hand toward her. "Ryan Baxter. Pleased to meet you."

"I'm Carrie," she said as she shook his hand. "Carrie Collins. Thanks for helping me with my bag."

"My pleasure, Miss Collins. I haven't been to the gym in almost a week. The weight lifting did me good."

"Now I'm really embarrassed," she said as the captain began his preflight announcements.

Her seat partner offered a dazzling smile. "Don't be."

By the time the plane leveled off to its cruising altitude and the seat belt sign went off, Carrie had learned that Ryan Baxter, a seminary graduate with a Harvard M.B.A, was the head of a nonprofit organization that used the proceeds from the sale of coffee grown on their Central American premises to fund improvements among the local poor. Headquartered in a small village on the edge of the Costa Rican rain forest, Heavenly Beans was in its third year of existence and already making a tidy sum.

Mr. Baxter claimed that, due to sound investment and numerous sources of funding back in the States, 100 percent of the profits were being reinvested in the company or distributed to an orphanage called Casa de los Niños. This fact, combined with the obvious incongruity of the man's style of dress, quality of briefcase, and choice of seating on the nearly empty plane, led

Carrie to one conclusion. This man was a feature story waiting to happen.

Possibly even the scoop that would make her boss reconsider his decision not to promote her to feature writer.

Carrie smiled and leaned back into the soft cushions as she made mental notes of the answers Ryan Baxter gave to her questions. Yes, indeed. If her reporter's instincts were correct, Carrie Collins was about to get the scoop of the decade.

The coffee scoop.

In her experience, big money plus high-profile ministry generally equaled fraud and deception on some level. A feature on bilking the brethren was long overdue.

The last time the *Times* had gone after a ministry like this the author had been awarded a Pulitzer Prize for journalism. While she did not aspire to that level of greatness, she could at least hope to get another crook off the streets.

Funny, but some sort of instinct deep in her reporter's gut told her Ryan Baxter was not that sort of creep. She ignored it.

Just because his dimples set her toes tingling and his passion for the ministry seemed genuine, that didn't mean the company was legitimate. Heavenly Beans could very well be a front for bilking big money out of innocent Christians instead of the means for showing orphans the love of Christ.

If only she could figure out a way to keep him talking well past the end of the flight. An interview in the airport would be rushed and probably wouldn't result in the depth of questioning she desired.

Did she dare ask him outright to submit to an interview? She cast a glance at her seatmate and noticed the restless look he now wore. Perhaps now was not the time.

Before she could blink, the seat belt sign above her flashed red, and the captain began to give the weather conditions in Austin. Suddenly there was no better time. *Think, Carrie. How can I get this interview?*

Chapter 2

Think, Baxter. How can I get her to interview me about the company?

Ryan Baxter had begun to fidget well before the FASTEN SEAT BELT sign went on. Now that he could feel the nose of the plane dipping toward Austin, he'd all but begun to feel a real panic. Carrie Collins was a delight, one of those rare young women with intelligence, classic beauty, and a sense of humor. She had also professed a love for the Lord and a desire to serve Him as a journalist.

A challenge she seemed well equipped to handle, since the newspaperwoman had certainly matched wits with him and come out the victor. Not that he claimed some great genius.

After all, if he had half a brain he would have already seized the chance to try and extend their conversation beyond the airport. Coffee somewhere, or ideally, dinner could very well get an interview that might garner Heavenly Beans and the precious ones it supported some much-needed publicity.

Ryan did many things for the company under silent protest, including this trip. While his body called on potential benefactors to the cause, his heart was back in Costa Rica where the real work of the Lord took place. A few hours with Carrie Collins, however, would be a welcome change from the rest of his stay here, namely his visit tomorrow with the head of Camex Incorporated, a likely source of revenue and distribution.

George Renfro, the international shipping and food service company CEO, lived on a ranch just west of Austin. This wasn't his first meeting with the corporate executive, but it would be the first time he sat across a table with him and discussed Heavenly Beans.

A Camex representative would be meeting Ryan at the airport to whisk him away to a downtown hotel where he had a breakfast meeting scheduled with Mr. Renfro himself before boarding a plane back home to Costa Rica tomorrow night. A whirlwind visit, to be sure, but one he hoped would make a large dent in the costs associated with running a coffee company and funding multiple ministries.

Just this morning the prospect of joining forces with Camex had made his mind spin and his heart race. Funny, but now the newspaperwoman to his left seemed to be having the same effect on him.

Somehow the plane landed, and he'd trudged all the way to the baggage claim area with her two-ton bag slung over his shoulder—at his insistence—without having found the courage to speak his mind. All the way there he'd tried to convince himself that dinner with Carrie Collins would be all about getting the word out regarding Heavenly Beans.

As he swung her bag off the conveyor and carried it to a cart, then dumped her carry-on atop it, he had to admit there was a bit more to it. Something about the auburn-haired journalist had him wanting to do an investigation of his own.

Just ahead, the line of dark-suited drivers holding signs beckoned. One of them surely bore his name. It was now or never.

Ryan gripped his briefcase and closed his eyes. *Don't be ridiculous, Baxter. It's not like you're asking her out on a date.* Heart pumping, he breathed out slowly. *This is for the company. For the ministry. For the kids at Casa de los Niños.*

"Are you okay?"

Opening his eyes, Ryan looked down at Carrie. She wore a concerned look. "I'm fine," he said. "It's just that. . ."

There it was—the card with his name on it. The driver wore a dark suit like the others, but an oversized lapel pin with the Camex logo set him apart from the crowd.

"I'm hungry." He swung his gaze from the driver to his companion. "Are you hungry?"

"I could eat," she said slowly. "Why?"

Why? Am I that out of practice? Truthfully he was, and she wasn't making his first foray into the dating world in over a year any easier.

It's not a date.

"Are you okay, Mr. Baxter?"

The second time she'd asked him in the span of thirty seconds. He was not making a good impression.

Ryan squared his shoulders and stared directly into eyes the color of the Costa Rican sky. "I've got a car here. What do you say we grab a bite somewhere?"

Was that relief he saw on her face? If so, he must have been wearing the same look.

What a relief.

Carrie allowed Ryan to push her cart toward the exit. The sheer bulk of her check-through bag combined with the weight of her carry-on and the precarious position of his briefcase and small overnight bag made the going rough, but the coffee magnate managed to reach the door in record time. To her surprise, he nodded toward a man in a dark suit.

"I'll be right back with the car, Mr. Baxter," he said before scurrying outside into the warm Texas night.

In short order, Carrie found herself being helped into a black limousine with tinted windows and a license plate that read, "CAMEX3." She'd made note of the plates, and the identification and description of the driver for the article.

Or, depending on the depth of Ryan Baxter's deception, for the series of articles.

Her cell phone rang the moment she turned it on. Molly, of course. She'd be wanting to know how the retreat went. She'd also be asking to come by and pick up the stack of books Carrie promised to have autographed by some of the more famous conferees.

Rather than answer, she hit SILENCE. Her host was speaking to the driver, and she didn't want to miss a word.

"Yes, I know the place," the driver said.

"Then that's where we want to go." A pause. "You sure it's okay?"

"Of course, Mr. Baxter. Mr. Renfro's orders are whatever you say goes."

Mr. Renfro? CAMEX3? Whatever Ryan Baxter says goes?

Carrie smiled. The plot had definitely begun to thicken.

Mr. Renfro had to be none other than George Renfro, CEO of Camex International. That would explain the license plates and the limo. But what possible explanation would Ryan Baxter, a man of God, have for taking up with a fellow who'd barely dodged one indictment after another in his long career as a businessman? Sure, there had been rumors that the Camex CEO had mended his ways. Why, he'd even been seen attending worship services at a rather large church near downtown.

While Carrie always hoped for the best in people, her journalistic instinct told her to expect the worst. And if Ryan Baxter, a man who obviously liked to travel in style, was mixed up with George Renfro, then there could only be one conclusion.

Big dealings were afoot.

A moment later, Mr. Baxter slid inside and closed the door behind him. As the limo blended into the traffic exiting Terminal C, Carrie began to plan her cross-examination. First she would ask her companion a few innocuous questions, queries about his home, his family, and his varies ministries. Maybe she would move on to ask him to speak about his adopted country, get him talking about the kids he claimed to be helping, and. . .

"Miss Collins, I hope you're hungry."

Carrie reined in her thoughts and focused on the businessman beside her. "What? Yes, actually I don't particularly care for airplane food."

"Then you're in for quite a treat."

Fifteen minutes later the limo pulled to the curb in front of a nondescript building in the shadow of downtown. Before the driver could exit the vehicle, Mr. Baxter jumped out and offered Carrie help in doing the same. The spicy scent of something yummy tickled Carrie's nose. Her stomach grumbled a protest at her slow pace as she and Ryan walked toward the humble facade of a restaurant called Ixtapa.

Funny, she'd driven within a few hundred yards of this spot and never noticed it.

A fresh coat of green paint covered the door and decorated the hand-lettered sign stating the hours of business. Inside, the dozen or so tables were covered with bright red cloth and filled with happily chatting diners. Mariachi music blared from a speaker situated behind an antiquated cash register, adding to the noise level.

Not much hope for a decent interview in this chaos. However, a wonderful meal did seem to be a distinct possibility.

A slender man dressed in a white chef's outfit picked his way through the crowd to meet them with a smile. Just above the pocket on his shirt the name JAVIER was embroidered in brilliant turquoise thread. "Buenas noches, Señor Baxter, Señorita." Javier swung his gaze toward Carrie, then back to Mr. Baxter. "Just the two of you?"

At Mr. Baxter's nod, the trio headed off toward the rear of the restaurant, weaving around chairs and people until they reached a surprisingly quiet corner. Javier held a metal chair out for Carrie, and she settled onto its cracked red vinyl seat in time to watch a waiter appear with a basket piled high with chips and a brilliant yellow bowl of poblano pepper salsa.

Javier and Mr. Baxter carried on a spirited discussion in Spanish while Carrie settled her purse beside her. A dark-eyed little girl peered at her from the booth to her left, offering a snaggletoothed smile before sliding down out of sight at her mother's insistence.

Carrie watched the men's faces go from happy to serious as their voices lowered. An envelope passed from the chef to his customer, then more discussion took place.

When Javier nodded, Mr. Baxter shook his hand. The chef gave instructions to a nearby busboy in rapid-fire manner, then scurried off to the kitchen, sparing Carrie a quick smile as he hurried past.

"I hope you don't mind, Miss Collins." Ryan settled the napkin into his lap. "I took the liberty of ordering for us."

She smiled rather than state her independence. Since when did men still order for their dates?

Dates? This was not a date. This was a business dinner, and no matter how wonderful the food or how charming the company, she intended to keep things all business.

After all, she had a story to get, a feature-writing job to land, and her Lord to serve.

Chapter 3

The food was as good as the company, and it nearly cost Ryan his promise to concentrate on the reason for his trip rather than the woman across the table. After all, his whirlwind visit to the States had one purpose: to find new outlets for distributing the coffee that funded Casa de los Niños.

It seemed bad form to come right out and beg the woman for publicity, so he endured her barrage of polite generic questions and waited for the chance to slip in some morsel of information on Heavenly Beans. He admitted his connection to Harvard Business School grudgingly but not because of any shame over graduating from the prestigious university. Quite the contrary. He felt humbled and in awe of the fact that the Lord had allowed him such a fine education, especially since he'd done very little to deserve it until recently.

But then that's why he kept his briefcase around. All it took was one look at the reminder of his former life and thankfulness overwhelmed him. To think he'd once believed that happiness could be found in faster cars, fuller bank accounts, and expensive toys.

Funny how much he had now that he'd given almost everything away. Maybe he would save that story for another day—should the Lord decide they were to meet again, that is.

She asked him something about California, something he barely heard for the memories. Pressing them back into the corner of his mind where they belonged, Ryan focused on Carrie.

"I've been lost in thought," he said. "Something about this place, I guess. Please forgive me."

"Nothing to forgive," she said with a shrug.

"I believe you were asking me about California." When she nodded, he continued. "Actually my business was up in Seattle. My direct flight to Austin got redirected, and the rest is history."

Carrie seemed to mull the statement over a moment. "So you got bumped, too."

"Yes, I guess so. Why?"

Again she seemed to be thinking. "Interesting," she said as her phone rang. Probably Millie. She'd called twice since the plane landed, each time leaving a detailed message regarding the speed in which Carrie should return the call.

Checking the caller ID, she frowned. "I'm sorry, Ryan, but I have to get this one. It's my boss."

"Of course," he said as she rose. "Go ahead. I should probably call my office and let them know I arrived okay."

He watched her sprint toward the exit, then picked up his own phone and dialed the main number of Heavenly Beans to leave a message for Alvaro on the voice mail. A second call, this to his home, produced the same result—the answering machine.

Tempted to call the housemother at Casa de los Niños, Ryan scolded himself as a worrywart instead.

Someone will call you back. It's nothing.

But it felt like something. With all the live bodies in the vicinity of those two phones, the odds of getting even a single voice mail were high. Multiplied times two gave him pause for concern.

Still, there was nothing he could do sitting here in Austin. He'd left the business in the capable hands of Alvaro, and the orphanage in the capable hands of Mamá Zadora. Someone would call him back.

He checked his watch. A quarter to eight. He'd call again in an hour.

Ryan looked up as his companion wound her way through the maze of tables to rejoin him. They had moved from the formal to the informal in the span of half an hour, and he now thought of her as Carrie.

As he watched her sidestep a crawling baby, he imagined her back in Costa Rica doing the same thing. When she stopped to lift the cooing baby into her arms, then return him to his mother, Ryan's heart melted.

She was a natural with children, this city girl. He sent a quick prayer skyward that the Lord would someday bless her with babies of her own.

"I'm sorry," she said as she allowed him to help her settle into her seat. "I've been away from the office for less than a week, but you would think I'd been gone a month."

"I understand," he said. And he did.

"What an interesting place." Carrie pushed aside the

half-eaten plate of flan to meet his gaze. "You seem to know the owner. Is he from Costa Rica?"

"Javier?" Ryan shook his head. "No, he's from Monterrey, I believe."

"Ah." She sipped at her water, then gently swirled the ice with a twist of her wrist. Her gaze held steady but several emotions seemed to cross her face. Finally she met his inquiring look. "I was wondering if. . ." She paused. "What I mean is. . ."

"Carrie?" He leaned forward and rested his elbows on the table. "Is there something wrong?"

"Wrong? No, nothing. . .actually, yes." She took a hasty sip of water, then set the glass down a bit too hard. "Look, I've made no secret of the fact that I'm a journalist. Asking questions is just something I do."

"So what's the problem?"

"The problem is I have all these questions I want to ask, and I'm afraid I might be overstepping my bounds. I mean, it's not like I'm doing a story on you."

Ryan could barely contain his smile. "Would you like to? Do a story, I mean."

"An article?" She pretended to mull the idea over. "Well, I don't know. What do you see as the focus?"

Carrie fought the urge to jump out of her chair and jump for joy. Only the fact that she might cause him to change his mind kept her seated. In order to get a serious scoop she would have to conduct herself as a serious journalist.

There was also the little problem of her boss. Mr. Scott

turned her down flat on her proposal to turn her scoop into a feature story. The idea of a series on fraud in religious circles was nixed, as well. He then began a monologue on crusading journalists and eligible bachelor subjects that she'd heard one too many times.

Her only retort had been a weak, "Are you going to tell me I can't date him either?"

She'd regretted those words the moment they escaped her lips and had spent the last ten minutes trying to talk her way out of them. Just about the time she had Mr. Scott convinced she was meeting Ryan Baxter under the condition of a serious interview, the front door of Ixtapa had opened, and a family numbering several dozen spilled out. The combined chattering, laughter, and mariachi music ruined her cover and her story.

Finally Carrie settled for a "maybe" on the story and a "watch yourself" on Ryan Baxter. She hung up knowing she'd lost the battle and praying she would win the war. Mr. Scott would see the value of her story, and the Lord would use her to rid the Christian community of one more bad apple.

Inwardly something jolted at the thought. Her deductive reasoning told her Ryan Baxter was up to no good with his fancy briefcase, first-class tickets, and connection to the folks at Camex. Something else, her heart perhaps, begged that the opposite be true.

And what if it were? What if Ryan Baxter really was a do-gooder with a heart of gold?

"Look, you're the expert," the object of her thoughts said. "I'd be grateful for whatever publicity our cause can receive."

He looked so sincere when he spoke the words that Carrie almost believed him. If he hadn't taken that moment to yawn, she might have suggested they begin their questions right then. Instead she watched in silence as Javier appeared tableside with steaming mugs of coffee.

Heavenly Beans Coffee, as it turned out.

"Oh, Ryan, this is really good," she said as she sipped at the truly heavenly drink. "I don't think I've ever tasted anything quite like it."

A smile tilted one corner of his mouth. "Do you really think so?"

"I do." Honestly it was the best coffee she'd ever tasted, bar none.

Her companion fairly beamed. "I'll see that you get a case when I return to the office."

Carrie leaned forward and narrowed her eyes. "Are you trying to bribe a journalist?"

Ryan feigned innocence. "Is it working?" Before she could comment, he leaned back and tossed his folded napkin onto the tabletop. "So," he said with a grin, "how long does an interview take?"

"Well, that depends on the subject matter and the depth of the investigation," she said as she studied him surreptitiously. "How much time do you have?"

Chapter 4

It turned out Ryan had much more time than he thought. After a frustrating evening leaving messages on voice mailboxes and a productive breakfast meeting with George Renfro at the Camex offices downtown, Ryan found himself at loose ends in his hotel room.

Thinking he'd be in meetings all day, he'd scheduled an afternoon appointment with the lovely journalist. Their venue? A coffee place in the shadow of the state capitol that featured Heavenly Beans, of course.

Pacing in front of what had to be the most glorious view of downtown in existence, he could only think of how the Lord's hand had been all over this morning's meeting. Over scrambled eggs and bacon, Mr. Renfro had offered the services of Camex distributors, as well as their expertise at selling. He'd even made a donation of a tidy sum to Casa de los Niños. The elderly CEO fairly beamed as he handed Ryan the check, then promised there would be more to come.

Ryan nearly fell over when he counted the zeros on the bank draft.

He could hardly wait to tell Alvaro the news. His Costa Rican counterpart and right-hand man would be thrilled. *No,* Ryan corrected, *Alvaro Gonzales de los Santos would be grateful.*

Alvaro was that way—thankful first, then excited.

Smiling, Ryan stared at the bustling city streets below. Like ants, the people moved, seemingly without direction or purpose.

How he missed home.

Not the two-story red brick colonial on the cul-de-sac in North Dallas, although that had been quite a nice place to grow up. No, he missed the wet, earthy rain forest with its perpetual sheen of dampness on glossy green leaves and the little room over the Heavenly Beans headquarters where he laid his head at night and spoke to God.

To be sure, the Lord could hear him wherever he roamed, but somehow Ryan always seemed to hear the heavenly Father a bit better in the quiet. He sank onto the neatly made bed and reached for the tattered leather Bible he couldn't seem to leave home without.

A page fluttered to the carpet, and by habit he returned it to its place in the book. Occasionally he would turn to look for a verse only to find that particular page had fallen out. Something about the fact that someone would find that page and possibly read it made him smile. He wondered if the fourth grade Sunday school teacher who had gifted him with the precious book realized what would become of his gift.

At this point Ryan estimated he'd left pages of that Bible in countless cities all over the United States, as well as in four foreign countries. And those were only the places he knew about.

Who knew where else he'd inadvertently dropped a page or two?

Today Ryan began his search for God's voice in the Psalms. His gaze landed on Psalm 84, and he began to read aloud, first in English, then translating the words into Spanish, again, out of habit. He'd once taught himself to speak the language this way. It only made sense that he continued with the exercise long after the necessity ended.

" 'Better is one day in your courts than a thousand elsewhere.' " He paused and let the words sink in. " 'I would rather be a doorkeeper in the house of my God than dwell in the tents of the wicked.' "

A doorkeeper in the house of God. . .not even on his best day could Ryan claim such an honor. Oh, but how he aspired to it.

He gave a cursory glance at the busyness that was downtown Austin as he set his Bible on the bed. The clock on the nightstand read half past eleven. Perhaps a lunch meeting was in order.

Rather than phone Carrie, Ryan leaned back on the bed and thought about it for a moment. Ultimately he decided to wait out the time until the appointed hour. The last thing he needed was for the savvy journalist to realize how desperate he was to see her again.

Funny, but if he were honest, he'd have to admit that publicity wasn't the only thing on his mind.

The phone rang and he smiled. Maybe Miss Collins was as anxious to see him as he was to see her.

"Ryan?"

The voice was unmistakable. His heart lurched in his chest as he sat bolt upright. "Alvaro? What's wrong?"

Carrie stood outside Mr. Scott's office, one hand poised to knock and the other clutching her cell phone. Her folder tucked under her arm, she carried all she needed to do battle with the unenthusiastic Mr. Scott. Surely once he saw her preliminary research he would be on board with the idea of a full-blown exposé on Heavenly Beans Coffee Company and its questionable connection to Camex International and George Renfro.

While her facts were solid, she had to admit there were holes in her theory—giant holes that could only be filled with more information. Information she hoped to get once she sat down with the head of the company to ask more questions.

She'd been fighting the urge to call Ryan Baxter all morning. Moving their appointment from this afternoon to an earlier time would have given her the excuse she needed. Now nothing stood between her and her monthly planning meeting with her boss, the one where they went over the articles she would be writing in the coming month.

Carrie lowered her hand and leaned against the wall, contemplating her options one more time. When Mr. Scott turned her down flat last night, Carrie told herself she just hadn't explained the story well enough. She decided that if he knew all the facts, if he could just see the angle as she did, then perhaps he would be enthusiastic as she.

Funny how that seemed so likely last night and so unlikely today.

The utilitarian clock at the end of the hall ticked loudly, signaling the half hour. Carrie pushed off the wall and straightened her shoulders. It was now or never. The only thing Mr. Scott hated worse than insubordination was tardiness.

While it was unlikely she would finish the meeting without being guilty of the former, she could knock on the door now and keep from being the latter. Still, she felt more like a misbehaving student heading for the principal's office than an up-and-coming journalist going to meet her mentor.

Two sharp raps on the door and Mr. Scott beckoned her to enter. Rather than look up from his desk, he motioned to one of the two chairs situated nearby. She took a seat and waited while he finished reading, then looked up and removed his glasses.

"I wondered how long you were going to stand out there."

"How did you know I was standing out there?"

Her boss leaned back in his chair and crossed his hands over his chest. "I didn't," he said. Still he did not look up.

She clutched her folder and tried to decide how to proceed. The direct approach always seemed to work best with Mr. Scott. Unfortunately, she'd taken that route last night on the phone only to be denied before her ideas had received a fair hearing.

"I'd like to see what your ideas are for this month, Carrie." He gestured to the folder in her lap. "I take it you've brought some things for me to look at."

With a gulp, she scooted her chair closer to his desk and set her folder in front of her. "Yes, actually, I have," she said, not quite meeting his gaze.

He leaned forward. "Go ahead then," he said as he reached for his coffee cup. "Wow me, Carrie."

"All right." She opened the folder and removed the first page, handing it to him. "These are my notes on the fire that destroyed that historic church near downtown. A homeless man's in custody, but there are questions as to whether he actually set the fire. I've got some sources who will state that before the fire there was a flurry of interest in tearing that old place down and building an entertainment venue."

"That sort of thing happens all the time. What's the big deal about one more old building being torn down?"

"It seems as though the parishioners were organizing a campaign to save the old church. If there hadn't been a fire, they might have managed it."

Mr. Scott scanned her sheet of notes, then handed it back to her. "Interesting. What's your angle?"

As she outlined her proposal for the story, she watched his look turn from bland to interested, and she knew she had him. Good. This story would be a go. Now if she could just get him to consider the one she really wanted to do.

The exposé on Ryan Baxter.

As they worked through her list of ideas, Carrie tried to keep her mind on the present and not let it go hurrying toward the last item on the agenda. They ticked off the items on the list one by one until the time stood at a few minutes to twelve.

"Well, if that's all, then I'll let you get to work." Mr. Scott rose and stretched, then offered her a smile. "I expect a preliminary draft of the church fire story by Friday. If I like what I see, we'll be running it in the Sunday edition."

The Sunday edition.

Carrie's heart soared. Thus far she'd only received the nod

for the Sunday edition twice in the three years she'd been at the *Times*. In both cases, she'd worked with a team to get the story. This would be her byline and no one else's.

"Really?" she said.

Mr. Scott nodded. "I've been pleased with your work, Carrie. I think it's time you start taking on bigger stories."

"Do you mean that?"

His thick brows narrowed, but his grin broadened. "Why wouldn't I mean that, Carrie?"

"I don't know. It's just that. . .well, what I mean is. . ." She paused to take a breath and consider her next sentence. She also prayed she could utter a complete one. "Mr. Scott, if you have confidence that I can get the church fire story, then maybe you'd consider taking one more look at the coffee story."

His smile went south. "Miss Collins, the discussion on that particular topic has ended. Was I not clear on that last night?"

"Yes, sir, you were. It's just that. . ."

That what? What else could she say to get her boss to understand how terribly important this story was?

The newspaperman brushed past her to open the door and step out into the hall. Gathering her notes into her folder, Carrie trudged behind him, defeated.

Her cell phone rang, and she ignored it. "Mr. Scott," she said as she stopped just inside the doorway, "if I can prove up my theory with hard facts, would you take another look at the idea of doing a feature on Heavenly Beans?"

"Miss Collins, I can't imagine what you could add to the information you've got. You have no connection between Heavenly Beans and Camex other than a possible charitable donation. Last time I checked, that was not illegal."

Once again her phone jangled. She hit the silence button and shoved it into her pocket.

"But there's more than just a charitable donation there," she protested. "I just know it."

"You just know it?" He gave her a hard look. "How?"

How indeed? Her phone rang a third time, and she answered it intending to tell whoever was calling to take a hike.

"Carrie, it's Ryan."

She held the phone against her chest and regarded Mr. Scott with a smile. "It's him," she said. "What kind of information do you need? What do I need to ask him that will make you change your mind?"

Mr. Scott seemed to consider the questions. She put the phone back to her ear to stall for time.

"Ryan," she said as she watched her boss, "could I call you right back? I'm kind of in a meeting with my boss."

"Well, that might be a problem."

Chapter 5

"Oh?"

"Yeah, there's been a slight change of plans. I'm on the way to Bergstrom to catch a plane home. I wondered if you might like to ride along. I know it's not the amount of time we planned for the interview, but it's the best I can do."

"He's leaving," she whispered. "If I'm going to talk to him, I have to do it now."

Her boss shook his head. "Concentrate on the fire, Carrie. That story is due Friday, remember?"

"Of course I do," she said, "but this one's much bigger. I feel it."

"Carrie?"

She returned her attention to Ryan. "Yes, I'm here. Sorry."

"Carrie, I'm downstairs. Are you coming with me or not?"

"He's downstairs, Mr. Scott," she said. "Won't you reconsider?"

Rather than answer, her boss turned on his heels and disappeared into his office. A second later the door slammed.

"Carrie?"

"I'm sorry, Ryan," she said as she raced to her desk to deposit her folder into the top drawer and grab her purse from the bottom one. "I'll be right down." She picked up a fresh notepad and tucked her tape recorder into her purse, then bolted for the elevator.

"Carrie, hey!"

Millie. Carrie slowed her pace to allow her friend to catch up.

"Where you headed, girl?" Millie Townsend's long-legged strides told the world her last job had been as a basketball player. Her smile and perfectly coordinated outfit, purse, and shoes marked her for a fashion writer.

Unfortunately, the *Times*'s fashion writer had come into the job during the Nixon administration and wasn't planning to leave any time soon. Swearing she would someday have that job, Millie toiled away in fact checking with high hopes and an eye for detail.

"Interview." Carrie pushed the DOWN button. "Ryan Baxter's leaving town, and I've got from here to the airport to find out everything there is to know about him and his company."

Her best friend smiled and stepped onto the elevator ahead of her. "Well then, we'd better hurry."

"What do you mean *we*?"

Millie feigned disappointment. "Do you mean to tell me you don't intend to introduce me to Mr. First Class?"

Carrie pretended to consider the question. "No, I'm not

introducing you. And his name is Ryan."

The doors opened and Carrie stepped out into the lobby with Millie at her heels. "All right," Millie said. "How about a quick introduction, and then I'm out of there."

"No."

"Carrie, girl, you owe me." She stepped in front of Carrie. "Remember the time you made that date with the guy who gargled his water? Who came and picked you up so you wouldn't have to ride the Metro home?"

She gave her friend a sideways look. "All right. I will introduce you, but that's all. He's in a hurry. He's got a plane to catch."

"And I've got a man to check out."

At the curb, Ryan's limo awaited. Carrie made the introductions, then, true to her word, Millie excused herself to go back to work.

Forty minutes later, she had the beginnings of a great feature article and an invitation to visit Costa Rica and the Heavenly Beans offices any time she liked.

Little did Ryan Baxter know, but before the limo left the airport, Carrie had already begun planning her trip.

When Ryan emerged from Juan Santamaria Airport into the overcast Costa Rican afternoon, Alvaro's face was the first one he saw. His friend enveloped him in a bear hug, then grabbed his bag and threw it into the truck.

"It's good to see you, my friend," Alvaro said. "I'm sorry you chose to end your trip so soon. We could have lasted a few more days here sharing the extra work."

Ryan shrugged. "I achieved what I set out to do. It's more important that I be here."

He pictured the geriatric force of nature whose injury had caused him to cut his trip short and tried to think of what would come of them should Maria Conchita Elena Zadora no longer live in the brightly painted cottage that served as headquarters for the orphanage. Among the locals, the *tico*, Mamá was revered as a woman whose love for children knew no bounds.

Most of the adult staff at Heavenly Beans had once rested in Mamá's care, but only Alvaro de los Santos could claim an actual relation to her. He was Mamá's grandson, the only child of Mamá's deceased daughter, and the reason Casa de los Niños had come to exist.

"If my Alvaro can grow to be a man of God and a pastor besides, then so can anyone," she was fond of saying. Always, the statement was punctuated with a chuckle and a wink. Mamá did have a sense of humor, although rumor held that Alvaro had not always followed the Lord so closely.

"How is Mamá?"

"Much improved," he said. "Asking for you, of course."

"That's a good sign. Any idea how she fell?"

"Answering the door in the dark again." Alvaro turned the key and the truck roared to life. "I tried to tell her she was lucky she only suffered a fall and not the blows of a robber's fist." He paused. "Or worse."

"You know Mamá," Ryan said. "She would never risk turning away a child in need."

"Sí. Perhaps now is the time to disconnect her doorbell."

"You know that won't work," Ryan said. "I wonder if we

can't figure out a way to have Mamá's route to the door lighted. What do you think?"

His friend smiled. "I think that's an excellent idea. I'll see what I can come up with."

The pair lapsed into a companionable silence as Alvaro wove his way around a collection of taxis and buses to point the truck toward the airport exit. Soon they merged into traffic heading west on the main highway toward San Ramon.

Layer by layer the city fell behind them until nothing lay ahead except the mountains, thick gray clouds shrouding their green peaks. The sign for Rio Rosales slid past, and soon the exit for home loomed ahead. Ryan's heart soared.

"I never get tired of this drive, Alvaro," Ryan said. "Look at those mountains, and tell me God didn't favor this little corner of the world."

His companion nodded. "Most certainly He did, my friend."

A few minutes later, they exited at Grecia and began the last leg of the journey to Rincon de Salas. The old truck rattled and shook on the poorly maintained road, but it was a welcome rhythm for Ryan. A ride in Alvaro's truck suited him much better than the extravagant transportation he'd been provided in Austin.

Austin.

The image of Carrie Collins came to mind. What would she think of this truck, of those mountains, of Alvaro and Mamá and the others? Perhaps someday soon he would know. For now he preferred to believe she would look favorably on each.

He also preferred to think she might miss him just a little.

After all, she had asked for his e-mail address.

Sure, she'd said it was standard procedure with all her interviews, but he wondered—no, he hoped—she wanted to get to know him better. He certainly would like to get to know her better.

"It's good to be back?" Alvaro shot Ryan a sideways grin.

"It is very good," Ryan said. As the truck wound its way down the last few kilometers of narrow roads under Alvaro's expert guidance, Ryan felt the last of the tension melt away. He noticed his friend giving him a sideways look. "What?"

"Nothing." Alvaro shook his head. "No, that's wrong. There is something."

"Okay. What?"

"I can look at you and see how not very glad you are to return to us." Again he paused, this time to navigate the over-large truck around a significant hole in the road. When they were rattling along again, he reached over and gave Ryan a playful jab in the arm. "You are here, and yet something tells me you left a bit of your heart in the States."

Ryan frowned. Had he?

Alvaro braked and made a right turn. "You did not answer. Am I wrong?"

Another three kilometers and they would arrive at the village of Rincon de Salas. Just past the crossroads was the dirt road leading to the humble collection of buildings that comprised Heavenly Beans headquarters. Beyond that lay the coffee plants that provided the best beans in Costa Rica.

Even at their slow pace, the entire drive would take less than ten minutes. If he kept his mouth shut and his attention focused on anything but Alvaro, he might get away with ignoring his friend's question.

If.

Alas, Ryan knew he could not.

"You are not wrong," he said in Spanish. "There was someone."

"The woman you mentioned? The journalist?"

Ryan regarded his friend with a mixture of surprise and fondness. How well Alvaro knew him.

"Yes," he said. "But I believe the Lord sent her to help us with the cause."

To his relief, Alvaro did not laugh. "What makes you think this?"

"She's a journalist, a newspaper writer in Austin. From the moment she sat next to me on the flight out of Los Angeles, I felt as though God meant us to meet. I knew this for sure when she interviewed me for an article."

"So this woman you're still thinking of, she's only on your mind because of some story she is writing for a newspaper? Is that all that keeps you from appreciating your homecoming? I don't have your Harvard degree, Ryan, but even I am smart enough to know that makes no sense."

Ryan chuckled. "No, I don't suppose it does."

"So, what is it that keeps this woman. . .what is her name?"

"Carrie," he said. "Carrie Collins."

Alvaro nodded. "So what is it that keeps this Carrie Collins on your mind?"

"I find her. . .interesting." He added the last word in English, unsure exactly which word in Spanish would give the proper meaning. "It's nothing, I'm sure, but I do wonder if a bit of free publicity for Heavenly Beans is why she and I crossed paths."

"Ah, the Lord, He will tell you if He means to," Alvaro said.

"I suppose so," Ryan said. "In the meantime, there's always e-mail."

"Ah, e-mail. I suppose that will work for a time."

Before Ryan could respond, Alvaro pulled the truck to a stop within inches of the gate to the property and bounded out to clear their way. The squeals of children at play floated toward them, mixed with the shrill call of birds and the sound of tree limbs rustling.

"Like music, the sound of a happy child," Alvaro said as he climbed back into the truck. "I pray you have many, my friend."

Ryan shook his head. "You know Mamá's set to marry you off first."

"Perhaps," Alvaro said as he inched the truck down the shadowed lane toward the clearing, "but Mamá's no match for the Lord, even if she sometimes forgets that. What Mamá wants may not be what the Father intends."

Chapter 6

Despite her promise to the contrary, Carrie pulled up her e-mails before she began her writing day. In the past, before Ryan Baxter entered her life, she spent at least an hour working before she allowed herself the perk of checking e-mails. The self-imposed rule had served to boost her productivity considerably, especially when the temptation to "just read a few e-mails" generally gave way to hours lost in following the links to sites or chatting with friends on Instant Messenger.

"C'mon, hurry up," she said under her breath as she waited for her slow-as-Austin-traffic laptop to pull up her e-mail program and chug through the process of downloading new mail. While she waited she glanced at the corner of her desk where a thick stack of papers awaited her attention. At the top of the stack was her rough outline of the Heavenly Beans story along with notes she'd added last night after a lengthy e-mail from Ryan.

Ryan.

Had it been just a week since she said good-bye to him at

the airport? Since then she'd traded at least a dozen e-mails with him, most on the topics of Heavenly Beans and Casa de los Niños. It all started with a short e-mail from Ryan asking if Carrie had any more questions for the interview.

She came up with a whole list of queries, not that she needed the answers to any of them. It seemed rude not to respond.

By the next morning, her in-box contained Ryan's responses, as well as a chatty discourse on an evening spent stringing night-lights to make the path safe for the elderly woman who ran the orphanage. Carrie inquired as to the purpose of this, and Ryan responded with a story of a knock in the night, a fractured ankle, and a fiercely independent senior citizen who loved children.

Carrie had laughed out loud at that one. Mamá Zadora sounded like quite a character—and an excellent candidate for a follow-up article.

In all, they traded four e-mails that day. By the time she went to bed that night, guilt had all but caused her to put a stop to their correspondence. After all, how could a man with a nefarious purpose seem so kind?

Ryan loved old ladies, children, and the Lord. Any other man would be considered near to perfect with those qualifications.

In her rush to serve the Lord in a big way, had she broken her ironclad promise not to go into a story with a preconceived idea about the people involved? Worse, had she allowed what she saw, namely the expensive briefcase, first-class seat, and wealthy contributor, color her opinion of the man and his mission?

It was certainly something to consider. And to pray about.

Seven days after that first flurry of correspondence, Carrie began each morning with a note from Ryan and ended each day with the same. Her responses to him were feeling more like friendship and less like work with each time she pressed SEND. Just last night he ended his e-mail with a note giving her his Instant Messenger screen name, "just in case you might want to chat sometime." Of course she quickly responded with hers.

While she waited for her e-mails to download, she signed on to her Instant Messenger program. There was Ryan's name highlighted in black, indicating he was also online. Sending a message might be fun. But what would she say? The familiar chime was followed in rapid succession by a pop-up window and the words, *Good morning, Carrie!*

"Thanks for making the first move." She giggled like a teenager. "Now, what to say back?"

Carrie typed a quick greeting in return and smiled as she pressed ENTER. In the background, her e-mails popped up. Among the ads for low-cost mortgage and health insurance was an e-mail from Ryan. She double-clicked on his name and watched as his note appeared on her screen.

It was a short note, one obviously written in haste, and the subject line read, "Costa Rican vacation?" Beneath the subject line he'd written the following:

Dear Carrie,

I should be attending to business, but instead I find myself wondering if you've had any decent coffee lately. After all, it wouldn't do for a professional journalist of your caliber to be writing about a coffee company and not be enjoying the beverage. I know I promised I would send a case, and I will do that today if you'd like, but I feel I must tell you I have a much better offer for you than that. Why not come get it yourself? Friends of the ministry who own a local bed-and-breakfast have offered the use of one of their guest rooms, and the Camex jet is at your disposal, with a few days notice, of course. I join these friends of the Heavenly Beans and Casa de los Niños in hoping—no, praying—that you will accept our hospitality very soon.

Ryan

How to respond? Carrie typed a clever line warning him to watch out what he prayed for, then quickly hit DELETE. It wouldn't do to sound silly or flirty. After all, this was merely an assignment, not a social situation.

She closed out her e-mail program, then sat pondering the situation. Her meeting with Mr. Scott loomed large on her afternoon calendar. The purpose of the meeting was to go over the final draft of the church fire story, or at least that was what she led her boss to believe. Her real agenda was to try one last time to interest him in the Heavenly Beans story.

In her briefcase, nestled next to the thick file with church fire research, was her data on Heavenly Beans, Casa de los Niños, and Ryan Baxter. She also added information on Camex International and George Renfro.

Her Instant Messenger program sounded a greeting, and Ryan's words appeared. "Did you get my e-mail about picking up your coffee?" she read aloud.

Carrie smiled. A simple yes should have been her response.

Instead, she typed *Make it two dozen cases, and I'm there,* then hit SEND.

As soon as she watched the words appear in the Instant Messenger box she longed to delete them. What happened to the professional journalist, the one who was sure Ryan Baxter was guilty of bilking innocent Christians just like the man who fooled Mama into giving away her savings?

She pushed the awful memory into the recesses of her mind and waited anxiously for Ryan's answer. To her disappointment, none came.

Ryan waved away Alvaro and continued to type. "Just one more minute and I promise I'll be there."

"Your caller isn't going to understand that a woman in Austin is what is keeping you from a conference call that may end with a sizable donation to our cause." Alvaro let the door close just a bit harder than normal, proof positive he held no understanding of Ryan's situation.

And what a situation.

First he'd managed to send a couple of polite instant messages to Carrie and then, just when the exchange started getting good, the line went dead, and so did his Internet connection. The moment he managed to get back online was the moment Alvaro barged into his office.

Surely his friend would manage fine without him. After all, Alvaro knew as much about the company as Ryan, probably more. What harm would it do to just send one more message to Carrie? After all, he wouldn't want her to think him rude.

Sorry about that, he typed. *Internet went down. So, as you were saying. . .double the amount of coffee?*

He could hear Alvaro pacing just outside the door, speaking a bit louder than necessary. Perhaps those cordless phones he'd brought back from the States weren't such a good idea after all. Keeping Alvaro in his office instead of walking the halls was a much better plan, at least right at this moment.

Yes, two dozen cases, came Carrie's reply. *Not a bean less.*

With glee, he typed a particularly bad reference from Shakespeare. *Two beans or not two beans.* He hit SEND and imagined the smile Carrie would wear when the words popped onto her screen.

Oh, that was bad, Ryan. She added one of those cute smiley faces after his name.

Forgive me. Ryan laughed. *When do you expect to take delivery of your beans?*

"Baxter," came the thickly accented voice from the hallway. "Line one. Now, please."

Line one? Since when did they have a line one? He rose and strode toward the door, then whirled around and raced back to the desk when he heard the sound indicating he had a new message.

Tomorrow if I could. You've ruined me for any other coffee. Seriously, I have to clear things with my boss. We're meeting this afternoon. Can I let you know then?

"Baxter." This time Alvaro's voice held more irritation than he'd ever heard. Perhaps he'd best end this conversation and get back to the real work of running a coffee company.

Ryan, are you there?

"Baxter, are you there?"

Yes, I'm here. He paused to edit his thoughts before settling for a bland response. *Of course you can let me know later. No hurry.* It wouldn't do for her to know how anxious he was to show her his part of the world.

The door flew open, and Alvaro stepped inside. Once in all the years Ryan had known the pastor had he seen the man that angry. "You are about to cost us a hundred-thousand-dollar donation, my friend. Now decide what is more important, speaking to the donor who is waiting for you on the phone or dallying with your girlfriend."

Ryan rose and closed his laptop. "I was not dallying," he said as he reached for the phone in Alvaro's hand.

"Interesting." A grin touched one corner of the Costa Rican's mouth. "You didn't deny she was your girlfriend."

Chapter 7

Mr. Scott leaned his elbows on his desk and peered over his reading glasses, his expression giving away nothing of how he felt. "Why are you so insistent on doing this story?"

Carrie took a deep breath and let it out slowly. The moment of truth had arrived. And the truth was what she would give her boss. Maybe then he would see things her way and assign her to cover the Heavenly Beans-Camex connection.

"The truth, Mr. Scott, is that I know firsthand what can happen when a Christian is taken in by someone claiming to be doing good deeds. Perhaps you know what I mean."

"No, can't say as I do." He continued to stare, so she pressed on.

"Well, okay, you see my mother was a wonderful Christian woman—still is, actually. Just after my dad died, a man showed up at her house claiming to be a friend of Dad's. He gave her a story about how he had this special deal just for her, an opportunity to donate money to the Lord and then make it back by the fistfuls. Suffice it to say, Mama never saw a dime of that money and neither did the Lord. The Feds caught up with that man living the high life in a beachfront condo in Florida. Meanwhile Mama lost her house and most of Dad's savings."

Again her boss just sat and stared. Carrie frowned. What else could she say to convince him?

Before she could speak again, he did. "So what you're saying is you've got an ax to grind with anybody who is claiming to raise money for religious purposes?"

"What? No, of course not."

Mr. Scott tapped the folder with the back of his hand. "I'm sorry, Carrie, but all I have here is circumstantial evidence. You've got a guy flying first-class, a nice briefcase, and a limo owned by George Renfro's company."

"The same George Renfro who was in trouble with the law not so many years ago."

"The same George Renfro who is now an elder at one of the largest churches in Austin. The same George Renfro who proclaims his faith in every interview he gives." He thrust the folder in her direction. "The same George Renfro who gives sizable sums of money to charity and refuses to accept publicity for it. Need I go on?"

She shook her head.

"Look, Carrie. I respect your ability to ferret out a good story. The church fire is a prime example. You went above and beyond to get the story. Is it true you posed as a homeless woman?"

Carrie shrugged. "Just for a few hours. I heard about this guy who might be involved, and I figured the only way to get an interview was to do it on his terms."

Mr. Scott chuckled. "I wish I'd sent a camera crew for that one."

Seizing the moment, Carrie pressed home her point. "So if you respect my abilities, then why not also respect my judgment on this one? I truly believe there is a story there."

Her boss rose and walked around the desk to head for the door. "So do I, Carrie."

She followed him into the hall and fell into step beside him. "You do?"

"Of course. Look at the facts. Missionaries, big business, orphans. You've got all sorts of angles to pursue." He paused at the elevator to push the DOWN button. "This could be huge."

"Then what's the problem?"

The doors opened and Mr. Scott stepped inside. "Your focus is all wrong."

Carrie jumped in just as the doors began to close. "What do you mean?"

Mr. Scott seemed to be considering the question. "You wrote the ending first."

The doors opened, and Mr. Scott stepped into the light-filled lobby with Carrie in pursuit. "I don't understand. I haven't written anything yet. I'm still in the research stage."

Her boss paused and turned to face her. "Carrie, you're one of the best young reporters on my staff, the operative word here being *young*. With age and experience comes a measure of impartiality. Cultivate that, and stories like this are yours."

"Wait!" she called as he exited the building. "What if I made a deal with you?"

"I don't make deals," he shouted over the roar of a Metro bus and the sounds of downtown traffic. "That's why I'm the boss."

"Fair enough." She raced to catch up to his long strides, the humidity and exhaust fumes thick enough to be almost visible. "But what if I work on this story on my own time? Say, on my vacation?"

"Vacation?" He stopped short and whirled around to face her. "You'd use up your only week of vacation for this story?"

"Yes," she said.

Mr. Scott shrugged. "I can't tell you what to do on your vacation, but I can tell you I'm making no promises on whether this story will ever see ink. Is that clear?"

"Crystal clear, sir." She paused a second to let his words sink in. "Does that mean you'll look at what I write about this?"

"I'm always willing to look at your stories, Carrie," he said. "Just don't disappoint me."

"I won't." She turned to race back toward the *Times* building.

"And this time wait until you have to whole story to write the ending," followed her inside.

In short order she secured a week's vacation and a decently priced round-trip flight to Costa Rica. The e-mail to Ryan took a bit longer as she agonized over every word, unwilling to give him the wrong impression about her visit.

And yet as she wrote the terse and succinct paragraph announcing her arrival date and flight information, she wondered if she could maintain the facade. Inexplicably, the thought of seeing Ryan made her smile.

He was nice, and he did have a wonderful sense of humor, so it was natural to believe he would be a good host. And the way he described his adopted country made her long to see it in person.

Yes, those were the reasons for her happiness. It had nothing to do with Ryan Baxter.

Carrie shrugged off the thought and set to work making sense of her notes on the Heavenly Beans story. The lunch hour came and went, and still she sat at her desk in the cramped windowless office. As the story unfolded before her, Carrie realized she'd missed an important detail: George Renfro.

While she'd concentrated on interviewing Ryan and learning about his company and the mission it supported, she'd neglected to ferret out details on Mr. Renfro's involvement. Beyond loaning Ryan a limo, she had no idea what Camex or its chief did to contribute to the Costa Rican coffee company and orphanage.

But would George Renfro do an interview with a lowly *Times* religion reporter?

"There's only one way to find out," she said as she reached for the phone.

After announcing her name and journalistic affiliation, Carrie was put through to Mr. Renfro's secretary and then to Mr. Renfro himself.

"So you're the girl Ryan ditched me for," he said when he came on the line. "What can I do for you?"

The girl Ryan ditched him for?

"Miss Collins, are you there?"

"Yes," she said, "I'm here. Actually, I'm working on a story about Heavenly Beans and Casa de los Niños. I was wondering if you would mind answering a few questions."

Carrie held her breath and waited for the rejection she knew would come. At least she would know she'd tried.

"I don't mind at all," he said. "The *Times* building is just around the corner from our offices, and I've got some spare time this afternoon. What say you meet me up on the twenty-seventh floor in half an hour?"

As it turned out, the twenty-seventh floor of the Camex Building was the helipad.

Following the dark-suited secretary's lead, Carrie emerged into the brilliant sunshine, then stopped short. A silver helicopter bearing the Camex logo sat tethered in the center of a bright orange circle. Inside was a man who looked suspiciously like George Renfro.

Chapter 8

Mamá Zadora sat in her rocker, a baby sleeping on one shoulder and another smiling up from a cradle at her feet. Around her a delightful symphony, the sounds of the children mixed with the call of the birds and the rustle of leaves in the breeze, echoed along the expanse of thatch-covered porch.

As Ryan approached, Mamá shifted the pink-clad infant into the crook of her arm and held her against her chest. With the toe of her sandal, the ageless beauty set the little cradle rocking again.

"So, my boy has come to visit, and it's not even time for a meal." Mamá punctuated the statement with a smile. "I was told you were too busy with that silly computer to speak to real people."

Ryan kissed the giggling Mamá on her cheek, then gathered the baby into his arms. A girl, this one, and soon to be adopted by a childless couple in Alvaro's Sunday services. Until all papers were in order, however, the *niña* remained in Mamá's care.

He held the infant close. She smelled like soap and sweet

milk, a combination that set him longing for a houseful just like her. The thought jarred him into picking up the lost thread of conversation.

"Alvaro speaks too much," Ryan said. "You should find him a wife to keep him busy."

"Alvaro speaks his mind, this is true." Mamá brushed a strand of dark hair off her face. "He also worries about his friend. I understand there was some measure of trouble with a certain person in Atlanta. A benefactor whose temper at being kept waiting almost cost the donation, perhaps?"

Ryan cringed. "I almost blew it," he said. "I admit I should have come to the phone sooner. I was wrong."

Mamá waved away the statement with a lift of her hand. "Wrong, perhaps. But those are the things that happen to a man when he is courting."

"Courting?" The little girl in his arms opened her eyes and frowned. "Nobody's courting here," he said softly. "Carrie and I just happened to be in the middle of an important conversation about a story she's doing on the company. And she's a friend, nothing more."

Smiling her knowing smile, Mamá remained silent. She knew better, he supposed, but the truth was he didn't have any idea whether he was courting or not.

"How's the leg, Mamá?" he asked as the baby's eyes closed once more.

"Fit and fine," she said. "I don't know why Alvaro won't just take this awful cast off for me. Surely he has something in that tool shed of his that will do the trick. Can you believe he's instructed the employees not to touch it either?"

"I can," Ryan said. "He loves you, Mamá, and taking off that cast before it is time will not be a good thing. Be patient."

"Patient? Bah!" She touched the cradle and set it in motion again. "Patience is wasted on the old. I am in a hurry—for walking again, for chasing my babies. This thing, it keeps me sitting when I want to run."

Across the lawn one of the workers called the children in for afternoon lessons. Ryan watched Mamá while Mamá watched the children. When the last one had filed inside, her attention returned to the situation at hand.

"So when will I meet this friend of yours?"

Ryan stared down into the baby girl's sleeping face and smiled. "Soon, I hope."

"Oh dear," Mamá said. "I hope so, as well."

He lifted his gaze to meet Mamá's. "Why?"

"I fear if this Carrie does not come to Costa Rica soon, you will be bringing Costa Rica to her."

"Come on aboard," Mr. Renfro shouted over the whine of the engine and the whirring of the chopper blades.

"Are you serious?" Carrie leaned against the wall and tried not to think about how high up she was. As far as she could see, the Austin skyline beckoned with not so much as a guard-rail to keep someone—or something—from falling between the buildings. The assistant who led her this far seemed non-chalant, but then she had known what to expect.

The Camex executive beckoned her with a wave of his hand. When she refused to move away from the door, he said something to the man sitting next to him, then removed his headset and jumped out.

George Renfro was taller than she expected, and lean without appearing thin. Striding toward her, the wind teased the coattails of his dark suit and lifted the end of his burgundy tie. His sparse gray hair, however, stayed in place.

He wore a look of concern as he approached. "I guess I should have mentioned we weren't meeting in my office."

Carrie looked past him to the helicopter and the uniformed man at the controls. Although he sat in the shadowy interior of the chopper, she could have sworn she saw him chuckling. No doubt at her expense.

Clutching her notepad and pen, she searched her mind for a reason to reschedule. Surely there was a standard response for being excused from helicopter rides.

"We can go on back downstairs," Mr. Renfro said. "I don't want you feeling uncomfortable."

His assistant leaned over to speak into his ear. Mr. Renfro shook his head. "Tell 'em I've been delayed," he said as he reached past Carrie to open the door to the stairwell. "Now come on with me, Miss Collins. I'll show you to my office."

"No, wait," Carrie said. "I'm terribly sorry for inconveniencing you. I just wasn't expecting. . ." She turned to point at the helicopter ". . .this. It will be fine if you want to be interviewed aboard. . ." Her voice cracked and she swallowed hard. "Aboard that," she managed.

Mr. Renfro squinted in her direction. "Are you sure?"

Carrie nodded and allowed him to escort her to the helicopter. Once inside, she went through the motions of buckling up while the pilot flipped switches and checked gauges.

George Renfro settled in beside her and adeptly fastened himself in. "You ever flown in a whirlybird, Miss Collins?"

"My flights are generally in something a little larger," she shouted over the engines. "Whoa!" The helicopter lurched and so did Carrie's stomach. A moment later the helicopter lifted, then, as they cleared the roof, abruptly tilted nose down.

Her companion offered a smile. "It's supposed to do that."

Soon the chopper buzzed past the buildings of downtown and headed off westward into the wide expanse of blue gray sky. Ten minutes later the pilot set down in a grassy field on the edges of what looked to be a farm.

Mr. Renfro released his restraints, then helped Carrie with hers. A moment later they both stood on the ground, the chopper blades kicking up a windstorm behind them.

"Over there," he pointed, indicating a modest barn painted dark red and circled by an odd collection of buses and vans. "I'd like you to see this."

Carrie followed her host, stepping inside to find a horse arena filled with children in various stages of riding or watching the horses. In the center of the barn, a half-dozen ponies stood at the wait while some children were helped onto saddles and others were eased off. The unifying factor in all of them, Cassie noticed, was their smiles.

"Special needs kids," Mr. Renfro said. "Inner-city girls and boys whose only contact with the country was what they saw on television. Now they get riding lessons and a picnic once a week."

"Hey, Mister George," a snaggletoothed girl called. "Watch me. I'm a cowgirl."

"That's great, Jenny," he said as he clapped.

As Mr. Renfro walked her through the barn, he stopped every few feet to speak to a girl or share a high five with a boy. In most cases, he knew their name. In all cases, they knew him.

Finally they reached the other side of the building. Mr. Renfro opened a wide door and motioned for her to go inside. He followed, snapping on the lights in what turned out to be a modest office. Three walls stood covered with pictures that looked to be drawn by the very children now populating the barn. The fourth wall was a large window that overlooked the interior of the barn and the scene unfolding there.

Carrie watched with a smile, then jumped when her host cleared his throat.

"Can I get you something before we begin?" he asked as he shrugged out of his suit jacket and settled behind the desk. "I have it on good authority that there's a fresh-baked peach pie to be had in the kitchen." He winked. "I think my housekeeper's got a thing for Sandy, my pilot."

"No, thank you." She sat across from him and pulled her notebook out. "I must say this is one memorable interview."

Rather than comment, her host lifted the receiver on an ancient black telephone. "No, nothing for us, thanks," he said. "But tell Sandy to get himself a cup of coffee and some pie. Miss Collins and I will be heading back in about half an hour." He hung up the phone and returned his attention to Carrie. "So, are we going to talk about my past, present, or future?"

Chapter 9

Do you have a preference?" Carrie balanced the notepad on her knees, her pen poised inches from the page. Her attention, however, was focused on the corporate executive on the other side of the desk.

Her reporter's eye went from the owner of the office to the details of the space. Other than the children's art, the lone framed item in the room sat directly behind Mr. Renfro. It was a page from a book. Upon closer inspection she noted that the book from which this yellowed page came was a Bible.

"No," Mr. Renfro said without the slightest hesitation. "Within limits, my life is an open book, some chapters better than others." He paused and seemed to be assessing her. "But then if you're any good as a reporter, you know all about the bad chapters. So why don't you start by telling me what you know?"

Carrie leveled an even stare at her host. "Born in Brooklyn, raised in New Jersey. Married. One son, two daughters," she recited from memory. "Influence peddling, stock manipulation, and a half-dozen white-collar crimes that added up to a stint in a minimum-security prison back east. How am I doing?"

"All true so far." He smiled. "Is that all you've got?"

She shook her head. "Born again after a visit from a prison minister. Left prison to start a company that eventually became Camex. Gives large but unsubstantiated donations to Christian charities." She paused. "Did I miss anything?"

He leaned back and the big leather chair groaned in protest. Swiveling to stare out the window at the merry scene unfolding beyond the glass, Mr. Renfro seemed to be deep in thought. Finally he whirled back around and leaned forward. Amusement danced in his dark eyes.

"Did you miss anything?" Her host asked the question with a contemplative tone, as if he, too, were wondering. "Miss Collins, if I may say so, you've researched me quite well."

"Thank you."

"As to whether you missed anything, if I might be so bold, I think you missed the most important thing." Mr. Renfro shrugged. "Haven't you wondered why I brought you all the way out to Wimberly today?"

Good question. Carrie pondered the possibilities. "My guess would be that you wanted to show me what a good person you are."

"I suppose I can see how it might appear that way." A smile tugged at the edge of his lips. "Unfortunately, you're wrong. I brought you out here to show you what a good person Ryan Baxter is."

Carrie dropped her pen, then scrambled after it. "I don't understand. What does Ryan have to do with anything?"

Mr. Renfro cast a glance out the window at the happy chaos going on inside the barn. "Miss Collins, do you see that mare right over there, the black-and-white one?"

She followed the direction of his stare to see a magnificent horse plodding slowly in a circle with two laughing girls on her back. "Yes, I see her."

"That's Mercy, and she's a real prize. If I hadn't been trying to outbid Ryan Baxter for that mare, I would never have come to really know Jesus. That prison minister gave me the head knowledge, but Ryan, well, I guess you could say he gave me the heart knowledge. Now that's the real story. I dare you to tell that one to your readers."

Carrie gripped her pen and formulated her question. "So you're saying that Ryan Baxter and a horse called Mercy caused you to find your faith? Would you mind elaborating?"

Mr. Renfro chuckled. "It would be my pleasure." He laced his hands behind his head and leaned back again. "It all started four years ago during the horse auctions at the rodeo. I had my heart set on that little filly. Saw her early on and knew I'd be taking her home. So I'm sitting there all confident, just waiting for her number to come up. Time comes to bid, and I figure it's a done deal. Next thing you know I hear someone in the back outbid me."

Scribbling as fast as she could, Carrie noted Mr. Renfro's description of the moment he turned around and saw Ryan Baxter standing behind the last row of seats.

"I looked right at him and doubled the bid. Well, he smiled real big and outbid me again. This went on a time or two more until I called a time-out to the auctioneer, then stood right up and asked the impertinent kid in the back row what it would take for him to cut out his foolishness and let me have that horse.

Would you believe he had the gumption to tell me he would let me win that horse if he could have an hour of my time?"

Smiling, Carrie nodded. "Yes, I can believe that."

Mr. Renfro paused and looked away. When he returned his attention to Carrie, his eyes looked misty. "I thought he was the biggest fool I'd ever run into. I took him up on his offer and told him I'd buy him dinner, too."

Carried turned the page. "I think I see where this is going."

"Maybe you do, but I sure didn't. I bought that snot-nosed kid a steak dinner, thinking I'd soon be seeing the last of him."

"Obviously that didn't happen."

"No." Again he paused. "No, it didn't. About midway through the best rib eye I'd ever sunk my teeth into, Ryan starts asking me questions. Well, I didn't like the answers, but he sure did. For everything I said, he had something in response. Pretty soon he'd given me more to chew on than steak."

"So was that the night you were changed?"

Her host stood and laughed. "Hardly, although I wish I could say I listened and learned right then. No, I'm a hardheaded man. I'd heard all about the Lord in prison, and I thought that religion was a nice thing for people with lots of time on their hands. Once I got back into the real world, I began to fall back into my old ways. Now I can see that the Lord used Ryan Baxter to head me back down the right road. Ryan didn't have any idea what he was doing that night. He told me later he was just being obedient."

"How so?"

Mr. Renfro touched the glass and seemed to contemplate her question. Outside, the muffled squeals of the children floated past. Behind her host, a large utilitarian clock ticked off the seconds.

"Seems as though your friend Ryan had something like a hundred dollars to his name: ten in his pocket and another ninety in the bank. He'd been working with a street ministry group in the parking lot when the Lord laid it on his heart to go inside that arena and bid on a horse called Mercy."

Carrie swallowed hard and rested her pen against the paper. "So you're telling me that Ryan Baxter is the reason. . ." She paused to clear her throat and collect her thoughts. "The reason for all the good you do?"

"No, Miss Collins," he said softly. "The Lord is the reason for what I do. Ryan Baxter was the messenger."

"Wow," she said softly.

"Wow, indeed."

The phone rang and her host picked it up. While he spoke, Carrie wandered to the window. Her gaze flitted from child to child, horse to horse, until it landed on Mercy.

What kind of man would walk into a horse barn and bid for a prize-winning mare with only one hundred dollars to his name? Perhaps there was more to Ryan Baxter than she anticipated.

Perhaps her instincts were wrong.

"Forgive me, Miss Collins, but it's time to head back to town."

Carrie turned to reach for her bag. "It's been lovely, Mr. Renfro. Thank you for being so candid."

"Yes, well, I don't see how being any other way serves any purpose. The Lord gave me the experiences I had to either teach me or show others. I'd like to think a little of both, really." He reached past her to open the door. Immediately the scent of fresh hay combined with the sound of happy children. The result stopped Carrie in her tracks.

An absurd thought occurred. If not for Ryan, this barn would be silent.

Interesting.

"Miss Collins, I understand you're planning a visit to see how the coffee business works. I suppose Ryan told you this already, but just say the word, and I'll have the jet ready."

"Yes, well, I appreciate your generous offer, Mr. Renfro," Carrie said as she followed him down the hall toward the noise, "but I really can't. It wouldn't be right under the circumstances."

He nodded. "I understand. Can't be accused of taking favors from someone you're writing a story about."

"I'm glad you understand."

"Of course," he said. "Now how about I get us a couple of pieces of pie to go?"

Chapter 10

A week later, Carrie climbed out of her mother's Toyota at the airport. As the recorded message regarding unattended cars fought for attention over the honking of horns and whine of jet engines, Carrie grabbed her bags from the trunk and kissed her mother's cheek.

"Remember Millie will be around to check on you. You have her cell number, right?"

"Yes, of course."

"Okay." Carrie handed her check-through bag over to the curbside porter, then slipped him a tip.

"Honey, are you sure this is safe?" Mama grasped Carrie's elbow, then turned the gesture of concern into a hug. "I'm already worried, and you haven't even left yet," she said into Carrie's ear. "I feel so helpless, what with you going off into the jungle and all."

Carrie held her mother at arm's length, her gaze traveling from Mama's perfectly styled blond hair to her expertly applied makeup, and then to her pink manicured nails. Mama looked anything but helpless. In fact, she looked fabulous.

Her mother looked her up and down, then stepped back to lean against the car door. She looked ready to speak and yet reluctant to say anything. Carrie recognized the familiar expression. Mama's worry extended beyond the usual concerns of air safety and lost luggage

"Mama. What is it?" She paused. "Look, I'm going to be fine, Mama. Really." She paused. "And besides, I'm not going into the jungle. This is a coffee plantation, and I have reservations for a perfectly respectable hotel in a nice village."

"Village?" Mama shook her head. "I don't like the sound of that."

"Okay," she said as she toyed with the zipper on her bag, "maybe I used the wrong word. It's a town, Mama, a nice little city with all the comforts of home. Feel better?"

"I suppose." The smile she offered didn't quite make it up to her eyes. For all her bravado, Mama still looked worried.

"Is there something else?"

"Actually, yes," she said. "I need to know something."

Carrie knelt down to dig her boarding pass out of her carry-on bag. "Sure," she said as she straightened and lifted the bag onto her shoulder. "Ask me anything."

"Are you doing this for me?"

Looking past Mama to where the security officer stood watching, Carrie feigned innocence. "Doing what?"

"Carrying on a vendetta against Ryan Baxter because of the mistake I made."

Carrie whirled her gaze around to collide with Mama's. "What are you saying, Mama?"

"I'm saying that I see how you act when you're sending computer messages back and forth with him. I also see a light in your eyes when you talk about him. That light disappears when you talk about this story you're doing." Mama touched her arm. "Carrie, pray about this. Ask God to show you not only what you are supposed to write but also why you're supposed to be writing it. I didn't do that and look what happened. All your daddy's money gone just because I didn't seek the Lord before I acted."

Carrie nodded. "All right."

Mama tightened her grip. "There's something else."

"What?"

"Don't you dare try to destroy a ministry the Lord is behind. I don't care what that newspaper pays you. Don't you do it."

Carrie glanced down at her watch, then stepped back. "I promise, Mama. I'm going to give Ryan a fair shake, and I won't let what happened to you color my impression of his ministry."

"Oh, Carrie, my sweet child." Tears brimmed beneath Mama's mascaraed lashes. "You already have."

Mama's words stung, following Carrie through the intricacies of boarding her flight and settling into a seat midway toward the back of the half-empty plane. Once the plane hit cruising altitude, she brought out her laptop and tried to make sense of her notes.

Another half hour went by, and she'd done nothing but demolish two bags of peanuts and a full can of soda. Finally she opened a new document and closed her eyes. Fingers touching familiar keys, she wrote a single sentence, then opened her eyes to read it.

If Ryan Baxter's the real deal, then all of this is for nothing.

Well, there it was right in front of her. The big conundrum.

Another statement tickled its way across her brain, and she

lifted her fingers to turn the thought into words on the page.

What if all of this is for something else or for Someone Else?

Carrie let her hands drop into her lap and stared at the blinking cursor and the sentence that preceded it. What did that mean?

She leaned back and closed her eyes, intending to ponder the question. When she opened them again, the plane had begun its descent into the San José airport. Carrie snapped her seat back into the upright position, then reached into her bag for her digital camera.

Cottony wisps of clouds hung on blue-green mountains and brilliant rays of sun glistened off dark green foliage, broken only in places by a ribbon of road that stretched off into the distance. As the plane's altitude decreased, the patches of green became tall trees with leaves that looked glossy and wet from a recent rain. The road became a ribbon of asphalt, or perhaps it was gravel. No, she decided, it must be concrete.

Closer still to the airport, the forest gave way to actual habitats, gatherings of small homes and buildings that looked to be villages. Carrie spied what looked like a soccer game going on in the center of one of these and snapped several pictures.

Finally, the villages became connected, forming an urban sprawl worthy of Austin. Carrie continued to take pictures until she felt the plane bounce onto the runway and lurch to a slow rolling stop outside the Number 5 Jetway. Beyond the mustard-colored Jetway, Juan Santamaria Airport unfolded in two identical wings punctuated with geometric cutouts and centered by a glass-enclosed control tower that looked like a three-layer wedding cake.

While those around her clicked open their seat belts and

began to reach for luggage, Carrie leaned back and exhaled slowly. *Father, let Your will be done here. As Mama said, don't let my feelings about what happened to her color my beliefs about Ryan. I confess that I haven't given him a fair shake. Please show me who he really is, Lord. Give me the right story to tell.*

Ryan paced the passenger waiting area watching for anyone with the slightest resemblance to the auburn-haired Carrie Collins. He tugged at the starched collar of his one presentable dress shirt and wished he'd worn something other than jeans and boots. He'd figured to make her feel more at home by dressing as he would in Austin or Dallas, but now that idea seemed silly.

At least he'd come alone. That had worked out nicely.

How he'd managed to slip away without Alvaro climbing into the truck with him was one of God's great miracles. His nosey friend had been after him all week for the arrival time of their guest.

His guest.

Alvaro had certainly teased him about that. Funny how many of the statements his friend made in jest were beginning to feel like the truth:

"You talk to her more on the computer than you speak to me in person, Ryan."

"She gets more of your attention than I do."

"You may say your intention is to publicize our work here, but I think there's something more to your invitation."

And finally, the worst—and most truthful of all Alvaro's comments:

"You're wondering if she's going to come to stay someday,

aren't you, my friend?"

The thought of Carrie as a permanent part of his life here had occurred on more than one occasion. While he wasn't prepared to give her his heart, he had given her a large chunk of his time—and his thoughts. If God intended more, He was certainly remaining silent on the subject.

No, for now, Carrie Collins was merely a reporter with the ability to tell the world, or at least her corner of it, about Heavenly Beans.

A glimpse of a woman with auburn hair caught his attention—and his breath. As soon as he saw her, he lost her in the crowd.

Ryan pressed gently past an elderly couple and a group of backpackers to emerge into a clearing. He looked first to the right and then to the left with no sight of Carrie.

Panic rose. What if she missed him and wandered outside? She could end up on a bus to another city, or worse, in an unlicensed cab heading for who knows where. Why, just last week a pair of female tourists were robbed and abandoned after accepting a ride from a supposedly reputable van driver.

"Ryan?"

A hand clasped his shoulder, and he jerked around. Carrie. *Thank You, Lord.* He wrapped her in a grateful embrace.

Then he smelled the scent of flowers in her hair and on her neck. And he realized he held her.

Ryan jumped back like a scalded cat. Heat flooded his face and his thoughts raced. For her part, Carrie looked merely shocked.

He looked into her eyes. She barely blinked.

A single thought occurred. *That was nice.*

Chapter 11

Carrie stared at her host, who looked quite flustered. While she'd expected a warm welcome, that degree of warmth was completely unexpected. It wasn't, however, completely unpleasant.

In fact, it was quite nice.

Nice wouldn't do, however. She had a job to do and getting too friendly with an interview subject was a bad idea.

Who was she kidding? She had already become too friendly with Ryan. All those e-mails and instant messages. All those Shakespeare jokes. But then who wouldn't like a guy who could take the words of the bard and turn them into the silliest jokes ever told?

Carrie shouldered her carry-on and looked past Ryan for the baggage claim sign.

"That way." Ryan slid the carry-on off her shoulder and hefted it onto his. He pretended to limp as he set off toward the far end of the building. "I see you packed with your usual thoroughness."

"Cute, Ryan," she said.

As they merged with the crowd headed toward the baggage area, Carrie took mental notes of the airport. Small but clean. Vintage sixties or seventies, probably, with the decor to match. Ropes much like those at a movie theater separated the baggage area from the rest of the airport. Ryan adeptly stepped around an older couple with a pair of suitcases and a wicker birdcage to secure a spot along the perimeter of the room.

"Stay here," he said. "I'll go get your bag."

Carrie watched her host amble over to join the crowd awaiting their luggage. With his attention focused elsewhere, Carrie felt free to take a good look at Ryan.

He looked freshly showered and shaved, and his dark hair curled slightly against the neck of his starched white shirt. Jeans and boots completed the picture, making him look more like a Texan than a resident of this tropical country.

Containers of every size and type began to roll off a conveyor belt. A pair of cardboard boxes was followed in quick succession by a zebra-striped duffel and a neon green cooler held together with duct tape. Thankfully her check-through bag appeared next, and Ryan snagged it with ease.

A few minutes later, he guided her and the luggage toward a well-used green pickup truck in the parking lot. With little effort, Ryan hefted the oversized bag, then ran around and opened Carrie's door for her.

Settling her inside, he handed her the carry-on and went around to slide behind the driver's seat. Despite Carrie's expectation to the contrary, the vintage truck roared to life when Ryan turned the key.

"Welcome to Costa Rica," he said. "This is as close to a

limo as we get here. At least where I live, that is."

Carrie smiled. "It's wonderful," she said, and she meant it.

Ryan guided the truck out of the parking lot and onto a freeway that looked as though it could have been in any major American city. Soon, however, he exited, and the terrain changed.

The road cut through a stand of trees and buzzed between collections of homes and sprawling fields. The occasional group of pedestrians, some looking like tourists with their backpacks and cameras and others obviously locals, slowed their progress, but generally their travel speed remained good.

Carrie made note of as much as she could. The exit sign for Grecia caught her attention, and she wrote the name in her notes. For long stretches, however, she would find herself staring out the window, so awed by the beauty of the countryside that she forgot her purpose in being there.

As they bumped along on a road that seemed too narrow for two cars, Ryan pointed out landmarks and told stories about the area. The higher they climbed into the mountains, the fresher the air felt. Carrie rolled her window down a notch more and inhaled deeply.

"You're not in Austin anymore," he said with a grin.

"No," she said softly, "I'm not."

"Up ahead is the road to Rincon de Salas." He smiled. "We're almost home."

Almost home. What an interesting way of putting things.

A soccer ball bounced across their path and Ryan braked hard. Carrie pressed her palms against the dash to keep from rocketing through the cracked windshield as the truck squealed to a stop just in time to miss a dark-haired boy of about nine or ten.

The child said something to Ryan in Spanish, then gave him a snaggletoothed grin. Ryan returned the smile and the comment.

"What did he say?" Carrie reached into her bag for her camera and took a few quick pictures of the retreating boy.

Ryan looked a bit uncomfortable. "He said you were a very pretty lady."

"And what did you say?"

He met her gaze. "I told him I had to agree."

Without thinking, Carrie lifted her camera and snapped a picture of Ryan.

"What was that for?" he asked as he found first gear and set the truck moving again.

Rather than answer, she turned to attempt a pieture of a softly swaying stand of sugarcane. It was only an attempt, and a poor one at that, for her hands were shaking so badly there was no way the photograph would be any good.

By the time Ryan turned the truck into the small parking lot of the inn and helped Carrie down the steep slope to the owner's office, he knew he was in trouble. The thought of leaving her here and not seeing her until tomorrow set so poorly with him that he decided to invite her to come out to the farm after she dropped off her bags.

Carrie paused at the wooden railing of the Casa Negrita's expansive eastward-facing deck. Her gaze swept the fields of

Negrita coffee, which gave the inn its name, and seemed to settle on the mountains beyond.

Ryan joined her, leaning his elbows on the rail. A movement in the trees caught his attention. "Look, Carrie, over there. See them?"

"Monkeys?"

"Howler monkeys, looks to be seven or eight of them. Probably a few more hidden in the foliage." He pointed to a ridge just beyond a cluster of mango trees where several dozen deer traversed the clearing. "Hey, look over there. Have you ever seen so many at once? You certainly won't see that back in Texas."

Out of the corner of his eye, he saw Carrie smile. "There are a lot of things here I won't see back in Texas." It was her turn to point. "What are those?"

He stared over in the direction of the canyon below them. "What? I don't see anything."

"Right down there, by those trees. Lemon trees, I think. See, there's another one."

Narrowing his eyes, Ryan leaned a bit farther over the rail and tried to see what caught her attention. All he saw was a lemon grove that stretched to the edge of the property and the coffee growing along its border.

"Don't you see them?" When he shook his head, Carrie grabbed his arm and pulled him to her side. "Come over here and look right down there. See? Oh, there's another one. A baby."

Rather than look at whatever caught Carrie's interest, he stared at her. Why hadn't he noticed before that the journalist wore a sprinkling of cinnamon-colored freckles on her nose and cheekbones? And when she smiled, when had she developed those dimples?

Surely those things had all been in place before she came to Costa Rica. Why were they so noticeable now?

Because you're seeing her in a new light.

"They look like foxes, but they're silver. How is that possible?"

"Silver foxes," he said as he continued to stare at Carrie. "In this part of Costa Rica, they usually shy away from people. You're lucky to have seen them at all, much less on your first day here."

The length of her lashes captivated him, as did the tilt of her chin and the way her earlobe had a single freckle where an earring should be.

"This is absolutely unforgettable, Ryan."

His heart skidded to a stop, then lurched to a gallop. "Yes, absolutely."

And in that moment he knew he'd lost his heart to the reporter from Austin. To be truthful, he'd probably lost his mind, too, because he barely knew her. And yet he felt like he'd known her forever.

He should tell her, give her at least a hint of what he felt. It made no sense; and it made complete sense. Better to be up front with his intention, especially since Carrie's purpose for coming down here was business and not pleasure.

Clearing his throat, he said a prayer that he might come up with something brilliant. As an afterthought, he asked the Lord to stop him if he should keep his peace about his feelings.

While Carrie continued to watch the silver foxes play below

the deck, Ryan waited for God to give him the perfect words. When nothing specific came to mind, he decided to step out in faith in hopes the Lord would meet him there.

"Carrie?"

She turned her attention to him and smiled. What a beautiful smile. He could stare at that smile and forget to breathe.

Stop it, Baxter. You're acting like a teenager.

"Yes, Ryan?"

"There's something I need to tell you." He paused. No, that didn't sound right. "I mean, I have something I should say." Again the words didn't quite fit the moment. Finally he decided to just blurt it all out, state his feelings flat out in plain language, and let the chips fall where they may.

"Carrie, look. I didn't have any idea this would happen until I saw you in the airport, and I wasn't really sure until just now, and I know we haven't known each other very long, but I need to tell you that I think I am beginning to fall in—"

"Ryan," came the familiar voice of the owner of Casa Negrita, "is that you?"

Chapter 12

Carrie sat at the small table in her room and opened her laptop. While she waited for it to power up, she walked to the window to watch the last purple fingers of twilight extend over the mountain. Already the night had come alive with sounds, some familiar and others distinctly unfamiliar.

As the innkeeper warned, the evening air had turned chilly. She reached to pull a sweatshirt out of her bag and shrugged into it, then closed the painted wooden shutters guarding her window. Tonight she would surely need the cozy quilt now folded on the chair beside her bed.

Her laptop sounded a greeting, and Carrie walked over to attempt an Internet connection. To her surprise, the little inn had a wireless network. In a modicum of steps, she opened a browser and retrieved her e-mails.

Deleting the junk mail came first, followed by a note to her mother detailing all she'd seen today. As an afterthought she added Millie to the recipient list, then clicked the SEND button. She was just about to sign off when the sound of an instant message rang out.

To be or not to be sleepy. That is the question.

Ryan and his Shakespeare jokes. Carrie smiled.

Not, she typed. *Wide awake, actually.*

Me, too, came the quick response. *Want to talk awhile?*

Sounds great! As soon as she typed the words, she deleted them. It wouldn't do to look overly excited. *Why not?* Again she hit DELETE as soon as she finished typing the last letter. Finally she settled for a more generic *Yes.*

What seemed like only a few minutes later, Carrie yawned. How strange to be tired so early in the evening. She typed an answer to Ryan's question, then hit the toolbar key, causing it to appear at the bottom of her screen.

1:27.

Carrie scrambled for the nightstand and the watch she'd removed earlier. 1:29.

Ryan, would you believe you're supposed to be picking me up in six hours?

After a brief pause, he sent another message. *Want to keep talking, or should we continue this conversation in the morning?*

Morning, she wrote, although she could have typed all night.

Alas, Ryan wrote, *parting is such sweet sorrow.*

Smiling, she sent one last message. *Upon the morrow then.*

The morrow arrived far earlier than she expected, leaving Carrie to believe the sun must rise on a different timetable in Costa Rica. She stumbled through the process of dressing and taming her hair, aided by the pot of steaming dark Negrita coffee and *gallo pinto* the innkeepers left on her doorstep.

Even in her sleepy state, she recognized gallo pinto—a bean, egg, and corn tortilla concoction—from the research she'd done in preparation for the article. While she'd frowned on the mix of ingredients when she read about them, the actual taste of the national breakfast was a pleasing surprise.

So was seeing Ryan waiting for her on the deck where she'd left him last night.

"Good morning," he called as he walked over to give her a quick embrace. "Did you sleep well?"

"Very," she said. "How about you?"

"Truthfully, I don't remember sleeping, but I'm not complaining." Ryan winked. "The conversation made the lack of rest worth it. So, Miss Collins, are you ready to see my corner of Costa Rica?"

For the next two hours, Ryan acted as tour guide while Carrie took videos and notes, as well as the occasional photograph. In Grecia, they stopped in the shadow of the iron church. Painted red with white fretwork adorning the roof, the church sheltered a tidy little park where Ryan set out a picnic lunch for them.

After lunch, they toured Sarchi, where they visited the oxcart factory and a furniture maker's shop, then stopped at a small zoo. After much coercing, Carrie allowed Ryan to take her picture feeding the toucans, but only after he posed with a feisty hair-pulling macaw. Before heading off for the mountains and the village of Rincon de Salas, Ryan pulled the truck over next to a sign advertising Heavenly Beans as the finest coffee in Costa Rica.

"Thirsty?"

"For your coffee, always," she said with a grin.

At a tiny table set on the edge of a lemon grove, Ryan surprised her by turning the conversation to the interview she'd all but forgotten about. "So, are you getting enough information to write your story?"

The idea of doing the story she'd planned set poorly. Speaking to him about it on this glorious afternoon in this idyllic spot felt even worse.

"More than enough," she said as she stirred a teaspoonful of sugar into her coffee. A thought occurred. Why not be honest and tell him of her concerns? If Ryan had nothing to hide, he wouldn't mind, would he? After all, Mr. Renfro was certainly forthright in answering her questions.

"Something wrong?"

She looked up to see Ryan watching her. "No," she said quickly. "Just thinking."

A child's laughter caught her ear. From around the corner of the little coffee shop, a quartet of raggedly dressed youths strolled toward them. Carrie watched Ryan set his mug down slowly, never letting the boys out of his sight. The tallest of the four, a lad of no more than ten or eleven, reached into the pocket of his cutoff jeans and pulled out a cigar.

He called Ryan by name, then said something in Spanish. Ryan rose, obviously tense, but said nothing. When the boy turned his attention to Carrie, Ryan walked over to stand beside her, casually draping his arm around her shoulder.

Ryan spoke, enunciating each word with care, then tightened his grip around Carrie's shoulders. A long moment of silence followed as he and the boy stared, neither moving, barely blinking.

Finally the boy shrugged and turned to walk away. As the others followed their leader, Ryan heaved a sigh. Abruptly the foursome stopped, and the older boy pulled something from his pocket. He handed it to a smaller boy, who raced toward the table.

Stepping forward to meet the little fellow, Ryan accepted what looked like a crumpled sheet of paper. As the foursome headed down the road toward the village, Ryan settled back into the chair across from her and stuffed the paper into his pocket.

"Carrie," he said slowly, "do you mind a change of plans? I'd like to show you something."

Twenty minutes later, Ryan stopped the truck in front of a tidy white picket fence. On the other side of the gate a group of children sat in a circle passing a ball between them. Situated on the porch of a whitewashed home was an elderly woman dressed in brilliant scarlet and holding a sleeping infant. Above her next to the open door was a sign proclaiming this residence to be Casa de los Niños.

"House of Children."

"Hey, I didn't think you spoke Spanish." Ryan came up behind her and grasped her hand. "I'd like you to meet someone very special. That's her up on the porch."

"Señor Ryan!" a little boy called, and soon the two of them were surrounded by dozens of children. The woman in scarlet stood and settled the infant in a cradle, then walked toward them.

With a few words and a clap of her hands, the woman sent the children scurrying back to their games. She extended her hand to Carrie and smiled.

"So pleased to meet you, Miss Collins," she said. "Ryan has told me so much about you. I'm Mamá. Mamá Zadora."

The trio moved to the porch where a neatly dressed young lady brought tall glasses of sweet lemonade. She smiled at

Carrie and disappeared inside. Moments later, heavy footsteps approaced the door.

"Mamá, I hear we have company." A tall, dark-haired man stepped out onto the porch and grasped Ryan's hand. Carrie recognized him at once as Ryan's best friend, Alvaro.

"Good afternoon, my friend," Alvaro said. He turned his attention to Carrie, brown eyes dancing with what looked like amusement. "So you're Carrie."

"Yes, I'm Carrie."

He winked at Ryan. "She's every bit as beautiful as you said, Ryan."

"Cut it out, Alvaro," Ryan said.

"Boys, remember your manners." Mamá shook her head. "Can you believe I must listen to this nonsense? And people think raising so many children is difficult. I tell you, it's the adults in this house that give me trouble. And to think this one is a pastor."

"Mamá, I saw the Gallego boys again."

The older woman frowned. "Up to no good, I suspect."

"The usual. Threatening the tourists and begging for money or a match to light his cigar."

Mamá shook her head. "If only the boy would see the error of his ways. His life would be so much better here."

"Some can learn by hearing and others must find their way by doing. That boy and his brothers, they fall into the second category," Alvaro said. "Someday they will ring the bell, Mamá. We cannot give up hope."

Ryan fished the crumpled paper that the boy gave him out of his pocket and handed it to Mamá. "He asked me to give you this."

Mamá opened the paper and smiled. A coin fell into her lap. "Look, he's sent payment for Angelina."

"Who's Angelina?"

Alvaro pointed to a little girl in pigtails. "The little one there, she's sister to the four you met in town."

"Mamá broke her ankle stumbling through the house to admit that one. The eldest, Jorge, he brought her to the orphanage last month while Ryan was in Texas. She was sick, barely able to breathe, and her mamá. . .well, let's say she's not so interested in her children as she is in the men she keeps company with. The brother said he would pay for her upkeep, and he does. I'm afraid to ask how though."

Mamá handed the paper to Ryan. "Look, son, at what the boy used to wrap the coin."

Ryan smiled. "Yes, I see."

"What is it?" Carrie asked.

"A page from Ryan's Bible," Alvaro said. "He leaves them all over the place. I keep telling him he needs to replace that book with one that's not falling apart, but does he listen?"

The men began to banter like boys, sending Mamá and Carrie into fits of laughter. "Is it always this way, Mamá?" Carrie asked.

"Yes, and I pray it always will be. Perhaps you will stay and find out."

"Mamá," Alvaro and Ryan both said.

"Fine, we don't talk about Carrie staying then. We talk about the weather and the cost of sugarcane and anything else rather than what I want to talk about."

"I'm glad you see it my way." Ryan turned to Carrie, a flush of embarrassment riding high on his tanned cheekbones. "Now that I've been thoroughly humiliated, maybe we ought to talk about the article you're writing. I'm sure you've got plenty to ask these two characters."

Carrie spent a delightful afternoon fielding questions and interviewing Mamá and Alvaro, then taking a guided tour of Heavenly Beans offices. Finally they ended the day with a drive to the coffee plantation where most of the coffee was grown.

"So by law we are only allowed to grow arabica beans," Ryan said as he perched atop the hood of the truck and pointed toward the field. "Some of the finest beans in the world, if I do say so myself."

Carrie leaned back against the windshield and watched the first stars of the evening appear. Never in all her imaginings could she have thought today would be so wonderful. She closed her eyes and mulled over all she'd learned.

According to Mamá, Ryan and Heavenly Beans were the reasons her babies, as she called them, were fed, clothed, and educated. She'd brought out a scrapbook of all the children who'd spent time in her care, and to Carrie's surprise, the book included doctors, lawyers, teachers, and even a politician.

And Alvaro, the pastor? He'd turned out to be the most interesting character of all. Why, to hear Mamá tell it, Alvaro kept the orphanage running and the coffee plantation producing during the week and saved souls on Sunday.

A feeling took root on that porch and grew until, just now, in the quiet of this place, Carrie felt the whisperings of the Lord. Ryan Baxter was the real deal. In her heart she'd known it all along.

It was her head—her stubborn and prejudiced ideas about men who raised money in the name of the Lord—that caused the trouble. Her article as she proposed it to Mr. Scott could no longer be written.

Carrie smiled. Oh, but she had another article in mind that would be much better.

"Now that's the prettiest smile I've seen in a long time, Miss Collins."

She opened her eyes to see Ryan looking down at her. "Yours is quite nice, too, Mr. Baxter."

He leaned closer. "Carrie," he said slowly, "I need to tell you something."

Carrie's heart kicked into a furious rhythm. Why, it looked for all the world like Ryan might just mean to kiss her.

"Oh?"

"Yes." Again he eased closer. "You see, there's something the Lord's been bugging me about, and I feel like it's time to come clean. See, I'm beginning to. . ." He frowned. "That is, what I mean is that after much thought I feel like. . . Oh, it's no use."

"What?"

"I'm trying to tell you that for some strange reason I've fallen in love with you, but the words just won't come out."

"Ryan," she said as she reached up to touch her palm to the rough skin of his cheek, "I think they just did."

Chapter 13

He said it. Ryan groaned and leaned back against the window, staring up into the night sky. Had there been enough light to see it, Carrie would have known he was blushing brighter than he had this afternoon on Mamá's porch.

"Ryan?"

"Yes?" he said as he closed his eyes.

"Open your eyes."

When he did he saw Carrie's face. "Me, too," she said.

"What?"

"I said, me, too." She resumed her position beside him and seemed to be staring at the first sprinkling of stars above the mountains.

"You, too?"

"Yes," she whispered. "*Et tu*, Ryan?"

Ryan chuckled at the poor reference to Shakespeare. "Oh, Carrie, you can do better than that."

She entwined her fingers with his. " 'Now join your hands, and with your hands your hearts.' "

"Oh, that's good," he said as he lifted her fingers to his lips. "How about this one? 'They do not love that do not show their love.' "

"Ryan?"

He shifted positions to see her better. "Yes?"

"That last one," she said as she looked into his eyes. "Was that from you or Shakespeare?"

"Both," he said as he leaned over to kiss her.

A moment later he settled her beside him as they stared up into the first stars of the evening. "Ryan, would you do that one more time?"

He happily obliged.

"I need to tell you something," she said softly. "And when I'm through, I'll understand if you never want to see me again."

Ryan listened while Carrie told him of plans to do an exposé on Heavenly Beans, all the while wondering at the amazing way the Lord had thrown them together. When she finished her confession, she swiped at her eyes with her sleeve. "So you see, I made up my mind you were just like that man who took my mama's money, but I was wrong. I was using you to get a story. Will you forgive me?"

"Oh, Carrie, honey, there's nothing to forgive." He sealed the statement with a kiss.

"Thank you," she whispered, "for understanding."

Ryan let the silence envelop them for a moment, then worked up the courage to make his own admission. "Carrie, I need to tell you something, too. See, I was using you, too."

"You were?"

He nodded. "I thought you were my ticket to free publicity.

I figured an article in a big Austin paper would get the word out about our little company and set the sales figures skyrocketing. The more time I spent with you, though, the less I thought about coffee, and the more I thought about you." He reached for her hand. "About us. I lived for those e-mails and instant messages. I don't know how I'll stand it when you go back to Austin on Saturday."

With that statement hanging heavily between them, Ryan drove Carrie back to the inn and saw her to her door. One last chaste kiss and he headed for the truck. He got all the way to the gate on the edge of the Heavenly Beans property before he turned the truck around and headed back toward town.

Carrie finished her e-mail to Mama and Millie listing the day's events, all but the kisses she shared with Ryan in the moonlight. Those were to be held in secrecy, sweet memories tucked away in her heart and brought out only in unguarded moments of solitude.

Moments when she would miss Ryan Baxter and Costa Rica terribly.

Her cell phone rang, and she dove to answer it. "Hello," she said, hoping the voice on the other end would be Ryan's. If only she'd checked the caller's number before she answered.

"Carrie, honey, it's Mama. How's Costa Rica?"

Carrie tried not to let the disappointment show in her voice as she chattered on about the land and people that had captured her heart. When Mama asked about Ryan, she fell silent.

"Oh, goodness, Carrie, you love him, don't you?"

She nearly dropped the phone. "How did you know?"

Mama ignored the question to ask, "When can I meet him?"

"Meet him? Well, Mama, I don't know. I mean, he's here in Costa Rica, and I'm leaving for Austin. It's probably not going to work out."

"Pish posh, Carrie. You gonna let a little something like location spoil a perfectly good romance? You think the Lord didn't know about that problem when He decided the two of you were meant to be a pair?"

"But, Mama, I. . ." Something hit the shutters and rattled to the floor. Carrie looked down and saw a pebble sitting there.

"Now that was odd."

"What was odd, honey?"

" 'But hark, what light is there in yon window?' "

Ryan?

"Mama, I'm going to have to call you back."

"Is your young man calling?"

Romeo's soliloquy from the balcony scene continued on the other side of the closed shutters. "I wouldn't exactly say he was calling. Actually, he's downstairs quoting Shakespeare right now."

"To you?"

"Yes, I think so."

"Don't let this one get away, Carrie," Mama said. "If he loves you and you love him, where you do the loving doesn't matter. Besides, my passport's good for another seven years. After that, well, we'll just see if you want me to stay and take care of the babies or just visit regularly."

"Bye, Mama."

She hung up the phone and strolled to the window just in time for Ryan to lob another pebble in her direction. The projectile narrowly missed her foot as it bounced across the hardwood floor and rolled under her bed.

Throwing open the shutters, she leaned out the window. "Ryan, what are you doing here?"

"It's about Saturday," he said. "Your last day here."

"What about it?"

"Well, I don't want it to be your last day here. I mean, Saturday's a nice day and all, but it just doesn't seem like the right day for you to leave."

"Oh?" Carrie looked up toward the moon and saw a shooting star trail across the sky. Her heart felt like that shooting star, burning bright and racing quickly. "All right then, what day do you think would be a good one for leaving?"

"Well, I've been thinking about that all the way back here, and I believe I've got an answer to that. I'd rather you came down here so we could talk about it without yelling though."

"And we'd appreciate that, too," came the voice of the innkeeper.

"Sorry," Carrie called as she closed the shutters and raced downstairs. Just before she emerged onto the deck, she slowed her pace and tried not to appear too hurried.

All reserve fled when she saw Ryan. She ran to him and fell into his arms. "So, what's the answer?"

"Don't go. Stay here, Carrie. You said yourself that you love it here. I can teach you Spanish, and you can write your stories from right here in Rincon de Salas. What with the Internet and phone service like it is, you don't have to live in Austin to make a living as a writer."

Thoughts swirled and danced across her mind, delightful images that flitted but refused to stick. Yes, she could pick up and move to Costa Rica, but why should she? What was he offering?

" 'Hear my soul speak: The very instant that I saw you, did my heart fly to your service.' " Before she could formulate the question, Ryan held her at arm's length then went down on one knee. "Marry me, Carrie Collins. Marry me and come to live in Costa Rica." He paused to grin. "And if it means anything, I promise a lifetime supply of love and Heavenly Beans coffee."

For a moment all she could do was stare. Then she smiled. "Oh, Ryan, I love you!"

He rose to let out a shout of glee, then lift her into his arms. "Tell the truth, Carrie. Was it me or the coffee that convinced you to stay?"

"Just kiss me, Ryan," she said, knowing it was a little of both.

KATHLEEN MILLER Y'BARBO

Kathleen Miller Y'Barbo is an award-winning novelist and sixth-generation Texan. After completing a degree in marketing at Texas A&M University, she focused on raising four children and turned to writing. She is a member of American Christian Romance Writers, Romance Writers of America, and Writers Information Network. She also lectures on the craft of writing at the elementary and secondary levels, and conducts distance-learning classes on the university level.

A Letter to Our Readers

Dear Readers:

In order that we might better contribute to your reading enjoyment, we would appreciate your taking a few minutes to respond to the following questions. When completed, please return to the following: Fiction Editor, Barbour Publishing, Inc., P.O. Box 719, Uhrichsville, OH 44683.

1. Did you enjoy reading *Fresh-Brewed Love?*
   ❑ Very much—I would like to see more books like this.
   ❑ Moderately—I would have enjoyed it more if ____________

____

____

2. What influenced your decision to purchase this book? (Check those that apply.)
   ❑ Cover ❑ Back cover copy ❑ Title ❑ Price
   ❑ Friends ❑ Publicity ❑ Other

3. Which story was your favorite?
   ❑ *An Acquired Taste* ❑ *Breaking New Grounds*
   ❑ *The Perfect Blend* ❑ *Coffee Scoop*

4. Please check your age range:
   ❑ Under 18 ❑ 18–24 ❑ 25–34
   ❑ 35–45 ❑ 46–55 ❑ Over 55

5. How many hours per week do you read? ____________

Name ________________________________

Occupation ________________________________

Address ________________________________

City____________ State__________ Zip__________

E-mail________________________________

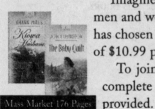